"My superior [would me] *wished to sp[eak] [about a] murder. Wh[ose?]"*

"Mine."

I looked up from my notebook. Blinked. Felt my eyebrows raise. "I beg your pardon?"

"I am reporting my own murder."

I stared. She didn't look crazy. In fact, the woman looked completely calm. Entirely in possession of her faculties. With President Dupont's orders firmly in mind, I said carefully, "Forgive me, Madame Villecourt, but you appear alive and well to me."

She laughed. "My dear, you have such a gift for understatement."

I was entirely lost here. "Tell me about… your murder."

She nodded. "Yes, indeed. Something has been stolen from me. It is of little value compared to the other works of art in my home, but without it, I shall die. Therefore, I can only conclude that whoever stole it specifically targeted it…and knew that doing so would kill me."

Aha. Now we were in familiar waters. A stolen piece of art. "What was stolen?"

"I can't tell you."

Haunted Echoes
CINDY DEES

MILLS & BOON®
Pure reading pleasure

First published in Great Britain 2007
by Harlequin Mills & Boon Limited,
Eton House, 18-24 Paradise Road, Richmond, Surrey TW9 1SR

© Cynthia Dees 2006

The Madonna Key series was co-created by Yvonne Jocks,
Vicki Hinze and Lorna Tedder.

ISBN: 978 0 263 85758 0

46-1007

Harlequin Mills & Boon policy is to use papers that are natural, renewable and recyclable products and made from wood grown in sustainable forests. The logging and manufacturing processes conform to the legal environmental regulations of the country of origin.

Printed and bound in Spain
by Litografia Rosés S.A., Barcelona

CINDY DEES

started flying aeroplanes while sitting in her dad's lap at the age of three and got a pilot's licence before she got a driver's licence. At age fifteen she dropped out of school and left the horse farm in Michigan where she grew up to attend the University of Michigan.

After earning a degree in Russian and East European Studies, she joined the US Air Force and became the youngest female pilot in its history. She flew supersonic jets, VIP airlift and the C-5 Galaxy, the world's largest aeroplane. She also worked part-time gathering intelligence. During her military career, she travelled to forty countries on five continents, was detained by the KGB and East German secret police, got shot at, flew in the first Gulf War, met her husband and amassed a lifetime's worth of war stories.

Her hobbies include professional Middle Eastern dancing, Japanese gardening and medieval re-enacting. She started writing on a bet with her mother and was thrilled to win that bet with the publication of her first book in 2001. She loves to hear from readers and can be contacted at www.cindydees.com.

How could this book not be dedicated to my
Madonna Key sisters? You ladies are, in a word,
phenomenal. Thanks...

To Lorna, for all the cool things you know
To Carol, for being so perceptive
To Sharron, for never failing to make me laugh
To Jennifer, for your unwavering personal grace
And especially to Von, for sharing your vision
with the rest of us.

Dear Reader,

When I got the call asking me if I'd like to come
play with several authors whom I greatly
admired, oh, and write a book, too, I was
delighted. What I didn't know was those authors
would grow to be some of my dearest friends or
that I would discover a world of ideas and
history that would utterly captivate me.

In fact, I had so much fun researching this story
that I had trouble actually hunkering down to
write the book! This has got to be one of my
all-time favourite projects to have worked on.
I got to combine my love of all things medieval
and my love of writing suspense thrillers into
one story.

And to any descendants of Queen Elizabeth the
First who happen to read this book, my
apologies for any fictional liberties I took with
her character or actions. Liz rocks!

Happy reading!

Cindy Dees

Chapter 1

Conceived in love and forged in stone,
Legend says in her belly alone
Lie the hidden seeds of eternity—
The Lady, the Babe, the Sword and Key—
And he who holds her safe from strife
Shall be rewarded with the Gift of Life.
—from the *Legend of the Lady*

The soaring notes of the aria washed over me, exquisite. Like Swiss chocolate melting into satin decadence on my tongue. Well, okay. Maybe not that good. But close. I have a few guilty pleasures in my otherwise bland life, and opera and fine chocolate are two of them. On my salary I can't afford either often, but when I do, I make sure to savor every last morsel.

The opera was close to ending when something vibrated against my right hip. Oh, hell. It was Saturday night for goodness' sake. I was off duty. But my cell phone continued to vibrate insistently. I leaned over to the side and made the guy beside me grumble as I dug out my phone and flipped it open. And gulped. Uh-oh. Armande St. Germain. My boss's boss. A big dog in the hierarchy of Interpol. Chief of the Stolen Cultural Property Group, also known as the Painting and Pottery Patrol.

St. Germain was calling *me* from Interpol headquarters in Lyon this late on a Saturday night? My voice message light blinked on, indicating I had a new voice mail. I slipped out of the theater, tromping on the toes of my neighbors and generally irritating an entire row of patrons in the process.

I stepped out onto the Grand Staircase and looked around. Chandeliers the size of small cars dripped crystals from the ceilings, and the matching marble staircases swept downward toward the main floor, guarded by two giant carved women in togas, reminiscent of the Statue of Liberty. Huge, cast-iron streetlight-type fixtures on tall posts lit the stairs. I tried my phone. As I expected, no signal in here. Too much steel and stone.

I walked toward the Grand Foyer to my right. It was possibly even gaudier than the cavern I'd just left. Ornate gold pillars rose to the painted ceiling, which was divided into gilt rectangles and ovals framing naughty-looking cherubs. Curly, cast-iron chandeliers lit this space with thousands of electric candles. I felt as if I was trapped inside a giant, turquoise-and-gold Fabergé egg.

I tried my phone again. Better. I called my voice mail service.

"Agent Reisner." St. Germain's clipped tones bit my ear. He took pride in his command of English and always used it on me, since I'm American. "An urgent situation has come up that requires your immediate attention. Call Littmann right away. He will fill you in on the details. This…problem…has come down from the highest levels of the French government."

High enough that he was calling me just to make sure I got on it right away? I *so* didn't like the sound of that. I'm an art historian. I catalogue works of art at museums and galleries in the Paris area. If one is later stolen, I'm occasionally called upon to verify the details I've entered into Interpol's master database of cultural property. But I don't get calls on Saturday evenings asking me to attend to urgent problems of national importance.

Thoroughly alarmed, I stepped outside into a triangular courtyard made up of rue Auber on my right and rue Halevy on my left. The limestone gingerbread facade of the Opera rose behind me, completing the triangle. The pavement was wet. It had rained while I was inside, lending a certain chill to the September evening. A steamy smell associated with wet worms rose from the shiny asphalt.

I dialed my boss, François Littmann, on his cell phone. I had no idea whether he'd be at home or the office at this hour of the night. You never could tell with him. He alternated between fretting over his blood pressure and giving in to his workaholic tendencies. He picked up on the second ring. Sounded more upset than usual, which was saying something. He was as hyper as a French poodle most of the time.

"Ana. There you are. Finally. I hope I haven't interrupted a romantic interlude?" The guy could not leave the subject of my nonexistent love life alone. Flatly refused to believe me when I swore there were no secret lovers lurking in my off-duty hours. Not since the bastard.

"I'm at the Opera. What do you want?" I asked brusquely.

"There's been a murder. And you've been asked to check it out."

"A *what?*" I squawked. I go to dusty old museums and write down the numbers on the backs of paintings for a living.

I've got just enough rudimentary police training to carry my Interpol badge, but a cop I am not. I don't *do* murders.

"Someone has requested you by name. Someone who's apparently friends with the president."

"*The* president? As in the guy in charge of France?" I choked out, for once even more flustered than Littmann.

"The very same. He requested that you personally look into this for 'a friend.' You'd better get over there right away." Littmann rattled off an address just off the rue de Bassano, a quiet and ultrachic street leading to the Champs-Elysées.

"Have the police been called?"

"No idea. The president called St. Germain to ask for you, and St. Germain called me. Now I'm telling you to get your derriere over there right now and take care of this."

Right. Whatever "this" was. A *murder?* Interpol had no jurisdiction in such a case. The Paris police did. Maybe some art had been stolen in the course of a murder being committed? In that event, our department usually got a call the following Monday morning. During business hours. The proper forms were filled out and the filched pieces were duly added to our database of recently stolen art. No self-respecting policeman fooled around with trivial details like that within the first few hours of discovering a murder. They had better things to do— like secure and collect evidence, and catch the murderer. Besides, it takes art thieves time to move a piece. There's no rush in reporting a theft to us.

Art thieves rarely resort to murder. It's a code of honor among them. They may take valuable objects, but they are not violent criminals. Who could've broken that code? I reviewed the list of Interpol's Ten Most Wanted art thieves. A thief called Dr. Moon had been tearing up Europe recently, but none of those thefts had involved any hint of violence.

Patrons were just starting to trickle out of the theatre. I'd have to hurry if I wanted to get a cab any time soon.

Why I happened to look over my shoulder just then, I have no idea. Maybe I felt Jean-Michel's presence at some subliminal level. At any rate, there he was, the ex-love of my life. Ex by nearly a year now. I probably ought to be over him, but I admit it—I'm the type to hold a grudge. The scumbag had dumped me like a bad stock investment the second he found out I couldn't have children the old-fashioned way. We were already engaged, for goodness' sake. His dragon of a mother even approved of me! But then I had to go and bring up the fact that I'd been diagnosed with a condition called polycystic ovaries—no big deal really. It just requires the use of in vitro fertilization to get pregnant—and boom, that was that. I was history.

Funny how the bastard hadn't forgotten for a second to be sure I'd signed the pre-nup, but had completely neglected to bring up the requirement that I be able to produce the next dynasty of LaRoche-Neuilly's in "God's way." What the hell was wrong with modern medicine's way? But there you have it. We were finished, and he was officially a jerk. And now he stood not twenty feet from me, wearing a piece of leggy, blond arm fluff as if nothing had ever happened between us.

I confess.

I hid.

I ducked behind a big, bald man and his equally corpulent wife. I scrunched down, keeping the couple between Jean-Michel and me like I was some sort of petty criminal on the lam. I couldn't trust myself not to smile politely at the blonde and pop off with something like, "I'm so pleased to meet you and your ovaries. And how is your uterus tonight? Fertile, I hope."

Rue de Bassano's north end runs right up to the George V Metro stop. But if the police were at the murder scene, which they were bound to be, I'd look more official arriving in a taxi instead of on foot and out of breath after hiking from the Metro. Interpol does have a reputation to maintain, after all.

I stumbled to the curb and waved half-heartedly for a taxi.

It wasn't that I felt inadequate as a woman or anything. I'm perfectly healthy. My ovaries are just too thick and hard to let eggs escape, and I happen to require in vitro egg collection.

In spite of the rain and people pouring out of the opera now, I rather miraculously got a taxi in under three minutes. I gave the driver the address and he smiled and sped off, no doubt anticipating a fat tip.

There were no police cars clustered out front when I arrived at the gray-white limestone building matching the address Littmann had given me. Odd. Absently I paid the driver—minus the fat tip, which I couldn't afford—and had a look up and down the quiet cul-de-sac. No discreet unmarked police cars. There wasn't even a bored-looking cop lurking in a doorway, smoking a quick Gauloise.

Despite the empty stillness of the street, I got a powerful sense of not being alone out here. It felt as if eyes were boring into the back of my neck, no matter which way I turned. Probably just my imagination. Either that or a nosy neighbor was peering out a window and sending these creepy chills up and down my spine.

There was, however, a burly man in a green doorman's uniform standing just inside the vestibule of my destination. He let me in and said politely, "Mademoiselle Reisner?"

I blinked, startled. "That is correct."

"Madame Villecourt is expecting you."

Never heard of her. But apparently, she'd heard of me. I prepared myself for the Madame to be an aristocrat. Achingly polite but tremendously demanding. Not exactly my favorite kind of person to deal with. Rubs my American sense of equality the wrong way. The French national motto might be "Fraternity, Equality and Liberty," but the unspoken—and more accurate—version was "Fraternity, Equality and Liberty in Direct Proportion to Your Wealth and Social Status."

The doorman led me to an old-fashioned cage elevator. He reached inside and poked the button for the fifth floor with a white-gloved finger, but did not join me in the elevator. It rose smoothly on silent pulleys to the top floor of the building.

I stepped out into the hallway. I expected a row of doors with numbers or nameplates on them like a regular apartment building. Instead, I was confronted with a single door. A massive, carved mahogany monster of a door with a brass lion for a handle. Well, then. A penthouse, apparently. Lots of *fraternité, égalité* and *liberté* going on here.

I crossed the gleaming black marble floor and lifted the heavy brass ring hanging from another lion's mouth. I dropped it with a thud.

A tinny voice spoke from beside me almost immediately. Out of an intercom with—crud—a doorbell button beside it. I was already messing this thing up and I wasn't even inside yet. My discerning eye was supposed to notice little details like doorbells. Duh.

The giant door before me swung open ponderously. A gray-haired woman stood there. Short. Squat. Bow-legged. Severe, steel-gray skirt, sensible shoes, white turtleneck. Steel-gray cardigan. Steel-gray hair pulled back in a bun. I'd peg her for a nun were it not for the absence of a wimple or collar.

"Madame Villecourt?" I asked.

Her dour face puckered in disapproval, and the abundant hairs on her chin waggled in indignation. "*Mon Dieu, non.* I am Madame Trucot. The housekeeper. Come in. We have been *waiting* for you."

Late, was I? Lovely. I stepped inside. And couldn't help but pause to breathe in the incredible ambience of the place. It was like stepping back in time seven hundred years. Gray travertine walls stretched away from me into a long, dim corridor with a tall, barrel vault ceiling. The only light came from flickering gas bulbs mounted in torches along the walls.

Heavy wooden doors with wide, iron hinges lined the hall. To my right hung a magnificent tapestry depicting a dark-skinned woman pouring water out of a white urn into the hands of several children. An unusual subject for such an old tapestry. It looked Belgian, maybe late fourteenth century. The picture was three-dimensional—also unheard of in a piece that old. Maybe my date was off. But the rich color, the *milles fleurs* border—I thought not. Regardless of its age, the piece was one of a kind. Had to be worth millions.

I was distracted by a giant floor mirror opposite the tapestry. It stood a solid six feet tall, and was dim and gray with age. The frame was intricately carved and decorated. For all the world it looked Arab, and every bit as old as the tapestry. If I were in the castle of a recently returned Crusader knight, I'd expect to see such a piece. It reflected the tapestry perfectly, except my image was projected into the picture standing exactly beside the woman. The effect was eerie. Like I'd been holographically projected into the woven image.

If the murder that had happened here was in conjunction with an art theft and this priceless tapestry had been left behind, the thief was a moron.

Glancing at my reflection again, I ran a cursory hand over my head, tucking a stray strand of hair behind my ear. My silver-blond hair was pulled back into a smooth ponytail. I wore a touch of makeup tonight because of the opera, and my cheeks looked a little less hollow than usual. I was startled at the effect a little makeup had on me. I might even be called attractive by some. My longer than fashionable nose was not so noticeable with a bit of lipstick to distract a person's attention. At least my teeth were white and even. My orthodontist could be proud of his work. I really ought to wear mascara like this more often. My too-pale blue eyes looked slightly less stark than usual now that you could see my eyelashes. Maybe I was finally starting to come out of my man-hating phase.

I'd spent the past year doing everything in my power to be un-attractive to the opposite sex, and given the monkishness of my existence, I'd apparently succeeded. Spectacularly. But for the first time in a long time, I got a little rush of pleasure at seeing myself look vaguely decent.

I tugged at my navy wool suit. By the functional—bor-ing—standards of my wardrobe, this was a colorful, even feminine ensemble. It was a sad statement about my wardrobe that it was perfect for interviewing witnesses at a murder scene.

Speaking of which… "Who has died, Madame Trucot?" I asked.

Her already thin lips pressed into an invisible line, the house-keeper said, "Follow me," without answering my question.

Farther down the dark hallway, we stopped in front of a set of double doors at least ten feet tall. Madame Trucot pushed them open and stepped aside, revealing a dark, wood-paneled library that made my blood sing. The room was large, dim, maybe thirty feet across. Every single wall was lined, floor to twelve-foot ceiling, with leather-bound books. It was a magnificent collection.

Statues stood on pedestals around the room. I spied a Greek ceremonial urn that, swear to God, looked like it came from Delphi. Had an offering urn actually survived the sack of the temple? My mouth watered at the idea of getting a better look at the piece. A Rodin bronze gleamed to my left. A marble statue across the room looked like an honest-to-goodness Mi-chelangelo—a small version of his *David*. The proportions were slightly off, as if this had been a study done hastily, but the lines were pure Michelangelo all the way.

Even the Aubusson carpet beneath my feet had me calcu-lating sales prices at auction and coming up with a stagger-ing figure. There was wealth, and then there were riches beyond imagining. From what I'd seen so far, the owner of this place fell into the latter category.

The doors closed quietly behind me. I glanced around and saw that Madame Trucot had not come inside. I stepped forward to have a better look at the Michelangelo. I must convince whoever owned this place to let me catalogue its contents for the Interpol database of great art. That, and I desperately needed to mark the contents of this room if they weren't already done, in case they were ever stolen.

A movement across the space caught my attention. Someone stood from a deep wingback chair in the shadows of a far corner. A warm, contralto voice said, "Come here, my dear. Let me see you. I've been waiting a long time."

I stepped forward, squinting past the pool of lamplight in the center of the room to see who'd addressed me. It was a woman. As tall as me and as thin. I'm five foot nine and spare of frame. The woman stood ramrod straight like me, too. Gray, lush hair in short waves around one of those faces you could guess the age of twenty years either way. I estimated early sixties, but I wouldn't bet a centime—a French penny—on it.

I said politely, "I am Agent Ana Reisner of Interpol. I believe you asked to speak to me?"

"I did. Come sit beside me." She gestured gracefully toward a second wingback chair angled toward the one from which she'd risen.

"To whom do I have the honor of speaking?" I asked. Surely this was Madame Villecourt, but I wasn't about to make the same mistake twice.

"I am Elise Villecourt." She waited until I'd sat down on the edge of my seat to deliver the coup de grace. "I knew your grandmother."

I blinked. "Gladys Roberson?" She and my Grandpa Ted live in a three-bedroom, brick ranch in Pennsylvania, a world away from this splendor. To my knowledge, they'd never been west of the Mississippi or east of Philadelphia, let alone visited the chic end of Paris. I was the only person in my family af-flicted by the wanderlust that had landed me in France.

"No. Your other grandmother. Ana Reisner."

An involuntary tingle shot down my spine. Whoa. Ana Reisner died over sixty years ago during World War Two. My father was just a baby when she disappeared and was never seen again. Years later, her name turned up on a list of people buried at an obscure cemetery in Italy, but that was all anyone knew—other than the fact that I look exactly like pictures of her at the same age.

I revised my age estimate of this woman well into her sev-enties. Dang, she was well-preserved. "You and my grand-mother were children together?"

"It seems like that now," Madame Villecourt answered with a small smile.

What was that supposed to mean? I forced my attention back to the business at hand and pulled a small notebook and pen out of my purse. "My superiors told me you wished to speak to me about a murder. Whose murder would that be?"

"Mine."

I looked up slowly from my notebook. Blinked. Felt my eyebrows rise. "I beg your pardon?"

"I am reporting my own murder."

I stared at her. She didn't look crazy. In fact, the woman looked extremely calm. Collected. Entirely in possession of her faculties. St. Germain and the president firmly in my mind, I said carefully, "Forgive me, Madame Villecourt, but you appear alive and well to me."

The woman laughed gaily, the sound incongruously young. "My dear Analise, you are just like your grandmother. Such a gift for understatement."

How did she know my full name? I'd only introduced myself as Ana. Besides, it was incredibly forward of a French person to use my first name with such familiarity.

As if she'd read my mind, she answered my unspoken question. "It is a long story."

I frowned slightly. "I have nowhere else to go this evening."

Her smile grew even wider. "I'd forgotten the fire in her eyes. But you have it, too. I'm so glad she is not entirely lost."

I was entirely lost here. "Your alleged murder?" I prompted.

"Have you not asked yourself why, out of all the law enforcement officials and agencies in France, I specifically requested to speak with you?"

"I have, Madame. But what does this have to do with your...death?"

"Please. Call me Elise. You're named after the two of us, you know. Ana and Elise."

Her casual remark was a punch in the gut. Threw me off balance all of a sudden. Out of kilter. My world is stable. Orderly. Free from surprises, the way I like it. I'm from a safe little town in central Connecticut, grew up in a German-American home of strict Presbyterians, went to Radcliffe University, majored in art history and minored in French literature. My grandfather, Otto, came to live with us when I was a kid, and never, not once, did he ever mention the existence of this fabulously wealthy French aristocrat in his dead wife's past. I bit back an urge to blurt, "Who *are* you?" to this mysterious woman.

Instead, I managed to mumble, "I didn't know I was named after you."

"Otto never said anything about me, did he? He always blamed me for her death. But it was not me. I swear. It was—" She broke off. "Well, that's a story for another time. I suppose he never mentioned—" a delicate pause "—a key?"

"I'm afraid not," I answered cautiously.

"Indeed. That, too, then, is a story for another time, my dear."

She kept calling me "her dear" like she was some elderly aunt of mine. It was disconcerting. And I still didn't know the first thing about this supposed murder—of the person who was speaking to me at this very moment.

"Tell me about…your murder."

She nodded. "Yes, indeed. To business. Something has been stolen from me. Out of this very room, in fact. And without it, I shall die. It is of relatively little value in comparison to the other works of art in my home. Therefore, I can only conclude that whoever stole it specifically targeted it…and knew that doing so would kill me."

Aha. Now we were swimming in familiar waters. A stolen piece of art. This, I could work with. My feet on solid ground for the first time since I'd arrived here, I asked briskly, "What exactly was stolen?"

"I can't tell you."

I stared at her, dumbfounded. Yes, she looked serious. "You can't tell me?" I repeated, my feet knocked right back out from under me.

"No. Its existence is the deepest of secrets, and I cannot reveal what it is to anyone. Not even to you."

The President of France clearly chose his friends in lunatic asylums. "What *can* you tell me about it? Has this item been catalogued for insurance purposes? Its identification markings photographed, perhaps?"

"No, no. I told you. It's a secret. According to the art world, it doesn't exist. I do not display it even when my closest friends come for tea."

"Forgive me, Madame Villecourt—"

"Elise."

"Elise," I repeated. "But what do you want from me? You want me to investigate a murder that obviously has not happened and a theft of something that doesn't technically exist?"

"It is a legend," she answered obliquely.

"Is it real?" I demanded. Whatever the hell "it" was.

Her voice took on the singsong tone of a mystic. "Who's

to say if a legend is real or not? We must each decide a legend's truth or falsehood based on the evidence of our own eyes and hearts."

Mumbo jumbo. Exasperation tickled my lungs. Time to try another approach. "Why me?"

"Because I knew your grandmother. I hoped you might have inherited some of her determination to succeed."

Oh, I had that all right. I never did anything halfway once I put my mind to doing it. Failures had been few and far between in my life. My love life being the notable and glaring exception, of course.

I felt as if I were pounding my head against a brick wall here, but it was my job, and I could practically feel the eyes of President Pierre Dupont drilling into my back. "Why is the loss of this item going to cost you your life?"

Elise looked at me for a moment. And then her eyes went blank as if she were looking right through me. She tilted her head, almost as if she were listening to someone speaking. Then she said suddenly, "Yes, I agree. She is not ready to hear the answer yet. She must learn the rest first. Then I can tell her about its special properties."

The woman blinked as if to shake herself out of a reverie and focused on me once more. "I'm sorry, my dear. I cannot tell you just yet why I shall die soon. But trust me. I will die."

"How soon?" I asked, alarmed. How in the world was I going to tell Littmann and St. Germain that President Dupont's friend was a complete nutcase?

"Oh, I should think I'll live only a matter of weeks, perhaps a few months at most."

"Have you been poisoned?" I tried, searching for something, anything, tangible to sink my investigative teeth into.

"Good heavens, no!"

"I'm sorry, Madame Villecourt, but I don't see how I'm

going to be able to help you if you can't give me more information to go on."

"We believe somebody obtained the security code to the alarm on the servants' entrance. He came up the back stairs this afternoon and let himself in that way. There's a fingerprint scanner on that door, and the thief must have gotten past it somehow. There were no signs of—how do you police say it?—forced entry."

"Where were you when this theft occurred?"

"Out. Attending an exhibition at the Cluny."

Ah, yes. A display of medieval tapestries, some from a century before the Cluny Museum's own Dame à la Licorne tapestries were woven. I catalogued the exhibit last month before it opened to the public. Nothing in it compared to the piece hanging in this woman's front hallway. Aloud I said, "So you were out of your home for several hours. Where were your servants?" It wasn't uncommon for a theft like this to be an inside job.

"There is only the housekeeper. My needs are not great. Madame Trucot was with me. And there's no possibility whatsoever that she had anything to do with this. We are…like sisters."

The sour nun and this obscenely wealthy and sophisticated woman? That was hard to picture.

"Did the doorman see anyone out of the ordinary?"

"Rudy saw no one. That is why we know the thief must have come up the back way."

Or paid off ol' Rudy to keep his mouth shut and look the other way. "I will need to question anyone with regular access to this apartment."

Elise shrugged, a graceful movement of supple shoulders. "As you wish. I doubt you will find any fingerprints or the like. Whoever did this knew precisely what he was doing."

"Nonetheless," I replied, "I will send over a crime-scene team to check things out."

The woman drew herself up and shot me a glacial look. "There will be no police in my home, pawing through my possessions. I will withdraw my crime report and deal with this in my own way if you insist on such a thing."

Maybe that would be for the best. She could hire a private investigator to run around on this wild-goose chase and take her money from her. Except the thought of some brownshoe taking this woman to the cleaners bothered me. Deep in my gut, I felt a low-level vibration of connection to this woman, a need to help her—even if the only thing missing was her marbles.

The door opened, interrupting my troubled thoughts, and Madame Trucot entered, carrying a sterling silver tea service that I'd swear was a Paul Revere original. I recognized the simple, clean lines from my college days in Boston. I took a sip of the tea Elise poured for me—no doubt it was the finest Darjeeling—but I'm a coffee kind of girl and all tea tastes like strained weeds to me.

"Would you consent to let me catalogue your collection someday?" I asked. "It really is remarkable. It should be listed in Interpol's database for safety's sake."

Elise glanced around the room and smiled gently. "These are only things, Analise. They are not important. Loyalty, friendship, family—those are the true treasures."

Her nonchalance about her collection startled me. "They may be only things, but they are valuable things. And based on the lack of security I saw on the way in, it's no surprise that you've been robbed. Frankly, I'm stunned that you haven't been before now."

Elise laughed. "I am not so defenseless as all that. I just don't like to look at cameras and sensors. They're here. They're just hidden."

They were hidden well, then. I hadn't seen any.

Elise continued, "Ask Rudy to show you the building's security system on the way out."

I nodded and made a note on my pad. My only note so far, in fact. I sighed. "Where was the stolen item kept?"

Elise's hand waved toward a corner behind me. "Over there."

An empty pedestal stood behind me, tucked into the corner next to a stunning, jewel-encrusted globe of the world, decorated with marvelous inlaid stones and a fine, irregular network of gold lines crisscrossing its entire surface.

Now we're talking. Must have been a three-dimensional object, a sculpture or pot perhaps that stood on that pedestal. Definitely not a painting, or anything wall-mounted, then. I looked more closely at the scale of the pedestal. Not wide or tall enough to support something large and still look proportionally correct. A small object, then. Maybe a foot tall, no more than two feet at the most. Probably slender, given the narrowness of the pedestal. A vase or a statue of some kind.

I asked Elise, "Can you tell me what it was made of? Its age, perhaps?"

The woman pursed her lips. Not going to talk, apparently. Damn. But then she surprised me by saying, "I took a vow of silence about it when it was given to me. If you can learn more of it yourself, then I suppose I could tell you if you're right or wrong without breaking my promise."

Who'd ever heard of a theft investigation where the police *guessed* and the victim told them whether they were right or wrong? I hoped to God none of the real cops at Interpol got wind of this or I'd never live it down!

I noticed that Elise was mumbling to herself again.

"…but I insist. She wouldn't believe me if I told her…it has to be you…I don't know how. Just show her. She's a smart girl."

Presumably, I was the smart girl in question. At the moment, however, my brain felt like oatmeal. Elise rejoined this space-time dimension and said firmly, "We will speak again when you have learned more. I am tired. It has been a long day."

And I was supposed to learn more *how?* On cue, the house-keeper came in to show me out. I was ever so politely getting tossed out of here.

"But I have more questions—" I started.

"The madame is tired," Madame Trucot said firmly.

Elise didn't look tired to me. She had a vitality about her that suggested she could party the night away and come home at dawn, fresh as a daisy. Yup, I was definitely getting thrown out. More confused than ever, I followed Madame Trucot back to the front door. The housekeeper pressed a small card into my hand that I vaguely registered had a phone number written on its back. I turned it over. The engraved card read simply, Mme. Elise Villecourt.

The heavy lion door swung closed behind me with a solid thunk. I stared around the black marble vestibule, my head spinning. I could just hear my report now. "Forgive me, Mr. President, but your friend is as crazy as a loon. She reports her own murder but clearly is not dead. She reports the theft of an item that doesn't technically exist. And as if that's not enough, she *talks back* to the voices in her head."

Not.

Now what the hell was I supposed to do?

Chapter 2

Robert Fraser slid the heavy backpack of books off his shoulders and set it on the stone floor with a solid thunk beside his motorcycle helmet. Letting his Scots roots show, he said, "Top o' the mornin' to ye, Lorraine. How goes it?"

The art department's blue-haired secretary and unofficial matriarch looked up from her desk. "You have a visitor. You'd better clean yourself up. Toot soo-weet."

Her bad French for "right away," liberally accented with the round vowels of Edinburgh, made him wince. "*I* have a visitor? Who is it?"

"Some old guy. Very mysterious. Came in the back door and disappeared into the chairman's office about twenty minutes ago. Professor McManus has been buzzing me to ask if you were in yet about every two minutes. Angus is in a fair tizzy over this gent, so he must be a personage with a purse, if you catch my meaning."

Angus McManus in a tizzy? The old geezer was usually

half-comatose these days. No retirement for that bloke, no sir. He'd die at his post, old Angus. The art history department he chaired at Edinburgh University was his life. Robert sighed. Sometimes he wondered if he was fated to end up the same way, shriveled and musty, hunched over tattered old books and half-assed papers from snotty graduate students.

"Go on in, luv, and rescue Angus before he has a stroke."

Robert sighed again. Schmoozing rich patrons—hell of a way to start the day. He dropped his black leather jacket on top of his rucksack, straightened his knitted tie and headed in to Angus's office. It was a spacious corner room with beautiful oak wainscoting on the walls and good light, although the books stacked absolutely everywhere ruined the sense of space entirely. Apparently, Angus didn't believe in that newfangled invention known as the bookshelf.

"Robert, my boy!" boomed a white-haired little gnome from behind a huge walnut desk that all but swallowed him.

Angus must've lost his hearing aids again. "Good morning, Professor McManus," Robert shouted as he wended his way between piles of books.

"Was just singing your praises. Come in. Come in. Sit."

Robert crossed through a shaft of dust-filled sunlight and headed for a chair in front of the desk. He sank down onto a humped leather seat so old and slippery he had to plant his feet firmly on the floor not to slide out of it.

"Professor Fraser, this is…errm, yes, well…a patron of the arts," Angus bellowed.

Robert nodded at the silver-haired man seated quietly beside Angus's desk. The man's face was hidden in shadow, but the hawk-nosed profile and strong jaw were visible. The guy's suit looked like Armani. A wealthy art collector, then. Looking for recommendations on a purchase perhaps?

"How d'you do?" Robert said.

"Fine, thank you," the man answered cordially enough. A

slight accent of the continent lurked behind the precise English, but its nationality eluded Robert. Too faint to identify. And the man didn't offer his name. Odd. The man just sat there, studying him.

"What can we do for you today?" Robert finally asked. He hated having to work at conversations like this.

"I need the provenance of an item traced. A work of art."

Ahh. That, he could handle. He nodded and said, "Then you've come to the right place. I teach both classes here at the university on tracing the history of artwork. Usually, it's a simple matter of accessing the Getty Museum's or Interpol's databases of registered works of art. Between the two of them, they maintain provenance histories on most of the valuable pieces of art in the world."

"This piece will not be listed with either," the man said with quiet certainty.

Robert kept his facial expression neutral. A stolen work, perhaps? Coming out of hiding after a long time? A Nazi piece? Maybe even a new find? An involuntary ripple of anticipation passed through him. He dreamed of unearthing a lost masterpiece someday. Aloud, he said, "If no provenance work has been done on a piece, the research requirements can be quite extensive. And expensive, I must add."

The shadowed gentleman waved a dismissive hand, and Robert saw that it was bony and heavily veined, mottled with age spots. The man was older than his profile gave away. "Price is no object," the stranger growled.

Well, then. Blokes usually wouldn't invest unlimited funds in tracing a work unless it was worth a great deal more than they were about to spend verifying its authenticity or ownership. He leaned forward in his seat. "Tell me about the piece."

"First, you must agree to trace it for me."

"You wish to pay the costs of the provenance search, then?"

The man didn't answer. Instead, he reached inside his suit to an interior breast pocket and pulled out a checkbook.

Robert did some fast math on how much money to ask for up front when this guy pulled out a pen and poised it over a blank check.

But the man surprised him by pushing the entire black leather checkbook across the desk to him. "That is a numbered Swiss bank account. It has fifty thousand dollars U.S. in it. If it runs out of money, it will be replenished. As I said, price is no object. Will you do the job for me?"

His palms itched to take the checkbook and get out of this jail. To hit the road once more in search of adventure and fortune. To toss off the yoke of classes and papers and the boredom of academia and do what he loved best. Chase treasure. On this guy's penny, no less.

But his last brush with the law slowed him down in accepting that checkbook. A year in prison will do that to a guy. Accessory to grand theft. Reduced sentence for testifying against the ringleaders, out early for good behavior and his police record sealed. But nonetheless, enough to still his hand at his side.

"Is it stolen?" he asked bluntly.

"Not by me," the man retorted.

Robert peered into the shadows. If only he could see the guy's eyes more clearly. No way to judge if the man was lying or not. He sounded genuinely indignant at the suggestion.

The man added, "All I want you to do is find out where it came from. Who has owned it before? Who made it?"

There was nothing illegal in that. Still, his internal radar was sending him red lights and warning Klaxons over this man and his secretive request.

"Who are you?" Robert asked.

"I am a patron of the arts. I wish for my identity to be kept secret. There are those who would try to kill me if they knew I was looking into the history of this object."

Object. Not a painting, then. Damned if his mind wasn't already spinning off on the possibilities of what the object was. Pre-Roman antiquities were hot right now. Lots of pottery and jewelry coming onto the market. Maybe something from the Far East. China was dumping a lot of old stuff onto the market at ridiculously inflated prices. The thing Westerners didn't seem to grasp is thousand-year-old trinkets are a dime a dozen in that ancient land. Just because it was old didn't make it valuable.

"If you take this job, you must not reveal my existence to anyone for any reason. You could, quite literally, cost me my life." The stranger surprised him by standing up abruptly and beginning to loosen his tie.

What the hell? The guy peeled back his crisply starched shirt to reveal sparse white chest hairs and dry, wrinkled skin. But that wasn't what captured Robert's attention. Rather, it was the fist-sized scar, angry red and nastily puckered directly over the old man's heart.

"This is what happened the last time my enemies caught up with me. You must promise to keep your silence about me."

Robert blinked. That was a bullet wound or he was the Easter Bunny! "Am I going to be in danger if I take this job?"

The man finished buttoning his shirt and adjusting his tie. He sat down, his face disappearing into the shadows once more. "Would it matter if you are?"

Hullo. How did this guy know that about him? Robert *did* love the rush that came with risk. But ever since he'd come to Edinburgh University, he'd been doing his damnedest to suppress it. Either the man was phenomenally perceptive or he'd done his homework on Robert Fraser. Either way, the adrenaline junkie in Robert was aroused. Hungry. Demanding.

Down, Tonto. We're not doing anything stupid anymore.

"How will I communicate my findings to you?" Robert asked. Had he just said that? Was he actually considering taking this job? A surge of adrenaline hit him almost as hard as an orgasm. Damn, the rush felt good. Had he really let himself go that dead inside for the last couple years? Somewhere, buried deep beneath the sexual thrill, was the tiny voice of his common sense telling him to get up and walk out of here.

"All in good time. First, you must accept the job. On my terms."

Robert stared at the man. Hesitated a few more seconds. *Aww, what the hell.*

He reached out and took the checkbook. The eel skin was cool and smooth beneath his fingertips. "What am I looking for?"

I looked around the alley and did my best not to wrinkle my nose. Sewage ran along the curb and a few pieces of paper skipped lazily across the uneven cobblestones. That creepy feeling was back from last night. Like I was being watched. I'm not the type to go in for paranoia, but I had to admit I'd been having feelings that I was being watched a lot in the last twenty-four hours.

René the Snitch was known to sleep in this alley, behind a gay bar called *Le Jeu d'Amour*. The Game of Love. René spent his days going through the club's trash, drinking the last drops from wine and beer bottles and scrounging food from the *Joue*'s Dumpster. Hard to believe that he'd been one of the premier art thieves in Europe in his day. If tales of his exploits were even half-true, he ought to be enjoying his old age in style, not lying in a filthy alley waiting to die.

I spied a pile of denim and black wool in front of me. That was my snitch. Damn. Passed out early today. It was barely midafternoon. I walked over and nudged him with the toe of my shoe. "René. Wake up. It's me, Ana."

An incoherent mumble is all I got. I poked his ribs a little harder.

"Stop tha'," he whined, batting at my shoe and burying his face deeper in his coat.

"Get up. I'm not going away. I need to talk. I'll pay." Assuming he was in any condition to answer questions.

An offer of cash always got him. He struggled to a seated position and stared up at me blearily. "Ahh. The toy cop. Whaddiya want, Anabelle?"

I didn't bother to correct him. He always called me that. "Let's go somewhere. Get a bite to eat. Some coffee." Which was to say, I wanted to sober him up before I questioned him.

"No coffee. Gin."

"No gin. Coffee. Take it or leave it," I retorted.

"And supper?"

"And supper."

"Agreed." He stood up, wobbling only a little. Good. Not so drunk, then.

I led him down the alley and turned into the first café we came across. The head waiter glared at René and puffed himself up preparatory to pitching a fit and tossing my companion out on his skinny behind. I did *not* need the hassle of a temperamental Frenchman today. I yanked my Interpol badge out of my coat pocket and flashed it at the waiter, along with an "I dare you" glare.

The guy deflated and seated us in the darkest corner he had. René ate a large steak, his baked potato, and mine, a salad and an entire baguette of bread before he finally slowed down. I ordered him a sandwich, and waited until he was partway through it before I leaned forward.

"Tell me, René, have you heard any good rumors recently?"

"What kinds of rumors?" he mumbled around a mouthful of sandwich.

"About a theft. Yesterday afternoon. A small object."

"Where?"

"In the Ninth arrondissement, off the rue de Bassano."

He tried to whistle between his teeth and only succeeded in spewing bits of lettuce and turkey at me. "High-rent district," he commented. "Lots of Impressionist masters hanging on those walls."

The guy actually was reasonably intelligent when he wasn't plastered. "I think this was a statue or a pot. It stood on a small pedestal."

"You don't know what was stolen?" he asked in surprise.

I squirmed uncomfortably. "I'm the one asking the questions. Have you heard any rumors?"

"Ahh. Not going to tell, are you? Waiting to see if my sources are right? Good plan. Not bad for a girl."

I rolled my eyes and didn't bother to rise to the bait.

He leaned back and signaled the waiter, who came over reluctantly. "A double piece of that apple tart I saw in the window when we came in. And a spot of—" René looked over at me guiltily "—coffee," he finished lamely.

"So?" I prompted.

"No, cherie, I haven't gotten wind of any such thing. I shall, without fail, hear of it when word does hit the street, however."

I didn't ask how he always managed to know the latest happenings in the art theft community in spite of his decrepitude. He just did. And, in return for a hot meal and twenty euros, he'd tell me. He'd figured out long ago that I wasn't really a cop, despite my employer. He seemed to think it was a grand joke to talk to me when he steadfastly refused to speak to the Paris police. In return, I didn't turn him in to those same police for some of the things he told me.

"Thank you, René," I answered him, "I am confident in your ability to find out what I need."

I sat back and watched him savor the apple tart as if it were his last meal. The guy knew how to take pleasure in the small things in life. "How did you end up like this?" I asked him abruptly. He looked up, startled. Never before had either one of us introduced anything personal into our conversations.

He shrugged. "Money, it comes. It goes."

"Did you drink away your fortune?" I pressed.

A faraway look came to his eyes. "*Mais, non.* It was a woman. Sweet Bernadette. She was worth every *sou.* I would do it again. The memory of her smile still warms me at night. Her eyes, they sparkled like the stars. Her breasts—"

"I get the point," I interrupted. "Why didn't you go back into the trade when you got low on cash?" This was a rare peek for me into the other side of the art world.

"I lost the use of my hands."

I glanced down at them, startled. He seemed to be handling a fork just fine.

He shrugged. "I was electrocuted on my last job and the nerves in my fingertips are gone. I lost the touch."

"I suppose the workman's compensation in your line of work isn't that hot," I commented dryly.

He laughed heartily. "I like you, Anabelle. I will find out what I can about your theft." He added wistfully, "You know, if it's dark enough and you tilt your head just so, you look a little like my Bernadette."

I smiled gently. What a sad little man. "Thank you," I said quietly. On impulse, I reached out across the table and squeezed his hand. He looked startled as much at the gesture coming from me as at the human contact. I suppose being touched is something a filthy, homeless old man doesn't get a lot of.

I delivered him back to his alley, and on impulse again, I hugged him. And damned if those weren't tears in his eyes as I turned away from him.

The piercing sympathy I felt for him came as a surprise. Somewhere along the way, I'd gotten hard. Cynical. I should work at being a little softer. A little more feminine. Maybe do something about my hair and clothes. Maybe meditate or something to release my pent-up anger.

I hailed a taxi to take me home, and the driver was rude enough to snap me out of the moment. I didn't know whether to curse him or thank him.

When I got out of the cab, thoroughly exasperated, I caught the faintest flash of…something…out of the corner of my eye across the street. It wasn't so much the sight of a tall figure wearing too heavy a coat for this fall evening as it was the furtiveness with which the guy ducked into an alley and out of sight that did it. Why would anybody follow me? If you look in the dictionary, a picture of my life is under the listing for *boring*. Heck, maybe a picture of me is in there under the listing *paranoid female,* too. I shook off the willies and went into my building.

My third floor walk-up faced the street, and I went immediately to the tall French windows in the living room and had a peek outside. I watched for several minutes, and there was no sign of anyone remotely suspicious out there. Man, I needed a vacation.

I headed for my desk on the other side of the room. The message light was blinking on my answering machine. Crud. I'd turned off my cell phone during dinner with René, and I'd forgotten to turn it back on. I hit the play button. Littmann. Twice. Jacked up enough to sound like the schizophrenic poodle he resembled with his big, sharp nose and frizzy halo of hair. Wanting a progress report.

I snorted. Everywhere I turned on this nonexistent case, I ran into dead ends. I wasn't even sure at this point that there was a theft. I spent the remainder of the evening working my Internet contacts, which isn't a bad way to do that sort of business. Today's breed of art thief is up to speed on the latest computer and electronic gear. But then, they have to be to beat the high-tech security systems out there. Most of my snitches are techno geeks I've never met. By my talking to them over the Internet, they stay entirely anonymous and are frequently much more willing to talk because of it. Yup, poor old René's time was past on many levels.

After four hours hunched over the keyboard and slurping down copious amounts of coffee, I was still exactly nowhere. I shoved back from my desk in disgust. Enough. Tomorrow morning I would tell Littmann and St. Germain that Elise Villecourt was a nutball and there was no crime. They'd just have to suck up the heat from the president's office.

The thief caressed the sweet, almost childlike face of the woman in the statue. It occurred to him that if he stared at her for a while, he could almost imagine that she began to smile back. If he'd have seen this statue on the black market, he'd never have guessed its true worth. It was pretty enough and nicely executed for its time period. At a glance, he'd peg it for a medium-value piece of interest only to a collector of Madonna statues.

But that was before a quiet rumor reached his ears about the real reason this piece was so highly sought after. Hell, if the whispers were true, maybe he oughta keep her for himself. He could use a little of the mojo this lady supposedly gave her owners—perfect health and long life. Really long.

Yeah, right. He snorted. It was all rumors and lies to push up the price, no doubt. No statue could make its owner immortal.

His cell phone rang. The disposable one his client had given him especially for this heist. It had a lot of minutes on it, but then, the guy who'd hired him was rolling in dough. Hard to believe he was going to collect a million bucks for stealing this little lady. But hey, if some obsessed bastard had to have her for himself, he was all about taking the dough.

If that whole long-life business were real, it would be a hell of a choice. Keep the statue and live an extra fifty or more years or take the million dollars and live a normal length life. How did a guy choose one or the other?

He answered his phone gruffly. "Yeah?"

"Do you have it?"

The client. Not long on niceties. "Yeah, I got it."

"Excellent. Bring it to the prearranged location immediately. A man will be waiting for you."

"Yeah, well, here's the thing. I mean, it was a pain in the ass to get this hunk of wood. You shoulda seen the electronic crap I had to wade through. I'm thinking maybe a million bucks isn't…uh…fair compensation for all the trouble I went to."

Silence from the other end of the line. It stretched out long enough that he started getting fidgety. He babbled, "I mean, if you got a million bucks to throw away on some old statue, then another couple hundred thousand ain't gonna put you out none. I'm thinking another fifty percent. A million five and we call it good."

More silence.

"She's real pretty. Kinda smiles back at ya," he wheedled.

The client's voice, when it finally came, was practically a whisper. Like the guy didn't want whoever was in the next room to hear him—or like he was really, really pissed off. "You bring that statue to the meeting place. Now. You take your million dollars and count yourself lucky to be alive. You hear me? You fuck this up and you'll wish all I did was kill you."

The line went dead in his ear. Goddamn rich people. Stingier than folks without two coins to rub together. Another half million in return for near immortality was nothing. Bastard. He could sit and stew in his threats.

Meeting place, schmeeting place. Let the bastard wait. The client would come around. He'd fork over the dough. Maybe next time they talked he'd ask for two million from the rich prick. Yeah. That was good. Every time the bastard refused to pay, the price would go up some more. Hell, if the client was stubborn enough, he might have the statue long enough to get the mojo from it and pocket enough cash to live on for a couple hundred years.

He kicked aside a pile of porn magazines and propped his feet up on the scarred coffee table. He picked up the remote and pointed it at the TV. And ignored the client's phone when it rang again an hour later.

I went to bed, but I had trouble falling asleep. Too much caffeine, dammit. I tossed and turned, my sheets hot and wrinkled. Twice I nearly got to sleep when the rising and falling wail of a siren passing by outside wrenched me back to full consciousness. People weren't kidding when they called Paris the city that never sleeps. And it was about to turn me into the art historian who never slept, either.

Sometime around 2:00 a.m., the cars finally stopped driving past, the television downstairs went off, and no more police cars came screaming by my window. My eyes gritty and my body aching with fatigue, I finally, thankfully, drifted off to sleep.

Torches flickered, throwing off more smoke than light. I squinted into the shadows and made out that I was in a lavish room, its stone walls covered with huge, brilliantly colored tapestries. An intricately carved table stood to my left, a gold-and-jewel-encrusted chest resting upon its greasy surface next to a small religious statue. Two high-backed wooden chairs stood against the wall at either end of the table. A strangely proportioned bed stood on the opposite wall. Mounded high with red velvet and elaborately embroidered pillows, it was only about three-quarters length and abnormally high off the ground. Wooden steps led up to it, in fact. More red velvet curtains were pulled back beside the headboard, which stood a good eight feet high and was carved and gilded into a replica of a giant crown.

It smelled in here. Bad. Like an outhouse. With a disturbing overlay of something floral and cloyingly sweet along the lines of roses mixed with cinnamon. The combination nudged my stomach well down the road to nausea.

A young woman stood across the room, staring out the diamond panes of a leaded glass window. Her red velvet dress was Elizabethan—wide skirt, narrow waist, elaborate starched collar that forced her chin up to a haughty angle. Her hair was red, her skin pasty, damp with a thin film of perspiration, as if she had a fever or was in distress of some kind. She might have been a statue except for her hand, which clenched and unclenched spasmodically in the folds of the red velvet drapes hanging beside her. She looked vaguely familiar, but I couldn't place her.

It was quiet. Really quiet. No cars. No television, no radio. Not even birds chirping. It was the dead silence of a tomb. And it was cold. See-your-breath cold. The woman's nose and fingertips were red with it.

Where was I? Or more to the point, when? The room could be anything from late thirteenth century to early seventeenth. I'd guess mid-sixteenth century from the woman's garb.

A door squeaked open on iron hinges behind me, loud in the silence. The woman whipped around and her chin notched up even higher. But then she seemed to recognize the intruder and her stiff posture wilted. "Where have you been, Jane? I need you."

A young woman, dressed well but not opulently in a black dress, hurried over to her. The newcomer dropped a small curtsey and then flung her arms around the redhead. "Oh, my lady, how do you bear it?"

"I bear it because I must," came the muffled reply.

Jane cried, "There is still time. The executioner has yet to climb the scaffold."

The first woman shot a steely look over Jane's shoulder

in my general direction, and her back went stiff. Jane pulled away from her as the redhead snapped, "Have his support-ers bribed you to sway my mind?"

As if she realized she'd made some sort of grave mistake, the one called Jane fell to her knees. "Never, Your Highness. You know my only loyalty is to you. Only to you. I only thought of your heart. Condemning your lover to death—"

She answered sharply, "I do not have the luxury of a heart, Jane. I am a queen before I am a woman. He plotted with the Papists, and the penalty is death." She paused, then added in an aching whisper, "I had no choice."

Abruptly I knew the redhead. Elizabeth I, Queen of England.

"The smell of blood does not agree with me. Fetch my pomander, Jane. It is time."

Jane suppressed a sob and opened a heavily carved trunk. She emerged with an orange stuck all over with cloves. The two women hastened toward the door. Jane stepped out, and Elizabeth paused for a moment. I watched her draw a shaky breath and release it slowly. In that instant, she looked like a lost little girl. Hurt. Vulnerable. Betrayed.

I thought that when she left, the room would dissipate, but it did not. In a few moments, a ruckus erupted outside the window. It sounded like hundreds of people out there jeering, whistling and shouting insults. As abruptly as the noise had started, it stopped. The silence drew out, like pain being stretched to the point of unbearability.

And then I heard a dull thud. Reminded me of a sledge-hammer hitting a log.

The crowd erupted again, screams mingling with the cheers and jeers this time in a macabre chorus. I heard a voice in the crowd shout, "Coins for the axeman!"

The axeman? The axeman? I'd just heard someone being beheaded?

Oh. My. God.

I lurched awake, startled to find myself sitting upright in bed already. My hands shook as I pushed my tangled hair back. What a godawful dream! That heavy, wooden thud still rang in my ears and creeping horror crawled up my spine.

I fell back to the mattress. Jeez, I felt like hell. As if I'd gotten about ten minutes' sleep all night. I cracked one eye open to peer at the clock—6:51 a.m. My alarm was set to go off at seven. No time to close my eyes and sleep off that bizarre dream. Nope, it was time to wake up, go to work, and ruin my—to date—undistinguished career. Oh, joy.

I staggered into my bathroom, which was approximately the size of a telephone booth. I pulled the chain on the overhead tank to flush the toilet and leaned over the sink, propping my hands on the cool porcelain. God, I was exhausted. It was as if that strangely real dream had totally drained me. I couldn't recall experiencing one that vivid before. I'm the kind of person who closes my eyes, goes comatose and wakes up the next day. Nothing fancy.

But this dream wouldn't leave me. I could still see that room, down to the dust between the paving stones. I'd had the distinct feeling I was there seeking something. What I'd have loved to seek right then was another couple hours of sleep.

I reached for my toothbrush and squeezed out some toothpaste. I stuck it in my mouth and let the rush of overpowering mint wake me up a bit. I looked up at myself in the mirror.

And lurched violently.

In the glass, just over my right shoulder, was a vague image of a woman and the top of her starched and pleated Elizabethan accordian collar.

Chapter 3

I whirled around, brandishing my foamy toothbrush like a weapon. The dingy, tiled wall of my bathroom stared back at me. She was gone. *What in the bloody hell was that?*

For all the world, that had looked like a ghost.

Yeah, right.

Not.

I turned around slowly, almost afraid to see what was behind me in that mirror. Reluctantly, I looked at it. Only my own wary eyes stared back.

I scowled at myself. Clearly, I had ingested way too much caffeine before I went to bed last night. But, God almighty, that transparent gray image had looked real—just like the woman in my dream.

The woman called Jane in my dream. Of course.

I breathed a huge sigh of relief. I had only been half-awake when I came in here to brush my teeth. Some part of my mind had still been stuck back in that Elizabethan room. I'd imagined the face in my mirror. It was nothing more than a leftover image from my wild dream. Sheesh!

Note to self: lay off the coffee in the evening.

Without further incident, I managed to get dressed in my usual brown tweed suit, cut too large and boxy. Part of my post–Jean-Michel, man-repelling wardrobe. I walked to work to help clear my head, and thankfully, no random afterimages of Jane popped up in any storefronts. I was more rattled by the dim image of that face in my mirror than I liked to admit. Maybe I ought to get around to taking that vacation I'd been talking about for the last, oh, four years.

All that staring in store windows was probably why I spotted the guy trailing along behind me. He was actually very good. The tail, I mean. Subtle. Blended in with the surroundings seamlessly. And I was not imagining this. I've had *some* police training, after all. Now why was somebody watching me? The timing made it patently obvious that it had to do with Elise Villecourt. Okay, so maybe the woman actually did have real enemies. But that didn't make her any less crazy.

The thing about Paris is that everybody walks everywhere. Because of that, it's easy to conclude that someone is following you, when perhaps they just happen to be walking in the same direction you are. Besides, it was a bright, sunny morning and the streets were crowded. I felt perfectly safe out here. No need to confront the guy. I memorized his face. If he showed up behind me again, then I'd take him seriously.

I walked into the Préfecture de Police, across the square from Notre Dame Cathedral, at 8:20 a.m. My meeting with St. Germain and Littmann was at 9:00 a.m. I took a few minutes to check the police blotters citywide for any stolen statues or pottery turning up. Nada. No e-mail messages from any of my Internet informants, either. Nobody had come up with even a hint of a stolen object overnight. Damn.

Ten minutes before nine, a detective stopped by the spare

computer workstation I was sitting at. "They're here," he said shortly. "Conference room five-oh-four."

Oh, Lord. My two bosses were so nervous they'd shown up early—a minor miracle for Frenchmen, who were more inclined to see meeting times as guidelines rather than deadlines.

I sighed. Time to face the music.

Carl Montrose laid his briefcase on the polished mahogany conference table and opened the black leather attaché. He pulled out his briefing notes, although he had the grim details completely memorized this morning. A quick hand through his short, graying hair to make sure it was in place, a brush of his suit's shoulders for nonexistent lint, and he was ready. Not a moment too soon, either.

The door at the end of the table opened, and his boss walked in. Alone. The significance of that was not lost on Montrose. The matter he was here to discuss today was of utmost secrecy and importance to the French republic.

Pierre Dupont, president of France, said gravely, "Good morning, Carl. I trust you have good news for me."

"I'm sorry, but the news is not good. Four more power outages occurred simultaneously last night."

"Four?" Dupont exclaimed. He swore violently.

Carl waited out the outburst and then answered, "That is correct."

The electrical power outages had started small a few weeks ago, happening in remote locations around France, not long after the freak earthquake in Paris. Nothing of any real concern. But then they started getting larger and more frequent. At that point, a conspiracy theory started circulating quietly within the highest levels of the French government. And it was then that Dupont pulled strings to put the lid on any press coverage of the incidents. He'd claimed there was no need to unduly panic the people of France by exaggerated reports of the nation's power grid being on the brink of collapse.

Except more and more, it looked as if that was exactly the case.

To complicate matters, a lone voice from outside the government—the president's old friend, Elise Villecourt—had predicted exactly this sort of attack weeks before it began. And now someone was trying to kill her. Which made her description of this as an *attack* all the more credible. Problem was, she also claimed the source of power for these attacks was...supernatural. That was the only reason the French army wasn't camped out at every power transformer station in the country right now.

Montrose reviewed the events of the weekend quickly for Dupont. "The Interpol agent Madame Villecourt asked for is on the case as of Saturday evening. Agent Reisner spent Sunday morning at home, working on her computer. Late yesterday afternoon, Agent Reisner went to the Latin Quarter and sought out a rather disreputable fellow whom I'd guess is one of her informants. They ate together. She spent last evening on the computer, as well."

"Any progress?"

"We will know shortly. She is due to brief St. Germain in—" he glanced down at his watch "—three minutes."

Dupont nodded. "Update me after that meeting. I've left instructions with my secretary that you are to be allowed to interrupt me no matter what if you have news to report. Understood?"

Montrose nodded crisply. He might worry that his boss was losing his mind for taking Elise Villecourt's claim seriously, except he'd talked to the woman himself, and she was arguably one of the sanest people he'd ever met. It was very difficult to discount her claims. Dupont believed her without reservation. But then, she'd saved Dupont's life on multiple occasions during World War Two. He was devoted to her.

Montrose reached for his notes with the intent to put them back in his briefcase when a door behind him opened. Dupont's secretary hustled into the room. Not good. The president took a single sheet of paper and began to read it. Looked like a fax.

Dupont looked up, his face grim. "We have a major transformer failure. Bordeaux region. Stopped the TGV."

Montrose winced. The *Train à Grande Vitesse,* high-speed train, was a huge source of national pride for the French people. No way would Dupont be able to keep it out of the news that the train had stopped without electricity to power it. "How big a region is affected this time?" he asked in resignation as he pinched the bridge of his nose. If and when word of these power problems became public, Dupont's distinguished forty-year career in public service would be in grave jeopardy of going up in smoke.

Dupont continued heavily, "Largest so far. Fifty thousand people affected."

Carl commented, "Each power failure is getting bigger, just like Madame Villecourt said they would." He traded looks with Dupont as they simultaneously took the next leap of logic. Elise Villecourt also said the entire French power grid would be destroyed before this was all said and done.

"Talk to her, Carl," Dupont said urgently. "Ask Elise if there's anything at all we can do to prevent this disaster."

"I already have, sir. Several times. All she ever says is to send her Ana Reisner. Ana is the key."

I followed the policeman quickly up four flights of stairs and down a corridor to the conference room in question. The long hall allowed me to catch my breath after all those stairs. Still, with each step my feet felt heavier. I had no choice but to tell the unvarnished truth. No choice at all.

We all have choices, Ana, a voice whispered in my ear on

a cool breath of air against my earlobe. I whipped my head around to see who was getting fresh with me. Nobody there. Jeez! I'm not touching any more coffee for a month!

The cop with me gave me a funny look as he held the door for me. That's one nice thing I can say about Frenchmen. Chivalry is not dead over here. I stepped inside, and was startled to see only two men in the room. Armande St. Germain and François Littmann. I'd naturally assumed they would bring along a posse of flunkies to witness my humiliation…and to cover their own asses, which were flapping in the wind right alongside mine.

"Ana, there you are!" François twittered.

Oh, boy. In full poodle mode this morning. "Hello, sir," I replied grimly.

"What have you got for us?" St. Germain blurted.

Yowza. Couldn't even wait long enough to say hello. Poor guy must have someone from Dupont's office breathing fire down his shorts. Sometimes I'm reminded that being a peon isn't such a bad deal.

I shook my head. No sense beating around the bush. "The President's friend is a certified lunatic. She reported her own murder to me. Something—which she won't describe to me, by the way—was stolen from her on Saturday, and she's convinced that without it she's going to die any day. She's also convinced the thief knew this and took the alleged item specifically to kill her. She won't allow a crime-scene team into her home, but wants Interpol, or more specifically me, to conduct a full-blown investigation into this theft and murder, even though she knows I'm not actually a police officer."

The two men stared at me, their jaws hanging slack. Good. I wasn't crazy to have reacted to this thing the way I had. They thought it was as nuts as I did.

St. Germain collected himself enough to start swearing,

and within a few seconds, Littmann was right there with him. After an impressive demonstration of words that didn't make it into my high school French dictionary, their attention swung back to me.

"What do you suggest we do now, Agent Reisner?" St. Germain demanded.

I took a deep breath. "Someone has to tell the president that this is a wild-goose chase." Like, oh, *him*.

Panic flitted across the guy's face. He huffed and he puffed, and opened his mouth to blow me down when the cancan song erupted from his suit. The cancan? Who'd have guessed the old guy would go for something so bawdy for his cell phone ring? St. Germain dug out his phone, scowling. But even more panic leaped in his eyes when he looked at his caller ID. "St. Germain here," he answered smartly.

He summarized my just completed briefing. And then listened for a long time. Long enough for whomever was at the other end of the phone to deliver quite a speech. Then, St. Germain said, "Are you certain? There's practically nothing to go on. Yes, sir. I understand, sir. Of course. We will do our best—" a short pause "—right. Rather, Agent Reisner will do her best."

Why did the mention of my name make my skin crawl?

St. Germain closed his phone and stowed it in his breast pocket once more. Then he announced ponderously, "That was the president's personal assistant. He reiterates that it is of utmost importance for you to proceed on this case with all possible haste, Agent Reisner."

I scowled. "What? Is it a matter of life and death that this crazy old lady be humored by me personally?"

St. Germain answered slowly, "Apparently, it is."

I blinked. The guy sounded dead serious.

"You've got to be kidding," I muttered.

"Dupont's man said this is a matter of national security.

He needs you personally to solve Madame Villecourt's theft and prevent her murder with utmost speed. She must not die."

"Good grief! The president buys into her nutty claims, too?" Dupont could forget getting my vote anytime soon. Of course, I'm not a French citizen and can't vote over here. Nonetheless, good grief!

St. Germain announced, "I've been ordered to put all of Interpol's resources at your disposal."

I smiled brightly. "Great! Then you can put a team of actual criminal investigators on this insanity and I can go back to cataloguing paintings."

"Dupont's man also made it crystal clear that you are to be the only agent to investigate this case."

"That's absurd!" I exclaimed.

He nodded, unmoved by my outburst. "It is thus at Madame Villecourt's express insistence. And apparently, what Elise Villecourt wants, Elise Villecourt gets."

Who *was* this woman? What hold did she have on Pierre Dupont? My frustration at that moment was boundless. What the hell was I supposed to do next? I parroted St. Germain's earlier question back at him. "Any suggestions as to how I proceed?"

He answered earnestly, "Interview the household staff. Find out what they know. Most thefts of this sort are inside jobs."

Duh. That was Police Investigation 101. When a single piece of art—not apparently valuable, but of great intrinsic value—is stolen, always look to the hired help and family friends.

"Why me?" I muttered.

Both of my bosses shrugged, imminently Gallic shoulder lifts that communicated both *I don't know* and *I could care less* all in one movement. Aloud, St. Germain said, "Why don't you ask the lady that?"

I nodded resolutely. "I will." *Again*. And maybe this time I'd get a straight answer.

Littmann jumped in, all but wringing his hands. "But be…tactful…about it, will you? We don't want to anger this woman. Her connections are, well…"

Yes, her connections went to the very highest level of a government that was convinced the woman *wasn't* crazy. Before the end of this case, I had a feeling I might be, though.

When I left the building, I didn't spot the tail again. Maybe I'd imagined the guy was following me, or maybe he'd been switched out for somebody better. Either way, I wasn't worried. I had nothing to hide. If someone wanted to waste his time following me, that was his business.

Rudy answered the door when I rang at Madame Ville-court's building. In the harsh light of day, he looked older than I remembered, maybe in his early sixties. He moved with a spring in his step, though, and a twinkle in his eye.

"Just the man I want to talk to," I said.

"Wantin' to see the security setup for the building, are you?" he asked.

"Exactly." Not at all what I'd had in mind, but it worked as a way to spend time with him and engage in casual con-versation. The good-cop interview technique, as it were. I would chat him up for a while, then work my way around to asking where he'd been on Saturday afternoon.

Except he beat me to the punch. He took me into a room just off the small lobby crammed with the fanciest surveil-lance setup I'd ever seen, with the exception maybe of the Louvre's. Rudy immediately began walking me through exactly how the equipment had been configured on Saturday afternoon prior to the theft. The guy was thorough. And at the end of his recitation, which included the fact that he'd been sitting at this very console at the time of the theft, my gut reaction was that no way had this guy been the thief.

That didn't mean he hadn't been the inside man on the job, of course. But you had to be there in person to hear the outrage in his voice at a theft on his watch, the guilt over letting down Madame Villecourt and the burning desire to help me catch whoever committed this crime. I'm not one of those people who goes around listening to my intuitions much. I believe in carefully gathering all the facts and making logical, sensible decisions. Nonetheless, my intuition shouted that Rudy didn't have anything to do with the theft.

One thing I did learn from him, though, was whoever did steal the thingamabob was a professional thief of the highest caliber. To have overcome this security system was quite an accomplishment. Bypassing the cameras alone must've been incredibly difficult. Not once did the thief show up on any of the surveillance tapes.

On the way out, I happened to ask Rudy, "So, how long have you known Madame Villecourt?"

His eyes did that thing where they glaze over and look into the past. "Let's see. Over sixty years."

Sixty? How old was this guy? Seventy-five? Man, I had to start drinking the water over here on the left bank. These people were better preserved for their ages than anyone I'd ever met before. "How old are you?" I asked.

"Sixty-seven."

"You've known her since you were children?"

Rudy shrugged. "I was a very little boy. But it was during the war. I have strong memories of that time, you know. One never forgets living through a war, no matter how young you are."

How true.

He continued, "Madame Elise, she saved my father's life at least three times. She stayed at our house once. Hid in the cellar for two days."

"Who was she hiding from?" I suspected I knew the answer to that one, though.

"The Nazis, of course."

"She worked for the Resistance during World War Two?" I asked.

He laughed. "Oh, no. She worked for the Nazis."

Huh? An ex-Nazi was a close friend of the French president?

Rudy laughed at my expression of surprise. "She was a spy. A double agent. She told the Resistance when and where the Nazis were going to raid Resistance targets. You cannot imagine the number of lives she saved. Hundreds. Thousands, perhaps. The risks she took—"

The guy actually choked up.

"—she is one of the great heroes of the war. I owe her everything. My life. My family's lives. This job. She has always been there for me." He dashed a tear from his cheek. "And I shall be there for her no matter what. You let me know if you need anything done to help her, Mademoiselle Reisner." He added significantly, *"Anything."*

I think the guy had just offered to bump off someone for me. I nodded my understanding. "I'll keep that in mind, Rudy. And thank you."

Okay. So this guy was fanatically loyal to Madame Villecourt. My gut was even more certain he had nothing to do with the theft. But I was more intrigued than ever with the woman upstairs.

My computer search on her the day before turned up the amount of her annual taxes—a staggering sum. Somewhere along the way, Elise Villecourt had become an extremely wealthy woman. She used a startlingly large chunk of her wealth to fund charities that helped mothers and children. She moved in the highest circles of European society. She was rarely photographed and managed to stay almost entirely out of the press. And all references to her whatsoever stopped entirely in 1942. It was if, prior to that, she'd never existed.

And given the revelation that she'd worked with the French Resistance, maybe she didn't exist prior to that. Most of the hardcore Resistance fighters had taken false names during the war to protect their families from Nazi reprisals. Many of them kept those identities after the war. They'd lost everything and everyone they loved, anyway. Why not start a new life altogether?

Rudy pressed the elevator button for the fifth floor and I rode up in silence. Even after six decades, the scars of World War Two were fresh in this part of the world.

Madame Trucot was waiting for me at the front door this time. No need to embarrass myself over the doorbell—which I had been planning on using, by the way. I'd been hoping to have a conversation with Madame Trucot alone, but the woman immediately showed me into the library.

Elise Villecourt stood up when I entered the room. "*Bonjour,* dear Ana. And how are you today?" she asked me warmly.

"I'm fine, thank you." It was hard not to get sucked into this woman's charm. But I was here today to get answers, and I was prepared to play hardball to get them. "Madame Villecourt, either you give me some concrete information to work with, or I'm terminating this investigation."

Chapter 4

Robert sat down at his computer. The standard method for tracing provenance on an object was to start with the current owner and trace the sale, gift or inheritance he or she got it by. Then after identifying the previous possessor, working backward to how that person got it, and so on. Few pieces of art were so famous that their whereabouts were a matter of public record in and of themselves. It was all about tracing the owners.

Problem was, he had no idea who owned the little wooden statue now. He had no starting point. His client had pointedly not given him a current location of the statue. Robert shrugged. And that's why the guy had put fifty grand in a bank account for him. This search didn't promise to be easy.

He started in the logical first place. The Getty Museum index of art. He checked out every hit for a wooden Madonna statue in the medieval style, but none of the photos matched the picture taped to the corner of his computer monitor. He tried the Cloisters and Cluny Museum indexes next. As two of the leading medieval museums in the world, maybe they had a record of his piece. It looked to be a finely crafted statue. And given that someone was willing to pay 50 Gs to learn about it, he had to believe it was authentic.

No luck.

He sat back and stared at his screen. What the hell. He typed in Edinburgh University's password to the Interpol database of stolen cultural property. It loaded for several seconds. He typed in a description of his statue. Another wait. His pulse started to pound. He couldn't afford to get tangled up in any way with another art theft. As the seconds ticked away, his gut turned to water. And then, finally, thankfully, *no hit*.

He typed in a description of the Madonna statue to a couple general Internet search engines and started sorting through the hits he got. After about a hundred mind-numbing references from various religious sites, he clicked on yet another link and sat up straight in surprise.

It was a newspaper photo spread of an art exhibition at the Cluny Museum last month of various images of the Black Madonna. The accompanying article had little to say about Black Madonnas in general, but it was a starting place.

His statue wasn't actually black. It was carved from a dark wood, possibly mahogany or cherry, that had aged with time to a deep, sable brown. At a glance in the right light it might appear black, though. Maybe someone at the Cluny could take a look at his picture and tell him more. His area of greatest knowledge was actually paintings by seventeenth- and eighteenth-century masters. He couldn't help but know a little about medieval art, living in Scotland as he did, but he was by no means an expert on the subject.

He picked up the phone. "Lorraine, Robert Fraser here. I need to go to Paris for a few days. Could you arrange for somone to cover my graduate seminar tomorrow and Thursday?"

The secretary, bless her, said she'd take care of it.

He threw some clothes and gear in a leather satchel and grabbed his motorcycle helmet. Given that fat bank account he could fly from Edinburgh to Paris, but he'd rather ride his Harley. The bike was the lone holdout from his prelaw-abiding days. It felt right as he set out on this adventure to take the old girl with him. He was way overdue for a road trip on Penny. She was a tricked out, 4-cylinder, split-exhaust, 1,500cc Harley-Davidson chopper he'd rebuilt and customized by hand, and she'd eluded more than one Scotland Yarder in her day.

He stepped on the kick-starter and reveled in Penny's powerful rumble between his knees. Oh, yes. Time for a road trip indeed.

Elise gestured me into a chair and I reluctantly sank into it. I would've preferred to remain standing, in a position of power, but my ingrained respect for my elders prevented me from ignoring her waved hand. Nonetheless, I resolved to stay strong. In charge of this conversation.

"Madame Villecourt—" I began.

"I insist you call me Elise," she interjected gently.

Fine. "Elise," I repeated, "I have spent all weekend researching your theft, and without more information I am simply not going to be able to help you. You *must* tell me exactly what was stolen and what it looks like."

Elise leaned back in her chair, studying me closely. Surely it can't have surprised her that I was here, asking this question. "You must understand, my dear," she began, "I took a vow of silence. A most solemn vow. A vow with untold consequences if I should ever break it."

"What sort of consequences?"

A shudder passed over her, visible even from where I sat. "I do not even like to think of it."

Curiosity momentarily diverted me. *Be strong, dammit. Focus.* I leaned forward and said urgently, "Tell me something. Anything. Give me a starting point. I truly want to help you, but I have nothing!"

"A starting point, is it?" she said slowly. "Yes, perhaps that would be the best place to begin." She smiled wryly at me, with that winning charm of hers. "You might want to relax and get comfortable, my dear. This could take awhile."

The rod of steel in my spine threatened to become a noodle. But I forced myself to remain perched on the front edge of my chair in an official pose. I was the interrogator here, after all.

Elise commented, "I will preface this story by saying that, in the interest of keeping it short, I am about to make several broad and not necessarily precise generalizations over which scholars have argued for centuries."

I nodded my understanding of the rules of this game.

Elise took a deep breath. And began.

"Since the dawn of the human race, there has undoubtedly been an inherent tension between the male and the female of our species. My field of expertise is not the prehistoric era, so let us skip over that first generalization without debate, shall we?"

I blinked. The woman's demeanor, even her language, had just shifted completely. Here was the powerful mind of a highly trained scholar at work.

She continued, "I mention prehistory because this is also where our first notions of religion came from. A few of those beliefs survived over a very long period of time and made their way forward into the recorded history of modern people. My point is that when you combine the male-female dynamic and religion, you have a recipe for trouble." She added almost under her breath, "And indeed, trouble we've had."

That sounded as if she were referring to something personal in her life. I propped an elbow on the armrest and leaned toward her, interested in spite of myself.

"Throughout history, people have approached religion in diverse ways. For the purposes of our discussion today, consider two schools of thought: those who see religion as a route to power, and those who see religion as a route to peace. Surely the conflict between two such belief systems is immediately obvious to you?"

I nodded, feeling like an obedient student.

"While I would enjoy tracing the history of each of these concepts for you, you've asked me specifically for information that will aid you in your search. So, I will limit myself to that."

I was actually disappointed. And I'm not usually the type who goes in for sitting around pondering the meaning of life for fun.

"Have you ever heard of the Huguenots, Ana?"

I shrugged. "I've heard the name, but I can't claim to know anything about them."

Elise smiled. "I suppose not everyone is a dusty old religious scholar like me. Hmm. Quick overview. The Huguenots believed that faith should be demonstrated by living a sober, godly life. They violently disliked forms of worship that emphasized ritual, images, saints, pilgrimages and church hierarchy. In short, they despised Catholicism. The Huguenots were a major force in causing the Reformation, which was mostly about the rise of Protestant religions. Are you with me so far?"

I nodded. "Huguenots versus Catholics. Led to the Reformation. Got it."

"The conflict came to a head by the mid-1500s. Henry the Eighth had tossed the Catholic Church out of England and formed the Church of England ostensibly because the pope wouldn't grant him a divorce. The Huguenots controlled large chunks of southern and central France. Martin Luther

was widely popular in Germany and other countries. The Catholics were beset on all sides. They began to fight back,
which provoked Huguenots to do the same. There were eight
civil wars in France in the last half of the 1500s. The
Catholic monarchy murdered Huguenots, and the Huguenots
formed their own army to raid and kill Catholics. It was a
bloodbath."

She looked at me expectantly, so I summed up again.
"Religious wars. Huguenots and Catholics killing each other
in France."

"England wasn't much better," she said, picking up her
narrative. "When Henry the Eighth died, his son, Edward the
Sixth, forced the protestant Church of England on all his
subjects. When he died and Mary the First took the throne,
she forced Catholicism on all of England, earning the
moniker Bloody Mary while she was at it. She eventually
died, and Elizabeth the First took the throne in 1558. Elizabeth herself was Protestant but understood the need to reduce
the religious unrest in England. Compared to her two siblings,
she was downright moderate in her views."

Queen Elizabeth? How creepy was that? Here I was, listening to a lecture about her when I'd dreamed of her so vividly
just the night before. It was no doubt just a coincidence. But
what a coincidence! I realized Elise was throwing me an in-
quiring look. I nodded at her to indicate so far, so good.

Elise continued, "Scholars still argue about how tolerant
Elizabeth actually was. But two factors forced her hand.
Mary Queen of Scots—an ardent Catholic—was implicated
in several attempts to assassinate Elizabeth. And in France
and Spain, Protestants were viciously persecuted, culminat-
ing in the St. Bartholomew's Day Massacre in 1572. Seventy
thousand Protestants were killed in Paris and across France."

"Including a bunch of Huguenots?" I interjected.

"Exactly!" Elise exclaimed in delight. "Elizabeth was

forced, reluctantly, to send an English army to the aid of the Huguenots after the massacre."

"Then what happened?" I heard myself asking eagerly. God, I'm a sucker for a good story.

Elise shrugged. "More persecution. Many of the Huguenots fled over the next fifty years or so to Protestant countries like England, Switzerland, the Netherlands, Denmark, Prussia and the American colonies. The first Huguenots in America settled in New York in 1624. But that takes us away from your original question. You seek a starting point."

I blinked. Right. Her stolen object.

"In the midst of all this strife, a few other religions—old religions—struggled to hang on. But, vilified by both Protestant and Catholic alike, they had a hard go of it."

I frowned. "Old religions? You mean pagan religions?"

Elise sighed. "If you will. I cannot confess to being fond of the term *pagan*. It has such negative connotations, thanks to our Christian friends during the Reformation. But yes. Pagan religions. Some female-centered and some male-centered. A few of them survived by allowing themselves to be absorbed by Protestants or Catholics. Some of the old religions went underground, some were destroyed by lovely inventions like witch hunts, and some just faded away."

Elise stopped talking. I waited for a moment, but it appeared that she'd said all she wanted to say. "So, what is my starting point?" I asked.

"I just gave it to you. Look to the old beliefs. The old ways. The ones that survived the crucible of the Reformation."

That steel rod was back in my spine all of a sudden. I snapped, "Will you, just for once, stop babbling mumbo jumbo and give me a straight answer?"

One of her eyebrows arched delicately, and I could swear that was amusement making the corner of her mouth twitch like that.

Whatever. "What *exactly* are you trying to tell me?"

"The thing you seek is old. Very old."

"Pagan?" I demanded.

A single reluctant nod. And then her lips pressed together in a stubborn line. She clearly wasn't planning to tell me another thing about her stolen thingamajiggie. And sure enough her next words, delivered lightly, were, "Have you eaten lunch? I'm a bit hungry."

Now that she mentioned it, so was I. "I haven't eaten," I answered stiffly.

Elise stood up. "I'll go ask Violette to make us a bite to eat."

Madame Trucot's first name was Violette? That old battle-ax? I snorted. It was like naming a pit bull "Precious." Elise stepped out of the room, and I seized the opportunity to take a look at the pedestal upon which the late departed "old, pagan item" had stood.

It had been dusted recently, so that was no help. But, as I examined it from just the right angle, a faint shape on the wood caught my eye. I bent down to take a better look at it. Bingo. Whatever had stood upon this pedestal had protected the wood beneath it from fading slightly, probably because of exposure to sunlight. It had left a slightly darker impression on the top of the pedestal than the surrounding wood. I whipped out my handy-dandy digital camera, which in my line of work, I never went anywhere without.

Quickly, I photographed the pedestal from several angles, praying that one of them would pick up the faint outline in the wood. The outline was oval in overall shape, but with small squiggles all the way around it. At one end of the rough oval, a second shape touched it, a perfect circle about the diameter of an American half dollar. So. I wasn't looking at anything round and regular in shape like an urn or container of any kind. Probably a statue of some kind, then.

I heard someone coming, and I rushed back to my chair, perching on it just as Elise swept back into the room.

"If I might impose on you," I asked, "would you consent to show me a bit of your art collection?"

Elise and I spent the next hour wandering around her penthouse, while she told me about her various masterpieces. Interestingly enough, she made no reference whatsoever to the magnificent tapestry in the front hallway. When I made to ask her about it, she hastily—and effectively, I must confess—distracted me by handing me an original Beethoven score. And I mean *original*. With notes crossed out and scribbles in the margins by the composer himself. Good grief. This thing was absolutely priceless.

My state hovered somewhere between shock and awe by the time Madame Trucot called us to the rooftop conservatory and wheeled in a serving cart. She laid out poached salmon *en croute,* fresh salads and mango slices. Man. It sure made my usual peanut butter and jelly on wheat bread look lame. Even if peanut butter was an exotic specialty food in this part of the world.

We ate quietly in the conservatory's lush greenery, savoring the delicious meal. Afterward, Elise took me over to one of the tall wrought-iron and glass windows to enjoy the view. The Eiffel Tower rose up majestically, not far away. I appreciated Elise's respect for silence. A fountain burbled among the tropical plants behind us, and traffic noises drifted up faintly from below.

And then a new sound shattered the quiet. Glass exploding.

A giant spiderweb of crazed cracks bowed the window inward, but the pane held. It took a moment for me to register that Elise was lying flat on the ground. A single thought pierced my brain. *Oh, shit.*

Robert emerged from the surreal, artificial daylight of the Chunnel into the bright sun of a French afternoon. Squinting, he handed over his passport to the French border guard and fixed his gaze on the guy's pillbox hat. It looked rather like a large, flat coffee tin perched on top of the man's head.

It had taken him nearly an hour to drive through the thirty-one mile long English Channel tunnel stretching to the north behind him. It was huge inside, a couple stories tall. But the idea of the vast, crushing weight of water above had done a number on his head. Nope. Not a fan of being buried alive. He took a deep breath of the salty air.

The border guard gestured him in to a guard shack to fill out customs forms. Robert parked Penny and filled out the questionnaire. Name, address, destination, purpose, no import items to declare. He stood in a short line, handed over the form and waited while the customs official—a woman whose jacket buttons strained over her barrel-shaped torso— typed in his information.

He went back outside, pulled on his helmet and swung his right leg over his bike as his identity entered the French electronic highway.

Unbeknownst to him, his name triggered an alarm in an obscure computer subroutine and sent a message to an obscure office in Lyon, France, and was then routed to an even more obscure computer on a desk in an apartment in Paris.

By the time he hit the road again and pointed Penny's nose southeast to Paris, the presence of Robert Fraser, former art thief and felon, was duly noted by the powers-that-be in Interpol…and by one other person to whom the name Robert Fraser was of greatest interest.

I dropped to my knees beside Elise. "Are you all right?" I cried. I raked my gaze down her body, looking for blood. What the hell had just happened? It had sounded like a gunshot, but the window hadn't broken. Whatever had struck couldn't have been a bullet.

Elise was breathing. But she was out cold. There was no apparent blood. I couldn't find an entrance wound or even the tiniest hole in her clothing to indicate she'd been shot. Perhaps in ducking a possible bullet, she'd lost her balance and hit her head.

"Madame Trucot!" I shouted. "Elise is hurt. Call an ambulance! And call the police!"

I heard a wail from the kitchen that assured me the housekeeper had heard me. My fingers pressed to the pulse in Elise's narrow wrist, I waited there, monitoring her heartbeat for lack of anything else useful to do.

Madame Trucot raced to join us in a few moments, brandishing a wicked-looking sawed-off shotgun. And she handled it as if she knew exactly what to do with it. She peered out through the conservatory windows, but to her apparent disappointment spotted nobody to shoot back at.

There was a faint pounding from behind us. The doorbell rang continuously as if someone were leaning on the button, and I heard faint voices shouting over the strident ringing of the door chimes.

"That's the police," I told Madame Trucot, who'd spun around defensively. "Go let them in."

She nodded and ran for the front door. Rudy and the police swarmed into the apartment, filling the conservatory with their blue wool and urgent questions. I wasn't able to tell them much. One of their men did a preliminary check on Elise and came to the same conclusion I had. She must have hit her head when she fell to the ground.

A minute or so later, a team of medics rushed in and verified our finding. Elise had a substantial goose egg forming on the back of her head and no other apparent injuries. Thank God. I sagged into a chair in my relief as they gently transferred her onto a stretcher and took her away.

But my relief was short-lived. About two minutes later, an

investigator dug a lead slug out of what turned out to be laminated, bullet-resistant Plexiglas.

She'd been shot at, after all.

And that changed everything. So much for this lady being a crackpot with whacked theories. Somebody was, indeed, trying to kill her. And one of the prime reasons to kill a person like Elise would be to silence her. All of a sudden, I had to take this woman seriously. And I gotta say, that gave me the willies.

I answered the barrage of questions that the police threw at me, but I could tell them very little. They declared the bullet they had recovered to be a relatively small-caliber slug, which meant the shot had to have been fired from close by. Most of the police dispersed to the apartment buildings across the street, and in surprisingly little time, the apartment was quiet once more.

After assuring myself that Madame Trucot would be all right there by herself, I headed out.

I had my starting point. Now I had to go use it.

Chapter 5

Old. Pagan. And a statue. I knew just who to talk to next. My friend Catrina Dauvergne, a curator at the Cluny Muesum and an expert on things medieval. And she'd made a few comments before that led me to think she knew a fair bit about pre-Christian beliefs. Just last month she had held an exhibition at the Cluny of images from a medieval cult of women from southern France. I had been there in my capacity as an Interpol cataloguer, though, and didn't actually pay all that much attention to the descriptions of the cult's significance. What I remembered most about that night was the fire alarm that forced the Cluny to be evacuated mid-exhibit, and a man dying afterward under rather questionable circumstances. The whole thing had been hushed up very heavily.

I was slouched in the back of a taxi, caught behind a parade of grizzled veterans from the French Foreign Legion, who were marching down the Champs-Elysées, when my phone rang. I dug it out and flipped it open.

"Agent Reisner," I answered when I saw the call came from the Lyon office of Stolen Cultural Property.

"Ana. Littmann here. I wanted to let you know that a major art thief has just entered France and gave Paris as his final destination. Name's Robert Fraser. He supposedly hasn't been active for several years, but he's been linked to some international heavy hitters in the past. Maybe he's coming to town to pick up our lost object and pony it to somebody. How's the investigation coming, by the way?"

That was the reason he'd really made this call. To check up on me. "I've figured out that the stolen object is an old pagan statue."

As Littmann commenced dithering in delight, I dropped the other shoe. "Oh, and someone took a shot at Madame Villecourt about fifteen minutes ago."

His dithers turned into an alarmed squawk. "A *gun*shot?"

I was tempted to let him sweat for a few seconds, but I was kind. "She wasn't shot, but she hit her head on the floor when she ducked. She's unconscious. Should have arrived at Val de Grace Hospital by now. She should be fine, though. Turns out her conservatory is made of bulletproof glass." As I said the words aloud, it occurred to me to wonder why. Next time I saw her I'd have to ask.

Littmann gasped like a dying fish. Sounded like he might need hospitalization soon, himself. I left him to his asthma attack and hung up since my cab had arrived at the Cluny. He could figure out how to tell the president that someone had tried to assassinate Elise. I had work to do.

I looked up at the tan and gray facade of the Cluny Museum. It looked like, and in fact was, the outer wall of a medieval abbey, complete with jagged crenellations topping the wall. A guard at the low, wide arch that led to the main courtyard informed me kindly that the museum closed soon and perhaps I'd rather come back tomorrow. I smiled at him and stepped into the intimate cobbled courtyard, anyway. It was like my dream last night, ripping me out of my own time and flinging me back eight centuries to a time so vivid, so real, that I felt as if I was actually there.

The abbey dripped in gothic arches, dark slate roofs, stone fretwork, and the Cluny's signature scallop shell designs brought back to medieval France by pilgrims to foreign shores. It even smelled old, with a faint musty odor of mildew permeating the stone walls around me.

Just inside the entrance, a large, incomplete circle with a dozen spokes was etched onto the wall. I glanced at the sundial. According to the shadow streaking across the partial bicycle wheel, it was quickly approaching 5:45 p.m. Closing time. Perfect. I wanted to talk to Catrina without interruptions.

I entered the museum proper, stepping into a room that had originally been part of the Roman baths over which L'Hôtel des Abbés de Cluny was built. The walls in here were stacked stone, the ceilings rounded vaults made for shorter folk than I, the windows tiny and high on the walls. A weighty sense of the place settled on me, and I could almost see men in leather sandals and togas strolling through this antechamber en route to the heated baths ahead. The sound of my footsteps was oddly muffled, lending the place an air of waiting mystery.

I stopped for a moment to look at the heads of the twenty-one kings of Judah, separated from their bodies at Notre Dame Cathedral during the French Revolution on the mistaken assumption that they depicted French kings. They might be statues, but there was an odd violence to looking at those rows of severed heads. Perhaps it was because the statues were defaced at the same time so many real people were killed that these stone visages connoted the victims of the French Revolution so vividly to me.

An odd shudder went through me as I pondered how many

innocents were murdered in cold blood in that mad time. It was as if someone else shuddered inside my skin, too. A strange and disturbing sensation.

Perhaps my imagination was just running away with me. Or perhaps it was the age of this place playing tricks on me. I walked through another dim chamber displaying various medieval weapons and armor. The light was dim to preserve the colors of the cloth artifacts, and shadows danced upon the elaborately fanned, gothic vaults of the ceiling. I could almost hear the shouts of knights, the singing clash of steel on steel as I looked at the collection.

I felt a stirring behind me and turned around quickly. No one was there.

I felt the stirring again, this time accompanied by a vague sense of—excitement maybe, or elation. *I was in the right place.* Was that damned afterimage from my dream still tickling at my brain?

I strode determinedly through the museum, ignoring all vague feelings, past the magnificent stained glass windows and tapestries, past the statuary and triptychs and jeweled trea-sures, to a door marked Employees Only in five languages. It led upstairs to the staff offices. I ignored the warning to keep out and climbed the stairs to the second floor.

Catrina's office door was open.

I stopped in the doorway. "Hi, Catrina."

She looked up, pleased. "Ana! Hello! What brings you here today?" She came around her desk and kissed me warmly on both cheeks, European-style.

"I'm afraid this is a business call," I replied.

That effectively wiped the pleasure off her face. Curators of museums never liked it when Interpol came calling on business. "What is wrong?" she asked seriously.

"I need some information. About a statue. It's old—pre-dates the Reformation—and is not Christian."

"Do you have a picture of it?"

I winced. "No. I have no idea what it looks like. All I have is this outline of its base. I think." I pulled out my digital camera and pulled up an image on the teeny screen on its back of the outline on the pedestal in Elise's library.

"Let's print that and blow it up, shall we?" she suggested.

I handed over the camera, and Catrina pulled the proper cable out of a desk drawer to plug it into her computer. In a trice the printer on the console behind her desk spit out an eight-by-ten photo of my outline. She used a magnifying glass and a magic marker to highlight the shape so she could see it clearly. The whole process took under two minutes.

The two of us stared down at the wavy oval with that odd little circle parked at one end of it.

"It looks like clothes to me," Catrina pronounced.

"It looks like a squiggle to me," I retorted. "What sort of clothes are that shape?"

She explained, "If the statue were of a person wearing long robes, their hems would fall on the ground in an irregular oval like that."

The second she said it, something in me surged with triumph. Somehow, I just *knew* she was right. It wasn't even a gut intuition. It was something else. Almost a—presence—in my head telling me that was it exactly. Clearly, if I was developing voices in my head, it was time for me to get more sleep and take a *long* vacation.

Clothes. Then that meant my statue was of a person. "Any idea how big this thing is?" I asked her.

"Let's take it downstairs and compare it to a few statues in the collection."

We went back down the narrow, dark staircase and into the museum. Visitors were making their way out in the wake of a loudspeaker announcement that the museum was closing. We walked against the flow of people to a room full of reliquaries, table-sized strong boxes, eating utensils, jewelry and other small trinkets of the Middle Ages.

Catrina used a key to open a locked panel on the wall. Inside the inconspicuous box, she keyed a long number into the electronic number pad there. A green light went on, and she swiped the magnetic card on a lanyard around her neck through the slot above the number pad.

"Planning to rob the joint, are you?" I quipped.

She retorted, "I'd love to have some of these pieces in my home, but I can do without the fifteen to twenty years in prison, thank you. No, I only wish to pick up a few statues and compare them to your outline. They all sit on pressure pads, so I had to disable the security system."

I was glad to let her don cotton gloves and handle the rare pieces as we moved from room to room, comparing various statues to our drawing. She tried a few statues that were around a foot tall, and most of them were noticeably smaller in diameter than my outline. She tried a statue nearly two feet tall next, and it was a little too big.

Cat commented, "I'm beginning to feel like Goldilocks. First too small, then too big. Maybe the next one will be just right."

She picked up a statue of a monk in long, Franciscan robes. It was about eighteen inches tall. Although the exact outlines didn't match, the size was just right. And, when Catrina turned him upside down, his robes did indeed form a wavy oval about the same shape as my outline. Catrina put the priest back on his stand. "If your statue is from roughly the same era, that's about the size I'd guess it is."

I examined the bald man's long face and slender form. I couldn't imagine Elise being so attached to a dour fellow like this. This statue might be the right size, but it definitely wasn't the right subject matter. That weird, internal vibration I'd developed concurred.

"What do you think the little round thing on my statue is?" I asked Catrina.

"It's not part of the person. It's something sitting at your person's feet. Could be a container of some kind like an urn or pot, or perhaps a pedestal of some kind."

I nodded. Logical. "Any further ideas on who my statue is?"

Catrina shook her head. "Depending on how old your piece is, portraiture might not have been that well-developed an art form yet. Prior to the Renaissance, wealthy and important people typically had small statues made of themselves instead of paintings."

She examined the drawing of the outline once more. "The profile of this clothing lies too close to the body to be Elizabethan. By then, women wore wide, round skirts, and men wore hoses and short pants. So, this has to be pre-Elizabethan. Assuming we've guessed the size correctly and the way these folds fall, I'd guess we're looking at a single-layer garment. That rules out most of the Renaissance, when noble women were swathed in multiple layers of cloth as a sign of wealth."

I let her continue to think aloud without interrupting.

"So that leaves us with a pre-Renaissance figure, or possibly a religious figure, since religious clothing tended to consist of simple robes."

I interjected, "One thing I do know is this is not a Christian statue. I was told it comes from an old religion, neither Catholic nor Protestant, that survived the Reformation."

Catrina's eyebrows shot straight up. "Practically no pagan religions survived that period. In fact, as early as the twelfth century, the wholesale Christianization of Europe was already in full swing."

She eyed the outline anew. "It could be male or female, although not many pagan religions made human statuary. If our hypothesis is correct that this is an outline of draped fabric, then we're definitely looking at a human figure. Let me do a little research for you. May I keep this picture of its base?"

"Of course. I'll make one for myself at home tonight."

Catrina nodded and we turned to leave the now deserted museum. We stepped into the chamber holding the incredible Dame à la Licorne tapestries. I was just admiring their rich cinnabar hues and intricate *milles fleurs* decorations when a man burst into the room.

Well, *he* didn't actually burst. *I* nearly did. His presence behind me filled me up, flooding me with sensations I couldn't even begin to name. And he didn't actually come into the room. He stopped in the doorway, framed by ancient, hand-hewn stone. He looked as if he would have belonged in that doorway when the blocks were new. There was something primal about him, an aura of recklessness, of seizing life by the throat, that spoke of older times than today's tame, modern era.

Our gazes jerked to one another simultaneously. Good grief, was I having the same effect on him that he was having on me? I don't know how long I just stood there and stared at him, but I'm sure it was too long to be polite or even remotely civilized.

He looked like an errant knight who just happened to be wearing a leather motorcycle jacket. Did I mention he was beyond gorgeous? Tanned skin. Intense eyes that were the most remarkable silver-grey. Stormy. Keen. Intelligent. They looked right through me. Dark brown hair pulled back into a ponytail, not a long one, but extremely sexy. Broad shoulders, lean hips, long legs with just the right amount of muscle beneath those snug black jeans. Taller than me by several inches.

Pick your favorite dark-haired, bedroom-eyed, bad-boy movie star. Now double his sex appeal. No, triple it. Then, put him in a mysterious, mystical room out of time. And then, have him stop in his tracks when he lays eyes on you, have his eyes widen, have him smile just enough to pop a dimple at you, and have him walk right up beside you, look you in the eye, and murmur in a soft Scots brogue…

"You are possibly the most beautiful woman I've ever seen. What are you doing for the rest of your life?"

I stared up at him. He stood far too close to be polite or even remotely civilized. His body heat wrapped around me like silken ropes, drawing me to him in an invisible embrace. My jaw undoubtedly was hanging open wide enough to catch flies. I mean, what's a girl supposed to say to something like that? It's not a line I'd ever had directed at me before. And certainly not from a man who exuded so much sexual appeal I could hardly breathe.

It might not be love at first sight, but it was definitely lust at first sight.

"Wow," I managed to breathe.

He smiled. And my knees about buckled.

Now, for the record, I am not a go-weak-in-the-knees kind of girl. I'd never reacted to anyone this way before. Ever. But there I was, in danger of collapsing into a moaning, writhing heap on the floor.

Thankfully, Catrina intervened tactfully. "I'm sorry, sir. The museum is closed. You'll have to come back tomorrow."

He barely took his eyes off me as he replied, "I'm not here to see the museum. I'm here to see the curator. Catrina Dauvergne."

"That would be me," Catrina answered dryly.

Was that a laugh I heard in her voice? Surely she wasn't missing the absurdly sexual vibes leaping back and forth between this incredible stranger and me.

He shook himself slightly and tore his gaze away from me. And just like that, I felt cold. Bereft. Like the sun had gone behind a cloud. I watched in unreasoning jealously as he turned to Catrina and held his hand out to her. I *know*

Catrina's deliriously happy with Rhys Pritchard, who came into her life recently. But she got to touch this man before I did, even if it was only to shake his hand. I wanted that hand on my skin!

It was at about that point that I began to think that maybe I was losing my mind. First the ghost in my mirror, then all those vague, inexplicable feelings and now my instant obsession with this man whose name I hadn't even heard. Wouldn't you know it, I actually heard laughter in my head then. A lilting, girlish sound. Like something—or someone—alien within me thought this was the funniest thing she'd witnessed in ages.

Catrina took his hand graciously. "And you might be?"

"I'm Robert Fraser."

Oh, crap. That thought echoed through my head on several levels. First, this was the art thief from England. Catrina hadn't reset the alarm system yet, and this guy was a crook. An entire museum full of priceless treasures was at his mercy.

Second, this was the art thief from England. And I'd just fallen like a ton of bricks for him.

Third, this was the art thief from England. I worked for Interpol to stop men like him, and...*I didn't give a damn that he was a thief. I wanted him.* The only reason I was suddenly contemplating detaining him and searching him had nothing to do with the safety of the museum and everything to do with getting my hands on him. Now.

Fortunately, I was shocked into immobility by his next words to Catrina.

"I saw a bit on the Internet about an exhibition here recently. It featured a number of Black Madonna images. I'm interested in learning more about them."

Could it be? Was he involved in the theft of Elise's statue? Why else would an international art thief show up within days of the crime and be asking questions on such a closely related subject? Black Madonnas, huh? From what I recalled, they were old. Not Christian. Religious, and probably wearing simple robes. Nah. Surely it couldn't be that simple.

Danged if that weird vibration of certainty in my gut didn't kick up again, though.

I spoke up casually. "Catrina, how about I stay with Mr. Fraser while you lock up?"

She ignored my hint, dammit. Instead, she said, "Come with me, Monsieur Fraser. Several of the pieces from that private exhibit are on public display now. They're this way."

Reluctantly, I tagged along behind the two of them, keeping an eagle eye on Fraser for many reasons and trying to figure out if anything was already hidden under that sloppy jacket. There was certainly room to have something squirreled away under there. Who knew how long he'd been in the museum by himself with the alarm system deactivated. Cripes.

Of course, if he were smart, he'd just move some object to a hiding place within the museum, like a restroom or a broom closet, where it was outside the net of security. Then he could come back later at his leisure and pick up his prize. Before I left I'd have to warn Catrina and suggest she do a complete walk-through of the collection to make sure everything was where it belonged.

The idea of an art thief wandering around this place after hours gave me a giant case of the jitters. Yeah, that was it. Jitters. That's why my stomach leaped and jumped like a gamboling fawn as I watched him saunter alongside Catrina. It had nothing to do with how well he wore a pair of jeans or my craving to get inside those jeans. The faded denim cupped his rear end just right…

…and I was *not* going to ogle said rear end! I *was* going to act like a professional!

I tore my gaze away hastily. And it alighted on his broad back. Hmm. That definitely wasn't padding holding out the broad leather shoulders of his coat. Nope, not gonna look at

those, either. My errant gaze went next to his right ear. I
stared fixedly at it rather than let my gaze roam an inch.

I tried to reason with myself. He was *so* not my type. I like
stable, upright, dependable guys. The kind who don't steal
art. I never have gone in for dark and dangerous men. I shuddered to think how my uptight German father would've
reacted had I ever brought home a guy with long hair and a
leather jacket. The words *tactical nuclear meltdown* came to
mind. And still, my body—my very soul—hummed with
need for this man.

Catrina filled in Fraser on the basics of the Black Madonna
cult. It dated back to the early Middle Ages. It was thought
to have been based on various, much older goddess cults—
some predating Christianity by a lot—that gradually combined over time. The black coloration of their Madonna
images had nothing to do with racial origin, but rather the
blending of all colors to form black. And the Madonna herself
was purely a mother image in their belief system and not a
Christian reference at all.

Catrina explained how some scholars speculated that, in
fact, the Virgin Mary image was lifted from the Black Madonna
cult as a way of incorporating the pagan imagery into Christianity. It was a common practice in the medieval Christian
church to assimilate the pagan beliefs they couldn't eradicate.

I listened avidly as Catrina outlined some of the stories and
rumors about biblical women fleeing after the crucifixion of
Jesus to southern Europe and bringing their goddess beliefs
with them. She ended by saying they were mostly legends,
though. That brought to my mind Elise's comment about
each person having to determine the truth of legends for themselves. Were these particular legends true? Yup, I had another
one of those vague feelings just then. Except it wasn't the least
bit vague, and it was more of a certainty than a feeling. And
it believed without a doubt that the stories were true.

I forced myself to tune back in to Catrina's minilecture. She was talking about how, by the Middle Ages, the Black Madonna cult centered itself in southern France, mainly in today's Languedoc region. The cult had left no written histories behind. At least none had ever been found. I was intrigued when Catrina commented as an aside that, just because there was no written record of a thing, that didn't make it untrue. So, she believed the stories about the Black Madonnas of Languedoc, too? Interesting.

The two of them stopped, and I almost ran into Robert's back, so busy was I avoiding looking at him.

"This is a typical Black Madonna image," Catrina was saying.

I looked at the statue. Ah, yes. I'd catalogued it last month. It came from the basement of a home Catrina had purchased not long ago. There'd been a provenance question of whether or not the artwork cached in the basement had been sold along with the house itself. That's how Catrina and I met, in fact. She'd called me to inquire after the legalities of it all. She'd wanted to make sure she definitely owned it free and clear before she displayed it at the Cluny.

The statue was made of a black, softly glossy substance that I knew from my previous examination of it to be highly polished ebony. The female figure was unnaturally slender, carrying an elongated baby that frankly, looked like a little old man. The piece was nearly four feet tall, an extravagant size for the medieval period, during which the Crusades emptied the coffers of most people in Europe who might have commissioned it. The statue was roughly the size of an altar piece for a small, private chapel.

At a glance, most people would probably confuse this for a statue of the Virgin Mary and baby Jesus. But the sword slung over the woman's shoulder was probably the biggest giveaway that this mother was different. Also, there were no halos adorning mother or child, which was the norm on Christian pieces.

My attention was snagged by Robert's's reaction to this piece. His eyes blazed and his body went rigid for a moment when he saw the lady. "Do you have any catalogues with more of these Black Madonnas in it?" he asked with thinly veiled eagerness.

My eyes narrowed. What was he up to? Suspicion rumbled in my gut, completely driving out for a moment the overwhelming attraction I felt for him. And in that second, I declared my reaction to him temporary insanity. A passing feeling.

The alien in my brain snorted in disbelief in the back of my head.

He paused in a doorway to let Catrina precede him, then looked back and put an arm out for me to go ahead. As I glided by him, my feet barely touched the floor. I held my breath, almost giddy with awareness of him. And then his hand touched the small of my back. Just a brush of his fingertips across my spine, but it robbed me of thought, of speech, of breath.

And my moment of sanity passed.

I concentrated with all my might on having only rational, logical thoughts and pointedly ignored the tug of need pulling me toward Robert. But it was hard, let me tell you. Catrina seemed prepared to take this guy upstairs and settle down in her office for a long talk, but my sane, professional self was having none of it. This guy was leaving the Cluny before me, or that wasn't an Interpol badge in my purse.

I tried to be subtle, but finally I had to come right out and say, "Catrina, it isn't good security procedure to leave the museum open like this after hours. You need to close up shop for the night, and the two of you can take your conversation elsewhere."

Catrina stared at me, shocked by my bluntness. A question shone in her gaze, something along the lines of, "Have you lost your mind?" But for some reason she bit her tongue and didn't voice it aloud. Thank goodness.

I ushered the two of them firmly out of the building. A shroud of night had fallen over the abbey, and its dark alcoves and stone walls seemed even more alive than ever. I could swear I heard horses' hooves clattering over the cobblestones as a tardy traveler arrived at the hostel, racing to beat the closing of the portcullis and the posting of the guards for the night. A line of monks paced across my mind's eye, their deep hoods drawn up over their heads, the leader of the procession swinging an incense burner, the deep, dark, male tones of a prayer chant echoing off the stone walls.

I blinked, and the image was gone. It was just a museum again. In downtown Paris. On a Monday evening. Cars whizzed past outside, and the air smelled of diesel fumes. Firmly planted in my own century once more, I followed Robert and Catrina from the museum. One of the night guards let us out and relocked the grate behind us. I turned quickly, bumping squarely into Fraser.

I did it intentionally, of course. Not because I was that desperate for sex—although in retrospect, maybe I was—but because I wanted to know if he had anything under his coat. He reached out quickly to steady me, his hands gripping my shoulders with easy strength. Damned if that wasn't knowing amusement glinting in his eyes. Unaccountably irritated at the idea that he might know exactly what I'd just done, I nodded shortly and stepped out from under his mesmerizing touch.

When I got home, I was going to make a call to the Paris police and suggest they keep a very close eye on one Robert Fraser. And then I was going to imagine him joining me in my lonely bed.

The unseasonably warm evening convinced me to walk home. That, and I do some of my best thinking when I'm walking. It took me a number of blocks to walk off my reaction to Robert and settle down to wondering exactly what he was up to. I made a mental note to warn Catrina about him tomorrow.

I turned west along the Seine. At night it was an enchanted ribbon of black, reflecting the twinkling city lights. A river barge full of tourists passed by, a party of some kind in progress aboard it. The street around me was dark and deserted by comparison. By day this area teemed with artists and pedestrians. But abruptly, I was aware of the deep shadows of the long line of linden trees following the bank of the Seine, the silence of the shopping district around me, closed down for the night. There weren't even any cars passing through here.

"Beware," someone whispered in my ear.

I lurched and spun around, my hands up in a defensive posture. Nobody was there. What in the *hell* was going on with me? I didn't think of myself as a person who spooked easily, but I was sure as heck spooked now.

I crossed the street in the middle of the block to get to the other side, closer to the river. There were more linden trees over here, but there were no storefronts or alleys for an assailant to jump out of, either. I sped up my steps, heading for the bright stripe of the Pont Neuf ahead of me. The wide stone bridge crossed over the Seine a few blocks in front of me.

Something scuffed behind me. I looked quickly over my shoulder and caught a glimpse of what might be a man back there. Sometimes I wished I carried a weapon. Maybe I ought to start. Fat lot of good it was going to do me now, though.

I cursed my two-inch heels as my calves began to ache from the punishing pace I was setting in shoes not meant for race walking. I began to keep an eye out for an improvised weapon. A stick or a big rock, anything I could use to defend myself. But this area was too clean for such projectiles. I settled for bending down, almost without breaking my stride and scooping up a handful of freshly spread sand from the square of dirt around the base of a tree. It wasn't much, but it was better than nothing. In my left hand, I clutched my key ring, slipping my middle finger through the large ring so the keys made a crude set of brass knuckles.

I thought I saw a movement across the street to my left. I looked quickly and saw a man. He had a hat pulled down low over his eyebrows and his hands were jammed in the pockets of an overcoat. It wasn't that cool a night.

I glanced over my shoulder. A second man was behind me. Coming up fast. Not good. By the time I could pull out my cell phone and call the police these guys would be on me. Sometime it's best to stand your ground and fight, and some-times it's best to flee and return to fight another day. Tonight I tucked tail and ran.

Immediately, I heard the slap of footsteps behind me. Uh-oh. These guys were definitely after me. I kept an eye on the figure across the street who was keeping pace beside me. One more block to the bright lights of the bridge. The guy across the street waited until a delivery truck passed by and then veered into the street.

Coming straight at me.

I dodged to the right of the line of trees and put on a burst of speed. Thank goodness I ran a little cross country in high school! It had been a few years, but I still had some get-up-and-go in the old legs. My arms pumped hard and I kept my chin up as I sucked great breaths of air into my lungs. Only a couple hundred feet to go. I lost sight of the guy to my left, but I wasn't about to waste any energy or speed looking around for him.

A steady stream of cars crossed the bridge, and I made out pedestrians leaning over the wide stone balustrades of the Pont Neuf. Craving the safety of lights and people I ignored the burning in my lungs, the sweat popping on my forehead, the fear twisting in my gut. I didn't know who those guys were behind me, and I wasn't about to confront them and try to find out.

I careened past the last tree and into the open. Still not out in the bright light yet. *Please* let them not catch me. Straining with every muscle I had, I sprinted for the bridge. I didn't stop until I was a good dozen yards onto the stone span and had charged past several startled-looking couples. There. I was right out in plain sight. Now if those bastards wanted to come after me, they'd have witnesses and cell phones and police to deal with.

I dropped my forgotten fistful of sand, letting it trickle out between my sweaty fingers. I planted my hands on my hips, breathing hard in the damp night air. There was nothing quite as unpleasant as the sensation of a silk shirt plastered wetly to my skin. The poor blouse was ruined. I unbuttoned my tweed jacket and twisted my hair up off my neck to try to cool myself after my impromptu sprint. I turned to look behind me, to see if the two men were still back there. Nobody was following me that I could discern. But then, a number of lone men were leaning casually on the railing, looking down into the river. Any of them could've been my tails.

I would stop at the other end of the bridge and hail a taxi to take me the rest of the way home. The stitch in my side was finally easing, although my clothes still clung disgustingly to me. I twisted around, trying to pluck my blouse off my back. And that's when I saw the headlights jump the curb behind me and head straight at me.

Pure survival reflex took over. I didn't stop to think. I turned for the bridge railing and jumped.

Chapter 6

At the last second before it slammed into the heavy stone balustrade, the car—a Peugeot—swerved back across the pedestrian walk and into the roadway. It sped off into the night. From my awkward position sprawled along the wide stone ledge, I couldn't make out the license plate number. A middle-aged couple rushed over to me, and the man helped me down off the bridge.

"*Mon Dieu!* Do you wish me to call the police, mademoiselle?" he exclaimed.

"I am the police," I replied wryly, brushing off my jacket with a trembling hand. Turns out being the target of attempted murder rattles me a bit.

I glanced around at the small crowd that had gathered, perhaps a dozen witnesses. "Did any of you catch the license plate number of that car?"

No one had, and the agitated bystanders quickly latched onto the idea that the driver had been a drunk who lost control of his car. I wished. Four or five men joined the back of the crowd. Were any of them involved in chasing me or that near miss on me moments ago? I tried to get a good look at their faces, but every last one of them either turned away or was placed so I couldn't get a good look at him.

I'd had enough of being a sideshow. After one last reassurance to everyone that I was fine, I resumed crossing the bridge. I *wasn't* fine, but I wasn't about to stand there any longer letting them fuss over me. I walked on wobbly knees to the far end of the bridge and hailed a taxi. It took several minutes, but one finally stopped. Thankfully I only lived a few blocks north. By the time the cab stopped in front of my apartment, the smell of my own sweat and fear was beginning to fill the confines of the vehicle most unpleasantly. No wonder these cabs smelled the way they did. People like me rode around in them.

I paid the guy an extra few euros to watch me enter my building and make sure no one followed me inside. I made it into the lobby all right and waved to him through the long window beside the door. The taxi took off and I was alone.

Not surprisingly, I had a burning desire to gain the safety of my apartment, lock myself in and get the heck out of my sweaty clothes. I rushed up the stairs and fumbled with the locks in my haste as I alternated looking furtively over my shoulder and swearing at the uncooperative dead bolt. I suppose it was stupid to have a panic attack after the fact, but my adrenaline was sky-high, and my pulse felt as if it were about to explode out of my throat.

Finally, the lock gave way. I flipped on the lights and breathed a sigh of relief at my empty living room. Quickly, I searched my apartment. And yes, I looked under the bed and in all the closets. But I figured I was authorized a little paranoia after my scare down at the Seine. I did stop myself from checking the front door locks a third time, though.

I stripped out of my ruined suit, took a quick shower and

crawled into sweatpants and a baggy sweatshirt. Comfort clothes. I even made myself a cup of hot chocolate. My comfort food.

And then I darned near spilled the whole scalding lot down my front when somebody knocked on my door. Who the heck was here to see me at this time of night? It was only a little after nine o'clock, but my friends didn't show up unannounced that late on a weeknight.

I have to admit the first thing that came to my mind, besides the thugs who'd chased me, was that Robert Fraser had followed me home and wanted to talk to me. I scowled at the accompanying leap in my stomach at the thought. He. Was. Not. My. Type. End of discussion.

Leaving on the chain, I cracked open the door and peeked outside.

A man stood there, all right. Middle-aged. Too paunchy to have been either of the guys who'd chased me onto the Pont Neuf, with washed out brown hair combed over a balding spot and kind, serious eyes. Definitely not dark, dangerous, bad boy Robert Fraser.

"Good evening, Agent Reisner. My name is Carl Montrose. May I come in?"

After my recent scare I wasn't about to let a total stranger into my home just like that. "Can I see some ID?" I asked.

"Of course. Forgive me." He pulled out his wallet and showed me his driver's license, a credit card and even a library card.

"Okay, so you're Carl Montrose. What do you want with me?"

"I want to talk about our mutual friend Elise. I work for—" He broke off, glancing up and down the hall.

Very cloak and dagger. I wasn't impressed. Just because he knew Elise's name didn't mean he wasn't one of the bad guys trying to kill her. But then he pulled out another ID badge of some kind and held it out for my inspection. Okay, now that impressed me. It was an access badge to Pierre Dupont's private offices.

He said quietly, "I work for this man."

"Who's been your contact at Interpol on this case?" I challenged. So maybe I was being a little paranoid here. But I didn't enjoy being followed or nearly killed.

"Armande St. Germain for the most part. Although I spoke to a fellow this afternoon by the name of Littmann. He called to tell me about the incident at the conservatory. Extremely nervous man."

That did it. This Montrose guy was for real. I stepped back, unchained my door and let him in. Gesturing him down onto my sofa, I said, "I apologize for my caution, but someone's been tailing me and a car nearly ran me down earlier." Just to gauge his reaction I asked, "Was it your people following me?"

Something flickered across his features. Uh-oh. Had I just let a bad guy in after all? And he was between me and my bedroom door—my bedroom being where my can of mace currently resided, not to mention my Louisville Slugger. Oh, and my service pistol, locked in a metal box and buried somewhere deep in the back of my closet. I'd have felt much better with some sort of weapon in hand.

"I did have you followed," he confessed. "My men tailed you over the weekend."

"Why?"

"To make sure you took the case seriously and actually started work on it. But they were called off once it became clear that you were pursuing it." He studied me for a long moment. "I should have waited until business hours tomorrow to see you at the police prefecture where you would be more at ease. But events are moving quickly and the president is very worried."

"Exactly what's got Dupont so worked up?"

"That is what I came here to discuss. As you no doubt know by now, Pierre Dupont has a personal interest in this case. But there is more to it than his old friendship with Elise Villecourt. Much more."

"And it's this other piece of the puzzle that makes it a matter of national security?"

Montrose nodded, then asked casually, "Would you mind if I sweep the room for bugs before we go any further?"

I blinked, startled. "Uh, go ahead."

The man stood up, laid his briefcase beside me on the sofa so I could see into it when he opened it, and pulled out a small black sensor. I watched, bemused, as he slowly circled my entire living room.

As he finished up, I offered politely, "Since we're both being so cautious, do you want to see my credentials?"

He closed his briefcase and sat back down on the other two thirds of the sofa. He leaned back and said solemnly, "No, thank you. I've seen photographs of you. Your extraordinary eyes are identification enough."

Like I said before, I don't think of myself in terms of beauty, so a comment like this caught me off guard. I had no idea what to say next, so I waited for him to pick up the reins of the conversation.

"How are you coming on your investigation?" he finally asked.

Whew. Solid ground once more. I answered, "Slower than I'd like. It does, indeed, seem as if Madame Villecourt's claims that someone is trying to kill her are true. Today's shooting leaves little doubt about that."

He nodded grimly. "The other reason I came here tonight is to impress upon you the importance of solving this case. Quickly."

"And what is it about this case that's so terribly important?"

Montrose sighed. "That is the question of the hour, is it

not? Monsieur Dupont hopes that by giving you all the information we have, you can help us more effectively."

Finally. Someone was going to give me something concrete to go on. No more smoke and mirrors. I hoped.

The thief frowned. Looked over his shoulder into the darkness. He slid deeper into the night, easing forward silent and fast. There it was again. That noise behind him. He wasn't one of the most accomplished burglars in Europe for nothing. He had hearing like a cat. It had already saved him once tonight.

He'd just been settling down in front of the television to watch a Jerry Lewis movie when he'd heard the faintest scratching sound at his door. In the vicinity of the lock, in fact. Somebody was very quietly, very deftly picking the lock. He'd leaped out of his chair and ran for his bedroom, locking the interior door behind him. He'd grabbed his rubber-soled shoes, the statue and a rucksack of gear, and sprinted for the bathroom. He'd locked that door, too.

Out the window fast and onto the windowsill. He'd balanced briefly, then made the precarious leap across a wide gap to the retracted fire escape hanging against the wall to his left. He'd practiced the move a dozen times just in case the law ever caught up with him and he had to get away fast. Except that hadn't been the law at his door tonight. It had been someone imminently scarier than the police—his client.

He'd executed his preplanned escape across the rooftops of his ancient neighborhood, taking running jumps spanning three different gaps that would thwart all but the most athletic pursuer. Then he slowed down, staying below the rooflines, creeping another several blocks in the steep, slate jungle that was the nocturnal home of a cat burglar. Down one of several fire escapes he could choose from and into the heart of the Latin Quarter, a place anyone could lose himself in if he tried. Its warren of narrow, winding streets and round-the-clock, eclectic mix of humanity was a no-brainer for a man like him to blend in to.

And that's why he was so surprised to hear someone behind him as he slipped into a residential street off the rue Cujas. His back should've been clean! Now what to do? He *had* to lose these guys. He had no doubt they'd torture him until he told them where the statue was, and then they'd kill him. Slowly and painfully. And speaking of which, he had to find someplace to hide the lady.

He needed a misdirection. Something to throw them off the trail. He looked around and the perfect distraction came to him. René ought to be holed up by now in his usual rat nest for the night. And it was just a couple blocks away. With renewed energy, he took off running.

He rounded the corner into René's alley and headed for the back end of it, behind the Dumpsters from the gay bar. Sure enough, the old man was curled up inside the wooden packing crate the Paris garbage department kindly never seemed to pick up. It really wasn't that uncomfortable looking. René was burrowed down into a deep nest of blankets with only the top of his head showing. Gentle snores emanated from the pile of wool.

"René," he whispered.

Another snore was the only reply.

"René!" he whispered louder. Still nothing. Oh, hell. He reached inside the box and poked at the pile of blankets. "Wake up you drunk old reprobate!"

A grumble, an elbow tossed at his prodding finger, and René's face emerged, bleary eyed. "What are you up to, Ives, waking an old man from a pleasant dream?"

Damn. Not as drunk as usual. Oh, well. He'd proceed with the plan, anyway. "Listen. Some men are after me. I need to lose them. Switch clothes with me, will you? They won't hurt you when they realize you're not me."

René's red-rimmed eyes narrowed suspiciously. "What kind of trouble have you gotten yourself into?"

He shrugged. "I nicked a souvenir from a job and the client's sent his goons after me to fetch it."

René's eyes narrowed even more. "What sort of souvenir? If you went into the Louvre to steal a cup, your idea of a souvenir could be the *Mona Lisa*."

"Naw, it's just a statue. Of a lady."

René snorted. "The *Venus de Milo* is a statue of a lady."

The thief looked over his shoulder nervously at the mouth of the alley. "It's nothing like that. I swear. It's just a woman carrying a kid. It's old, but I checked the Internet and it's got no provenance at all. As far as I can tell, it's never even come up for sale, let alone for auction. Can't be worth much."

"Then why are these guys chasing you?"

Damn. René was a sharp old bastard when his back teeth weren't awash in gin. "Principle of the thing. C'mon. Help me out. Trade clothes with me. I'll let you keep my threads."

That perked up René. "Permanently?"

"I suppose," he answered grudgingly. "Just swear you do not have lice before we do this."

René reared up indignantly. "I take a shower every week at the Catholic mission." With a hint of the agility that had earned him his reputation as one of the great ones in his day, the old guy extricated himself from his blankets and began to strip off the various layers of mismatched clothing adorning his emaciated body.

The thief was somewhat heavier and in better physical condition, and René's pants were uncomfortably snug on him. He pulled on a shirt that didn't fit much better. René might bathe, but clearly he had no use for deodorant. The shirt stunk to high heaven. Ah, well. It lent the disguise credibility.

He pulled René's secondhand ski sweater down over his shirt and shrugged on the ratty, black wool jacket René passed him. It smelled as greasy and filthy as if it had just come off the sheep who donated the wool to make it. The thief handed over his own handmade, Italian leather jacket with a pang of regret. The coat could be replaced, though. His neck could not. He pulled a black knit watch cap out of the pocket of René's coat and yanked it down over his ears. They kept their own shoes.

René murmured, "If you climb the wall behind me, you'll be in another alley. Turn right at the end of it and left at the next intersection, and the Maubert Metro stop will be in front of you."

The thief grinned. Old habits died hard. No cat burglar worth his salt went to sleep at night without an escape route in place. Not even decrepit, out-of-business René.

"Thanks, my friend. I owe you one." He flipped his rucksack into the Dumpster, then turned and jumped for the wall. His fingers caught the top lip of the eight-foot wall and he used his toes to climb the rough brick surface. His rubber soles caught easily on the mortar joints, and he straddled the wall in a matter of seconds.

As he swung his leg over the wall, René called after him, "Bring me a case of gin, and we'll call it square!"

With a nod, he slid down the wall.

Just as his face disappeared behind the bricks, he glimpsed a pair of big, dark shadows rounding the corner of René's alley and advancing. He swore violently under his breath. He released his handhold and landed softly, bending his knees deeply to absorb the noise of his landing.

And into that moment of silence before he pivoted and took off, he heard another faint noise. A thick, liquid gurgling. The sort of sound an old man might make if fingers wrapped around his throat, choking him.

Holy Mother of God. He turned then and ran like he'd never run before.

* * *

I looked up sharply as an abrupt cry sounded outside my window. It sounded like a woman half screaming. Montrose lurched to his feet and moved to the window, peering outside. The man was nearly as jumpy as I was. The sound came again, this time rising into an unmistakably feline yowl. I let out a relieved breath. It was just an alley cat in heat. My guest moved once again to the sofa and sat down.

"Okay, start talking," I said grimly.

"As you know, this has been a strange year. It started with that bizarre earthquake here in Paris a few months back. Elise Villecourt was the first—and only—person to propose that the earthquake was not natural in its cause."

"Meaning what?" I asked in alarm. How in the world did someone manufacture an earthquake from *un*natural causes?

He shrugged. "I'll explain in a moment. But suffice it to say that Monsieur Dupont had her claim investigated and found reason to believe she was correct."

What in the heck had I stepped into the middle of?

Montrose continued. "Soon after the quake, Madame Villecourt suggested to my boss that another form of attack from the same source was likely. This time, she anticipated that it might involve the draining of electrical power from the French power supply—"

I interrupted, "The TGV. There was a big blackout in central France this morning."

He nodded. "That is only the latest of a number of inexplicable blackouts we've experienced since Madame Villecourt made her prediction."

"I haven't heard anything about other power failures."

He pursed his lips. "It was deemed alarmist for the press to report on the blackouts. There was no need to panic the populace over a phantom threat to the French power grid."

"Which is to say, Dupont put the kibosh on news coverage of the electricity problems."

Montrose frowned at my comment and opened his mouth, undoubtedly to defend his boss, but I cut him off.

"Except there really is a threat to the power grid, isn't there? And whoever's trying to kill Elise is mixed up in it. No, wait. They're trying to kill her to shut her up, aren't they? She knows something about these power outages the killers don't want to become public. What is it she knows?" I demanded.

Montrose sighed. "She has suggested a possible source for the power outages."

When he didn't continue I said, "And that is?"

He looked me square in the eye and said the last thing I ever expected to hear come out of his bureaucratic mouth. "Magic."

I stared. Gave a laughing snort of disbelief. "You've got to be kidding."

"I wish I were."

"You're telling me the president of France believes the French power grid is under attack from *magic?* What sort of magic, pray tell?"

Montrose winced. "That is exactly how I reacted when I first heard about it, too. And to answer your question, I suppose earth magic would be the best way to describe it. The theory goes that a net of energy covers the surface of the earth. Some people say it comes from the Earth's magnetic field, others believe it's tied to deposits of certain ores underground. Some say the lines are created by cosmic energy of some kind being collected by the Earth and stored like a battery, and others believe they represent the Earth's chi. Take your pick."

At about that point, I realized I was staring. I blinked a couple times while he continued.

"Regardless of what they are or where they come from, there is a measurable network of areas with increased energy readings that spans the Earth's surface. The threads of that net are called ley lines, and the knots where the ley lines intersect are called nodes. Large nodes where many ley lines come together are referred to as nexus points. Are you with me so far?"

I nodded, speechless.

He continued crisply. "With proper…sensitivity to such things…mankind has been able to sense these lines of power and their intersections. Not surprisingly, great religious and ceremonial sites around the world sit upon ley lines and their intersections. Notre Dame Cathedral here in Paris sits on a large nexus point, I'm told. Stonehenge, Angkor Wat in Vietnam, the Forbidden City in China, Machu Picchu, the Temple Mount, they all sit atop of some of the largest nexus points on the planet."

"And what does all this have to do with earthquakes and power outages?" I asked.

"The Paris earthquake was caused by someone attempting to manipulate a ley line running underneath the city."

"May I compliment you on managing to say that with a straight face?" I commented dryly.

"Actually, I saw proof with my own eyes that this is the case. I must warn you that what I am about to tell you is highly classified information. Were you to leak it to anyone, you may rest assured that you would be thrown into the deepest, darkest dungeon we could find and the key thrown away."

His eyes twinkled when he said that, but I got the distinct impression he wasn't kidding, either.

He continued in a hushed tone. "We have positive proof that the Paris earthquake was created by a scientist. He used a machine—a pulse bomb—to send a burst of energy down a ley line. That's what triggered the Paris earthquake. He was apprehended and his machine seized while attempting to cause another—larger—earthquake."

"How much larger?" I asked cautiously.

He nodded as if to confirm my suspicion. "Much larger."

"Then why aren't you talking to him? He's the scientist, after all."

"He's dead."

Of course. The guy who jumped off Notre Dame Cathedral after Catrina chased him out of the Black Madonna exhibit last month. I recalled her saying something about the deceased being a geologist. "And what does all of this have to do with the power grid?"

He glanced around furtively and leaned in close to me, his voice even lower. "We suspect that someone else knew about sending power down the ley lines. Now they're trying to activate the ley lines by some other method. A method that requires enormous amounts of electricity."

"Why are you telling all this to me? I'm an art historian you don't know from Adam." I added flippantly, "For all you know, I might get a wild hair to go out and create my own earthquake machine for fun."

That garnered a little huff of exasperation out of him. "I know this sounds…bizarre. But I assure you, I am not crazy and what I am telling you is the God's honest truth. At any rate, Madame Villecourt first suggested that another possible way to power up the ley lines would involve channeling electricity through them. And, soon after she did so, the attempts upon her life started."

I asked in alarm, "You mean there have been several?"

He blinked. "Oh, yes. There have been a half-dozen attacks. But her luck—it is uncanny. It is almost as if the gods are looking out for her."

"What do you want me to do about the power grid?"

He shrugged. "Find out who is trying to kill Elise, and we believe you will find who is using the ley lines. As soon as we know who they are, we will apprehend them. Before they knock out the electricity to us all."

Suddenly, I felt trapped in a bad episode of *The Twilight Zone*. "So I'm supposed to track down a bunch of magic-using, ley-line manipulating, would-be murderers for you and save the entire French power grid?"

Montrose responded wryly, "Actually, much more than just the power grid is at stake. The French economy depends heavily upon electricity, and the safety and livelihood of the French people depend upon the economy. So, for simplicity's sake, let us just say the fate of France rests in your hands."

I absorbed that one for long moments in silence. And then I said the only thing that came to mind. "Gee. Isn't that special?"

Chapter 7

I suppose I shouldn't have been surprised when my dreams that night landed me back in that stone-walled Renaissance bedchamber from my previous dream.

It was night this time and colder than sin. A thick pall of smoke hung from the ceiling, probably from the giant fireplace and a sluggish blaze that looked to be putting out little, if any, heat. The red velvet bed throw was in a heap on the floor, and furs were piled high on the short, wide bed. I started as the pile heaved.

I looked more closely and made out a man lying on his back. Not a bad-looking guy. Faintly like Robert Fraser with dark hair and dark, intense eyes. But then I spied a pale, female form rising up above him, sitting back on her haunches. She reached down with her hand, and the guy groaned with what sounded like discomfort. He gasped something about being allowed to finish, but she repeated what-

ever she'd done before, and he groaned again. Demanding woman. Definitely making this guy suffer a little.

Finally, she swung a leg over him and sat astride him. Didn't take a lot of imagination to figure out what was going on there. An almost animal energy enveloped the lovers. It was arousing in an uncomfortable, voyeuristic sort of way that I didn't especially like, but couldn't prevent, either. The sounds and smells of their sex rolled over me, pungent and primitive. The lovers became more urgent, their movements becoming jerky as their bodies slapped together. An image of Robert Fraser and me doing that flickered through my mind and my breath quickened sharply.

The woman sat up, straddling the man. She bounced up and down ridiculously fast on top of him and he moaned dramatically. Good Lord. Is that what sex really looked like? The guy partially sat up and gave a theatrical shout. He fell back on the bed, flung his arms out wide and broke into a monologue about the transports of ecstacy to which his lover had just lifted him.

A log broke in the fireplace, sending up a shower of sparks and shooting up a new burst of flames. In the sudden glow, I got my first good look at the woman. Queen Elizabeth again. No surprise there. The Virgin Queen, eh? Not.

What truly shocked me was the look on her face as she leaned back, panting. Her features were icy cold fury incarnate. That was one pissed-off woman. The guy must be some sort of dimwit not to be aware of it. But he prattled on about the firmament moving and started into something inane about roses. I wished he'd shut up already. That's about how Elizabeth looked like she felt, too.

Finally, the guy squinted up at her. And stopped cold. "What ails you, my rosebud?" he wailed dramatically. "I shall plunge a dagger into my breast if I have displeased you. What can I do—"

Thankfully, ol' Liz cut him off, snapping, "Cease and desist! You have done quite enough already."

He looked perplexed. And alarmed.

She climbed off him and snagged a fur robe absently as she crawled down from the high bed. She strode over to the fireplace naked, dragging the throw behind her. She ran to the bony side, her shoulders narrow and her hips unattractively wide. Her breasts were pancake shaped, her skin snow-white but sprinkled liberally with unfortunate freckles. And her armpits were hairy. Definitely too much information for me. I'd never look at a painting of her the same way again.

Elizabeth planted herself squarely in front of the fire and turned to face her lover. "What is different about me?" she demanded.

The poor guy looked panicked. Didn't know the right answer to that one, did he? "You—you—" he stammered. But then he gathered himself. "You are more beautiful than ever. The stars shine in your—"

"Shut up," Elizabeth snapped. "I am increasing."

"Increasing?" her lover repeated stupidly.

"Can you not see it, you fool? I am with child."

Now that she mentioned it, she did have a bit of a belly forming. That distinctive swell low in the abdomen that can mean only one thing.

The guy reared back in horror, all but climbing the head-board. "It cannot be! We took every precaution! The sheep's intestine sheaths—"

"Did not work. My lady-in-waiting says I am at least three months along."

"What shall you do?" the man gasped.

Elizabeth's face went hard and closed. I was right there with her. The jerk hadn't said, "What shall we do?"

With great interest, I turned to see what she had to say on the matter. She wrapped the fur about her and stared into the

*fire for a long time. Meanwhile, the scumball crept out of the
bed behind her and dressed in total silence.*

"Fleeing the scene of your crime, are you, Winchester?"
Elizabeth asked coldly.

The guy looked about ready to puke. "I thought to give you
time to ponder what you will do."

"I shall not lop your head off if that is what you fear," Elizabeth retorted. "I will not make an orphan of my child. At
least, not without provocation," she added direly.

Winchester halted his inching progress toward a large
tapestry and the secret passage I assumed must be hidden
behind it. He blurted, "Then what will you do?"

She flung off the fur and leaned toward the fire, pulling out
a stick of burning wood. She carried it over to the big desk
across the room and lit a tall candle. Finally, she answered
bitterly, "I shall abase myself as I vowed never to do again
in this lifetime. I must write a letter."

"To whom?"

My question exactly. I watched Elizabeth intently as she
sat down, naked, and pulled a piece of parchment out of a
drawer. She sharpened a quill with quick, angry strokes of a
small knife. She looked like she wished that feather she was
carving up so violently was her lover's private parts. Eventually, she looked up at Winchester and bit out, "I shall write
to the pope. Offer him a deal. I will allow the Catholic faith
to be practiced freely in England if he will recognize this child
as the heir to my throne."

Winchester's jaw dropped. "But the pope has steadfastly
declared you a bastard all these years. And your parents
were wedded. Why would he reverse course now and recognize this child when we are not—"

The guy stopped speaking abruptly, as if he'd just realized
the life-threatening folly of bringing up the illicit nature of his
relationship with the queen. A little slow on the uptake, he was.

Elizabeth glared at him from the desk. "Leave," she ordered imperiously.

At least he wasn't dumb enough to disobey that command. He skedaddled, slipping behind the tapestry and disappearing.

The queen's shoulders slumped. I thought she might cry, but she didn't. Strong woman. After a moment, she lifted her head, staring straight ahead at the statue on the desk before her. "Damn you!" she burst out. "Why didn't you tell me this was the other part of the gift?"

What gift? I tried to ask her, but instead, the dream evaporated....

And I was sitting up, my mouth trying to speak, staring at the walls of my own bedroom. What was *up* with these dreams of mine? They were like nothing I'd ever had before. More like visions of some kind. And speaking of visions, I gave a quick glance around my room. Whew. No sign of the ghostly woman from my bathroom mirror. I flopped back down but had trouble going back to sleep. Elizabeth's anguished cry kept echoing in my head. What gift?

I knew exactly where I had to go when I woke the next morning. To see Elise. When I stepped out of the elevator at the hospital, the desk directly in front of me was crowded with what looked like some sort of morning staff meeting breaking up. I inquired after Madame Villecourt, and a doctor separated himself from the crowd right away.

"Who are you?" he asked me in a borderline rude tone.

Every now and then I really love having an Interpol badge, even though I usually feel like a complete fraud for flashing it. I pulled it out now, and the good doctor thawed considerably.

"Come with me," he said.

I followed him through a set of double doors into a much quieter ward and was pleased to see that I had to show identification, sign in, get patted down and have my purse searched by a gendarme before I was allowed to see Elise. A nurse told me she was asleep, but gestured me to come along, anyway. Apparently, it was time to wake Elise to check her vital signs.

On the way down the hall, the nurse commented, "Ah, to have inherited your grandmother's genes. She is in spectacular health for a woman of eighty-eight."

I was distracted enough by the nurse mistaking Elise for my grandmother that I almost missed the eighty-eight bit. Good grief! *Eighty-eight?* And to think I'd guessed she was sixtyish when I met her!

We stepped into Elise's private room. She was awake, albeit groggy. Her face lit up when she caught sight of me, though. I could swear those were tears of gratitude glistening in her eyes.

"How are you, my dear?" she murmured.

"I believe that's my line." I smiled back. She grasped my hand, and her grip wasn't as firm as I remembered. Must be the concussion making her weak. "How are you?" I asked.

"I'll live. So. What have you come to ask me today?"

At her dry remark, I felt more than a little guilty. I was, indeed, here to interrogate her again. But it would have to be in private. I waited while the nurse injected something into Elise's IV drip and then announced that I could only stay a few minutes. The nurse left the room and shut the door behind her.

I looked down at Elise. Her hair seemed whiter than I remembered, her skin more fragile. Must be the stress of her injury and being in the hospital. I said quietly, "I had a visitor last night. Guy by the name of Montrose. He spun an interesting tale."

"Pray tell."

Cautious of the policeman sitting in the chair outside her door, I said only, "He talked about some interesting lines."

Elise nodded immediately.

"How did you learn about—all of that?" I asked.

She smiled. "I am a scholar."

I frowned. "I thought you studied the history of the Catholic Church."

Another nod and a firm answer. "I do."

I stared down at her. Was she trying to tell me the Catholic Church was somehow mixed up with the use of these supposed ley lines? Her eyelids sagged to half-mast. The nurse must have put a sedative of some kind in her IV.

"You will need my jet. The pilot knows where to land in Rome…." her voice trailed away.

Rome? What the heck was in Rome that had to do with ley lines or the Catholic—Of course. Not Rome. The Vatican. "Elise!" I said sharply enough to pop her eyelids back open a millimeter. "Do I need to go to the Vatican?"

She gave the faintest of nods and whispered, "Go into…the…wind."

And then she was out cold. Dammit. I was really sick of all these innuendos and puzzles. What the heck did "go into the wind" mean? I left her room, thinking. The Vatican, huh? I was waiting for an elevator when my cell phone rang. I pulled it out and was relieved to see it wasn't one of my bosses calling to pester me.

"Ana Reisner," I said.

"This is Madame Lebec at the city morgue. I have a body that came in early this morning. We have a tentative ID from a wallet, but procedure requires me to attempt to find someone to make a positive ID on him. The police suggested I call you."

Robert Fraser's face flashed through my mind, and the thought of him pale and lifeless made me miss a breath. "Who is it?" I asked in alarm.

"We believe it is René Hallibert."

Oh, no. Not René. I felt punched in the stomach. "I'll be right there," I said heavily. I suppose it was inevitable. Living out in the elements was hard on a person, not to mention the inherent dangers of the humanity a soul was exposed to on the streets.

When I arrived at the morgue—an appropriately grim structure on the outskirts of Paris—I was directed to an empty waiting room holding a few tattered issues of the *Paris Match* magazine and uncomfortable plastic chairs.

A second before the waiting room door opened, I felt who was about to walk through it. I looked up in anticipation, my breath catching in my throat. Sure enough, Robert Fraser strolled in. His presence was a physical thing upon my skin. I could all but feel his body against mine, inside mine, surrounding mine, and I instantly ached to make it real.

He stopped cold when he saw me, too. His pupils dilated hard and fast, and I felt my own eyes go wide as he stared down at me. The heat in his gaze nearly brought me to my feet. He moved then, stepping fully into the room and letting the door close behind him. He eyed the chair beside mine, and then moved carefully to the one across from me. For a moment I was crushed, but then the advantage of this arrangement became clear. We could look at each other to our heart's content this way.

He sat down, leaning forward, his elbows planted on his knees. And stared at me. Intently. Enough to send what little breath I had whooshing out of my lungs. I told myself I was sitting in a morgue and this wasn't the slightest bit appropriate, but darned if I could tear my gaze away from him.

"What is your name?" he murmured. "I lay awake half the night wondering what to call you in my thoughts."

I was in his thoughts? I pressed my thighs tightly together against the lust raging in my loins. "My name is Ana. Analise,"

"Lovely," he murmured. "It fits you." His gaze touched me all over and he nodded in affirmation. "It's elegant. Classic. Timeless."

He thought I was all those things? My initial pleased reaction gave way to dismay as it dawned on me that *elegant* and *timeless* sounded like my grandmother's jewelry, not sex. I wanted to be hot and irresistible to this man. Misery washed over me. Why hadn't I done something about my wardrobe before now? And why hadn't I put on more makeup this morning and fixed my hair in something other than a boring, sexless ponytail?

Robert shifted in his seat and I focused on him once more. He spoke in the lilting rhythm of Scotland that sounded more like song than speech. "I apologize for staring at you. I'm afraid I canna' take my eyes off you."

"Why not?" I blurted. The words were out of my mouth before I could stop them. Dull heat crept up my neck and spread over my face.

He laughed quietly. "No need to blush for me. At least not yet."

The sexual undercurrent of his words about knocked me off the chair. I squeezed my thighs even more tightly together.

The waiting room door opened, and a sniffling woman came in and sat down at the end of the room. Periodically, she erupted into full-blown sobs, and then they'd trail off to nose-blowing.

Robert leaned back in his seat, his eyes twinkling as if we shared a hilarious secret between the two of us. And maybe the fact that he actually seemed attracted to me was just that. At any rate, we sat there in silence, looking at each other. I can't even begin to describe the things I imagined while I looked at him and he looked at me. I felt another blush begin to climb my neck, and his mouth twitched up into a quick grin with a flash of dimple. Praying he had no idea what I was thinking about doing to him, I succumbed to yet another blush, and the rest of my face burned fiercely. I must look like a tomato.

I don't know how long we sat there. But eventually, my

befuddled mind finally unwound enough for it to dawn on me to wonder why he was here. The sniffling woman had pulled out a cell phone and began sobbing into it.

Under cover of her commotion, Robert leaned forward as if to speak, and I matched the motion. In unison, we both said, "What are you doing here?"

We laughed awkwardly, and he motioned for me to go first. I complied, saying, "I'm here to identify the body of a friend. You?"

"The same," he said in that rough voice that sent chills down my spine. "I'm sorry for your loss."

"And I for you," I replied, frowning. Was it possible that Robert knew René?

He leaned back once more, propped a leather boot on his opposite knee and draped an arm across the back of the plastic chair beside him. I couldn't strike a pose that casual and sexy if I practiced it for a year. I was painfully aware of my primly crossed ankles tucked underneath my chair and my hands clenched together in my lap. God, I was a stick-in-the-mud. But for the life of me, I couldn't uncoil my body into something approximating relaxation. The very presence of Robert Fraser tied me in knots.

"How's your search going?" I finally managed to choke out.

His eyebrows shot straight up and he didn't look thrilled that I'd brought it up. With a glance at the woman on the phone he answered, "Slowly." Then silence. Not going to help me maintain a conversation, was he?

Problem was, I was nervous. Not only was I in grave danger of making a complete fool of myself over him, but I'd never seen a dead body before and I didn't know how I was going to react to it. I'd have been okay by myself, but with him here, now I had to worry about throwing up or fainting or something else equally embarrassing. An urge to babble nearly overwhelmed me, but I managed to bite it back.

I was surprised when he spoke again. "Do you work in the art world, or are you just a lover of art?"

Grateful for the safe topic of conversation, I replied, "Both, I suppose. I'm an art historian. I catalogue and mark pieces of art." *So guys like him couldn't fence their stolen pieces.*

"Do you have a favorite time period?"

A harmless enough question, small talk, really. But it occurred to me to turn it into a minor fishing expedition. I replied lightly, "I love statuary. Pre-Renaissance. And you?"

He jerked upright in his seat. "Really? Are there any good private collections in Paris?"

Well. That certainly had hit a nerve. He was looking for private collectors, was he? Perhaps looking to acquire Elise's stolen statue on the black market for a private buyer? He had been asking Catrina about Black Madonnas, after all. I didn't *know* that was what Elise's statue was, but the coincidence was hard to ignore.

I shrugged noncommittally. "There are a few collectors here and there." And given his past, I couldn't in good conscience reveal who any of them were to him.

His unwavering gaze held mine captive, weighing my vague response. Good Lord, the man was looking straight into my soul.

Partially to distract him, and partially to see how he answered, I casually asked, "Who did you say you were working for again on tracking down the provenance of that statue?"

"I didn't."

Damn. His face closed up tighter than a bank vault. And all those lovely sexual vibes abruptly ceased rolling off him. I felt their loss acutely.

An interior door opened just then, and a woman wearing green surgical scrubs stuck her head out into the waiting room. "Ah, good. You are both here."

I jumped about a foot straight up in the air. Tearing my

gaze away from Robert, I looked up at her. "We are both here?" I echoed, confused. That sounded as if we were supposed to have come here together.

"Yes," she said briskly, "To view Monsieur Hallibert. If you will follow me."

I looked quickly at Robert, but he beat me to the question. "How did you know René?" he demanded.

"He…worked…for me now and then."

Robert frowned. "You mean he snitched for you?"

I shrugged and said, "For what it's worth, I liked him. We had dinner together this weekend. How did you know him?" I suspected I knew the answer to that one, but I wanted to hear it from his own lips.

"We worked together a number of years ago."

"Stealing things."

"As a matter of fact, yes," he answered evenly. But his shoulders went stiff and his jawline looked as if he were biting down on something hard.

God, why had I gone and said that? Stupid, stupid, stupid! It was a surefire way to kill any attraction between us. Plus, I felt like a complete heel for bringing up the guy's past. He'd done his time and was out of jail now. For all I knew he'd turned over a new leaf. Silently, I followed him into the morgue, cursing myself with every step I took.

The smell of formaldehyde permeated the air. I supposed the antiseptic smell was better than the alternative, but it was enough to make a person faintly nauseous. I braced myself when the woman in front of us opened a small door in businesslike fashion and pulled a long tray out, holding the covered body of a corpse. She flipped the rubber sheet back.

The first thing that captured my attention were the vivid purple marks around the dead man's throat. They were garish against the blue-gray pallor of his skin. I steeled myself and lifted my gaze to his face. And stared. Robert's hand gripped my shoulder all of a sudden as if to steady himself against the nearest solid object.

But his voice was strong as he spoke aloud the exact words ringing in my head. "That's not René Hallibert."

That knocked the bored look off the attendant's face. Startled, she glanced over at me. I shook my head in the negative.

"There was a wallet with identification in his clothing," the woman insisted.

I looked down at the clothes the dead man was wearing and nodded. "I saw René two days ago, and that is what he was wearing. And trust me, he only had one set of clothing to his name. Maybe this guy robbed René and was killed later."

"Or maybe Monsieur Hallibert killed this man," the woman retorted.

Robert flared up. "René is an art thief. Not a murderer. Art thieves do not kill people."

And he should know. But I didn't say that. Yet again, the question ran through my head. What art thief broke that code and stole Elise's statue with the intent to kill her? He or she was likely a lone wolf. Other art thieves working in the same ring would never stand for the violence. Of the most wanted thieves in Europe at the moment, only Dr. Moon was thought to be a solo operator. Whoever Dr. Moon might be.

I piped up. "I have to agree with Monsieur Fraser. René Hallibert is no murderer."

The woman shoved the tray back into the refrigerated wall and led us back out to the waiting room, muttering all the while about the hassle of having to retag this guy as a John Doe and all the extra paperwork it was going to cause her.

Robert and I made our way out of the building in silence. We stepped out onto the sidewalk, squinting in the late morning sunlight. Then he turned to me and asked, "Do you have any idea where to find René?"

I shrugged. "He usually stays in an alley behind *Le Jeu*

D'Amour in the Latin Quarter. But, given that those were his clothes on that dead guy, I'm betting he's hiding somewhere only a rat could find him right now."

"I heard he'd fallen on hard times."

A silence fell between us. Awkwardly, I said, "Well, I must be off. Good luck." I have no idea what I was wishing him luck for, but it had just come out of my mouth. I turned away and hurried off down the sidewalk, cursing myself for being such a social klutz around him. Clearly, I'd been out of the dating pool far too long. And darned if that guy didn't make me think about diving back into its shark-infested waters.

I walked for a couple blocks to clear my head. Why had René's clothes shown up on a dead man? Where was René? Could this have anything to do with my investigation of Elise's stolen statue? I had asked René to check it out, after all. Had he run into some sort of danger and had to make an escape that involved leaving his clothes behind?

I hadn't been kidding when I told Robert I was certain René would not be at any of his usual hangouts. I was also certain that, until the man decided to surface, nobody had a prayer of finding him. He hadn't been a top-notch cat burglar for nothing.

Now what was I to do with myself? Elise's offer of her jet came back to me. I looked around. I was in a residential area. Just ahead, I spied a small park. It was enclosed by a tall, wrought iron fence and was bursting with an array of autumn-colored mums and yellow-leafed trees. I opened the gate and stepped inside the oasis. I found a bench in a secluded area surrounded by tall shrubs and sat down.

I dug around in my purse, found the calling card Madame Trucot had given me and dialed the number on it. If I were lucky, maybe the housekeeper would pick up the phone.

"Allô?" Madame Trucot said in my ear.

Thank goodness. "Hello. This is Ana Reisner. I just visited Madame Villecourt, and I thought you'd like to know she's resting comfortably. We spoke for a few moments and her spirits are good."

"Thank you for thinking of me!" The woman sounded genuinely pleased. "Madame Elise, she is such a fine lady."

"Indeed she is," I agreed warmly. "I actually called you to ask about something else, as well. Elise offered me the use of her private jet just before she fell asleep. Was she likely to have been serious, or was that perhaps just the medications talking?"

Madame Trucot laughed. "Oh, no. She was serious. She is an extraordinarily generous woman. She is also intent on helping you as much as she can in your search. One moment. I will get you the phone number at the airport."

In a moment, I had copied down the number on the back of my electric bill, which was stuffed into my purse. I hung up with Madame Trucot and dialed the new number. Sure enough, I'd reached the company that managed Elise's jet for her. I wasn't entirely surprised when the man told me Madame Trucot was on the other line and had verified that the Villecourt jet was to be placed at my disposal.

"Where do you wish to go, Mademoiselle Reisner?"

I didn't hesitate. "Rome. The pilot knows where to land."

"When do you wish to depart?" the man asked me.

"How soon can the plane be ready?"

"It will take the pilots approximately an hour to get here and file their flight plan."

Wow. I didn't need to leave *that* fast. I'd like to have a look around for René and make sure he was all right. "How about tomorrow morning? Say, eight o'clock?"

"Very well. I will schedule an eight o'clock departure. You will need your passport to enter Italy."

Dang, that was easy! I stowed my phone in my purse and stood up to leave.

And fell flat on my face, plowing my cheek hard into the dirt, as something incredibly heavy slammed into me and knocked me to the ground.

Chapter 8

I don't know how other women react to getting tackled by strange men, but I sort of freaked out. The idea of getting raped or killed brings out the violent side of me, it turns out. I twisted in the grasp of whoever had me around my thighs and hit and clawed at everything I could get my hands on. And, of course, I screamed my head off.

My assailant swore and called out, *"Un poco d'aiuto qui!"*

That was Italian. He was demanding help. Oh, crap. Sure enough, a second guy leaped out of the bushes, clapped one hand over my mouth and wrapped his other arm around my neck from behind. I twisted and squirmed, lifting my hips off the ground as I fought their grips. I was not going down without a fight! I bit at the guy's hand and managed to get a little flesh between my teeth. More swearing in Italian erupted.

And then all of a sudden, there was a third man. Dammit. I was hosed now.

Except this guy came roaring into the fray and slammed his fist in the face of the guy who had my neck. Both of my assailants let go of me and jumped to their feet to face this new threat. I took the opportunity to kick the guy who'd had my legs as hard as I could in his shins. He howled and jumped back from me. I leaped to my feet, my back to that of my impromptu rescuer.

"Keep screaming, lass!" the third man ordered me—in a Scots brogue.

Robert. What in the world was he doing here? No time to think about it, though, because my two assailants rushed us. I ducked as my guy grabbed for me and jerked my knee up hard and fast. The guy'd been ready for the move and got out of the way. But it made him step back. I heard the crack of knuckles on flesh behind me and prayed Robert was handling his guy all right. Then I felt the warm body at my back spin away. Crud. I hoped I hadn't just lost my backup.

I watched my guy warily, my hands up defensively, and my weight on the foot I'd just lifted. I figured if I threw the other foot the next time, I might catch the guy off guard. But then my Italian attacker took another quick step back, pivoted and took off running. His buddy joined him, wiping at his nose, which was pouring blood.

Hands grabbed my shoulders again, but this time in concern, not aggression. "Are you all right?"

While heat flooded me from the shoulders outward, I did a quick body inventory. "I'm fine. Where did you come from?"

"I was following you."

"Why?"

The wail of police sirens started in the distance and got louder quickly. "Later," he bit out. "You'll forgive me if I don't stay to make nice with the coppers."

Frankly, I was more interested in knowing why he'd appeared out of the blue to rescue me than I was in dealing with the police right now. "Did you get a good look at those men?" I asked him.

"Yeah."

I replied quickly, "Good, because I didn't. Let's get out of here. We can make a police report later."

He stared at me in surprise.

I took a couple steps back toward the gate, but he put a restraining hand on my arm. "This way. There's another exit from the park."

I followed him as he walked toward the back gate. Why didn't he run? Maybe it would draw too much attention? I trusted his experience as a criminal to best know how to flee the scene of a crime. Sure enough, just as the police cars drew up on the other side of the park, we slipped out of the park unimpeded and blended in to the flow of pedestrian traffic.

We walked for a couple blocks and then Robert swore under his breath. Without warning he grabbed my arm and yanked me down the steps to a Metro stop.

"Have you got a pass for the tube?" Robert bit out as we all but ran for the turnstiles.

I nodded. I bought a monthly unlimited usage pass for the Metro like most native Parisians did.

"Get it out." He dug in his wallet and came up with a Metro ticket. We shoved through the iron posts and Robert grabbed my arm again. In a few seconds, we lost ourselves in the stream of people flowing through the dim underground tunnels. He checked over his shoulder every few seconds. Clearly he thought we were being followed. And given that he was the one who knew what my attackers looked like, it was up to him to spot these guys.

We stopped on a platform to wait for the next train, and Robert dragged me into a dark shadow behind a cement post. He backed me up against it and crowded close, using his body to shield me from view. At least that's what I thought he was doing. It could be he was making a blatant pass at me and I was too dense to catch the hint.

His head tilted down toward me, and for all the world it looked as if he were about to inhale my tonsils in a blistering kiss. Except his gray eyes were nearly black with concern and there wasn't the slightest hint of sex in them. Damn.

He murmured, "Your face is dirty. Let me wipe it off."

His hands were gentle as he used his handkerchief to wipe off my cheek. Pleasure speared into me, and I caught myself swaying forward into his touch, as impersonal as it was. My eyelids wanted to drift shut so I could savor the moment. This was definitely turning into some sort of unhealthy obsession, but darned if I could do a thing to stop myself from reacting that way to him.

"You've got a few scrapes that could use more thorough cleaning. Where do you live?"

"Near the Opera."

He nodded. "Good. Penny's not far from there."

"Penny?" Oh, God. He had a girlfriend. Jealousy and grief flared in equal parts in my gut, both of them white hot in their intensity. Sheesh! I'd just met the guy! He was authorized to have a prior life of his own. Nonetheless, I went rigid with regret and humiliation at the way I'd thrown myself at him.

"Yeah. Penny. My hog."

Huh? "You have a pig?"

He grinned. Lord, I loved his dimples. "No. A motorcycle. Penny's my Harley-Davidson."

The slang term for the iconic American brand of motorcycles came back to me all of a sudden. I'd been living in France for so long that such euphemisms from my homeland were all but lost. I cannot describe how good the cool flood of relief rushing through me felt. It left me feeling almost limp.

A whoosh of cool air from the tunnel on my left and a squeal of brakes announced the arrival of the train. Robert's arms caged me in place till the very last second before the train pulled out, and then we leaped for it. He yanked me down to a crouch beside him, well below the level of the windows. When the tunnel's blackness had closed in around us, he finally let me stand up.

"Well, that was fun," I commented.

I was rewarded with another flash of those delicious dimples.

We exited the subway near Notre Dame Cathedral. Robert kept a sharp eye peeled out around us but didn't spot our Italian friends again. Nonetheless, we hurried quickly enough to where his bike was parked to leave me out of breath. The black-and-chrome chopper fit him. It was dark, and dangerous, and sexy.

"Hop on," he said casually.

"I'm wearing a skirt!"

"So?"

"So, I'll have to hike it practically up to my waist to ride that thing."

He shrugged. "You've got great legs. What's the problem?"

He thought I had great legs? Well, then. Not to mention I'd get to wrap them around his hips. Sign me up. I nodded, capitulating.

He swung a strong leg over the bike and kicked up the kick stand. He looked at me expectantly. My heart about to burst out of my chest, I hitched up my skirt—not quite to my waist but nearly to my hips—and swung my right leg over the back of the bike.

Oh, God. His buttocks nestled against my crotch, and my thighs tucked under the full length of his. He started the engine and I lurched straight up in the air. It vibrated against my loins and I nearly came apart on the spot.

Robert murmured over his shoulder, "Hang on to me."

Weakly, I wrapped my arms around his waist. The leather of his jacket was cool to the touch, but the man beneath it burned me alive. I tried not to cling too tightly, but I probably failed. What little control I had left was completely finished off by the four-hundred horsepower vibrator between my legs. He steered the bike out into traffic while I descended into a nearly orgasmic state and stayed there for the entire—unfortunately short—ride to my house. It was all I could do to remember my address and shout it into his ear over the traffic noise.

At least the noise prevented him from hearing how fast I was breathing as I tried not to writhe around like some over-sexed snake. It was a killer to sit still and let all those sensations of man and machine roll over me. But I managed. Barely.

Robert parked the bike across from my building and slid off from in front of me. He looked down at me. His eyes were black and hot as if he knew how his motorcycle had affected me. And I was too blown away to care. Silently, he held out a hand to me and helped me off the bike. I tottered across the street on shaky legs and managed to let us into my apartment without collapsing.

I stepped inside. Stopped. Stared. The place was a shambles. Drawers were pulled out and overturned, cushions were thrown off furniture, not a single book was on a shelf where it belonged, and even my clothes were strewn in the middle of the floor. Somebody had ransacked the place!

"I swear, I'm not this messy a housekeeper. Someone's been in here."

Robert went into the kitchen to pour me a cold drink while I called the police. Heck, after that motorcycle ride, a cigarette was probably more appropriate.

I got through to the detective I wanted, a guy I'd worked with a number of times before. And a big softie.

"Someone's gone through my apartment, Victor. But here's the thing. I don't have time to stick around while you guys do your forensic thing on it. Can I just seal the place up and have someone come over here tomorrow? I promise I won't touch anything vital. Please?"

"It's not standard procedure, you know."

"I know. But you'd be doing me a huge favor," I wheedled.

He sighed. "All right. But leave right away. And don't put anything back where it belongs. Just leave the mess."

"No cleaning. Got it. Oh, and I was assaulted in a park a little while ago."

"And I suppose you fled that crime scene, too," he commented sarcastically.

"Well, yes. But it's really important. I'm investigating something huge and my bosses are breathing fire down my neck to solve the problem yesterday."

"What happened, in which park, and what did your assailant look like?" Victor asked heavily.

I gave him a quick report of the assault and relayed Robert's descriptions of my two attackers. The detective said he'd enter it in the crime reporting system for me.

I went into the bathroom, which was relatively undestroyed, and washed off my face. The scrape on my right cheek wasn't too bad. It was red and angry, but there were only a few scratches deep enough to bleed. In a day or two, it would be mostly gone.

I stepped out into the living room. Robert was looking over the mess with a critical eye. "They were looking for something. Too many valuable items were left behind for this to be a robbery."

And he ought to know.

Robert asked, "Why did those men in the park jump you? Is it related to this?"

"I have no idea."

He shot me a skeptical look. "Two middle-aged, well-dressed men don't just randomly attack a woman in the park in broad daylight. Don't you have any clue who they might be?"

"Well, I might have a vague notion of who they are."

He stared at me expectantly.

Where to begin? I couldn't tell him about the power grid. Montrose had sworn me to secrecy on that one. I dared not tell him about my weird dreams, or the ghost I'd seen. He'd think I was nuts. Although on second thought, he probably already thought I was crazy. I mean, how many women would sit in a morgue and make goo-goo eyes at some guy they've barely met?

"It's complicated." I sighed and plowed on. "There's this woman. Something was stolen from her recently and I'm trying to help her get it back."

"What was stolen?"

"I'm not sure. I think it may be a statue."

He frowned. "You don't know what was stolen? Why don't you ask her?"

"She won't tell me."

Sure enough, he stared at me for a moment, as if he were weighing my sanity.

I blurted, "I know it sounds bizarre. But she made a vow never to talk about whatever was stolen. I do know that it's very old and probably a human figure wearing simple robes. Catrina Dauvergne—you met her at the Cluny—guesses it's around eighteen inches tall."

"How did you know about me and René?" he demanded.

The abrupt shift of topic startled me. It took me a moment to figure out he was talking about my earlier reference at the morgue to him and René working together. I thought fast. I ought to lie. Tell him that René had mentioned it. Although, thieves took their code of silence nearly as seriously as they took their code of nonviolence. Robert wouldn't buy it for a second if I told him René had spilled the name of one of his old partners to me.

And so, I told him the truth. "When you entered France, a message was generated by the Immigration service and sent to my office."

"And you work for?"

I winced. "I'm not a police officer. I'm an art historian."

He stared at me expectantly. He was going to make me say it. And it wasn't hard to guess how a convicted art thief was going to react to it. So much for having met a man who fired my soul. I exhaled heavily. "I work for Interpol."

Air sucked in between his teeth and his eyes narrowed.

For lack of anything else to say that might diffuse the sudden tension permeating the space between us, I said, "I also know you helped MI-6 with several other investigations, you did your time, and you got out early for good behavior. As far as I'm concerned, your slate with society is clean."

"It's one thing to say the words. It's another to believe them," he retorted with a touch of bitterness in his voice.

I suppose I couldn't blame him. In general, if I met someone I knew to be a convicted felon, I'd feel a definite caution where that person was concerned. However, the few genuine art thieves I'd actually met were not bad sorts at all. What really made me suspicious was that both of us were suddenly tracking down old religious statues. I'm just not a believer in that big of a coincidence. Was I looking for a Black Madonna, too? His Black Madonna, maybe?

Since we were being honest here, I fired off a salvo of my own. "What are you doing here in Paris? And where did you get that picture of the Black Madonna?"

He stared at me for a long time. Long enough that I figured he'd decided not to answer. Hence, I was surprised when he actually spoke. "It's a legit job. I've been hired to trace the provenance of the statue in that picture, and I'm in town to see what I can find out about it."

Provenance, eh? I had a fair bit of experience at tracing works of art, myself. "How's your search going?" I asked with genuine interest. Okay, so I was officially an art geek. I could stand in the middle of the carnage of my house and get caught up in an interesting provenance search.

He answered animatedly, "I've hit a dead end. I need to find out more about the cult of the Black Madonna in southern France. But the medieval Catholic Church destroyed most of the records about it."

He was an art geek, too, apparently.

I had a sudden thought. One that made my heart race and my body tingle. "I know someplace where the Church doesn't destroy its records on anything."

"Where?"

"The Vatican archives."

He frowned. "Don't you have to have some sort of letter of introduction and permission to get into those?"

I nodded. "I work for Interpol, remember? I've got access. And furthermore, I'm going to Rome tomorrow."

Disbelief flickered in his gaze. "Are you offering to take me with you?"

"I guess I am."

"I don't have a plane ticket, and flights these days book up pretty solid."

I grinned. "I happen to know there's an extra seat on the plane I'm taking."

He didn't hesitate. "Well, then. I guess I'm going to Rome tomorrow. When does the flight leave?"

"First thing in the morning. We can go together."

He nodded. And then he smiled. The sort of slow, sexy smile a man gives a woman whom he's anticipating seducing in the very near future.

And my heart nearly stopped. Apparently, he'd already overcome his objections to the identity of my employer. Who'd have thought when I got that phone call from the morgue this morning that I'd end up jetting off to one of the most romantic cities in the world tomorrow with the sexiest guy I'd ever met?

The morgue.

René.

My house.

My hormone-charged daydreams finally gave way to a burst of logic. "Do you have any idea where René might be hiding? I have reason to believe the same men who attacked me today and did this—" I gestured at the mess at our feet "—might be after him."

"Why's that?" Robert asked.

"The stolen statue I told you I'm looking for? I asked René to poke around a bit and see what he could find out about it. I think the men who jumped me did so because I'm investigating that statue. And if René's been asking questions about it, too…I'm worried about him. I need to find him. Warn him that he could be in danger. Maybe I can arrange for Interpol to take him somewhere safe for a little while."

Robert shrugged. "If René knows he's in danger, he's probably safer on the loose in Paris. He knows this city better than anyone I've ever met."

"Do you have any idea where he might go to hide? I still want to warn him if I can."

Robert added dryly, "And, if someone's after him, he obviously poked the right nerve. You'll want to find out what he's learned, too."

Honestly, I hadn't even thought about that. But as soon as Robert mentioned it, it made sense. "Good point."

"I might have an idea where he went. He had one particular hidey-hole that was his favorite. He called it his refuge of last resort. Said nobody would ever find him down there."

"Down where?" I asked eagerly.

"I don't even know if I could find it again. I'd have to show it to you myself."

"Let's go, then!"

Robert's gaze raked down my body. "You'll need to change clothes. Put on slacks you won't mind getting dirty. And walking shoes. If you have a flashlight and chalk, bring them, too."

Flashlight and chalk? It sounded as if we were going on an expedition of some kind. I went into my bedroom and, disturbing as little of the mess as I could, located appropriate clothes for our expedition. I certainly had no shortage of utilitarian clothing and slipped into rugged khaki pants, a cotton turtleneck and a sweater vest. I grabbed a rucksack and picked my way into the kitchen for the flashlight and chalk. I also grabbed matches, candles, a couple bottles of water, a tube of crackers and a can of almonds I happened to have in the cupboard.

I don't know why I threw in the extra stuff. I suppose just because I had the room in the rucksack. But in truth, it was more than that. An intuition, I guess. Something strange was happening to me. Ever since Armande St. Germain called me at the Opera, my world had been turned upside down. It was as if I'd been caught up in some sort of invisible current that was carrying me along, tossing me about like a leaf. And I had the feeling I was rushing toward an unseen cataclysm of Niagara-sized proportions.

"Are you ready to see the underbelly of Paris?" Robert asked me.

And all of a sudden, that cataclysm was close enough to hear. The silent sound grew and grew in my skull until it roared in my ears and made my head ache. And I had no power to stop it, no power to hold back the flood. Whatever it was held me firmly in its grasp and I was just along for the ride. And I didn't like that sensation one little bit. "Uh, okay."

Robert's mouth tightened into a grim line. "Let's go."

Gratefully, I closed the door on the chaos of my apartment—of my life, really—and followed him outside.

Chapter 9

Robert spent nearly an hour dragging me all over Paris, ducking in and out of storefronts, and sprinting down alleys I'd never known existed before, all in the name of making sure we weren't being tailed. I humored him. After all, my right hip was bruised from where I'd slammed it into the stone balustrade of the Pont-Neuf bridge, and my cheek still stung from the two guys who had jumped me earlier. Maybe next time I wouldn't be so lucky.

We wound up in the Montmartre district, a trendy, artsy neighborhood on the slopes leading up to the Sacré-Coeur Basilica, which topped the eighteenth arrondissement like a snow-white crown. I huffed up the steep streets beside Robert, who turned out to be one of those insanely fit people who doesn't even get winded climbing uphill briskly for nearly a half hour. I was going to be damned if I asked him to slow down—or, heaven forbid, stop—to let me catch my breath.

Thankfully, we arrived at the majestic staircase leading up

to Sacré-Coeur itself before I collapsed. But it was a close thing. Robert stopped then and looked inward to his memory. He glanced around as if to get his bearings, and then took off to the right.

"The entrance is this way."

"To what?" I replied.

"The catacombs."

Of course. When Sacré-Coeur was built on the spongy limestone mountain top, enormous pilings were sunk hundreds of feet into the hillside to stabilize the entire mountain enough to bear its weight. In and among those gigantic pillars, a series of catacombs were constructed. Rumor had it they connected secretly to the ancient catacombs beneath older sections of Paris. But that was all I could remember about the warren of tunnels and chambers beneath our feet.

I followed Robert into an innocuous-looking building. A small brass placard announced it to be the offices of the Sacré-Coeur Family Counseling Service. More to the point, it had a basement with a low, wide, rusty iron door tucked way back in a dark corner. An oversized, antique padlock held together a shiny new length of chain that locked the door shut. The two looked incongruous together.

Robert pulled out a small flashlight and had a look at some odd shapes scratched on the door itself. They looked almost like runes. They must have been a code of some kind, because after a few seconds of studying them, Robert turned briskly, reached up high to the left of the door, and from a tiny niche I would never have seen on my own, extracted a big, old rusty key.

The padlock opened and the door swung back with a silence out of all proportion to its age and rust. A rush of cool, musty air escaped as I peered at the rough, gently hollowed stone steps leading downward. It smelled like dirt and old age. The walls were rough-hewn stone, damp in the gloom. It looked like a passage into the very womb of the earth. I only hoped we didn't run into any of the millions of skeletal remains exhumed from ancient graveyards and stored down here under the city. Fortunately, the crypts were over in the Montparnasse area in south central Paris, far from where we were. Just last spring, my friend Catrina and her boyfriend, Rhys, had fallen into an old section of the catacombs and walked around here for days. They'd nearly died. Fortunately, Cat had stumbled across a tour group at the last minute and they'd been rescued.

Robert threw an apprehensive look over his shoulder at me. "This isn't the best time to mention this, but you probably ought to know. I'm not particularly keen on small, dark spaces."

"You're claustrophobic?" I exclaimed under my breath. "How bad? Are you going to faint on me?"

"No, I, uh, tend to sweat and breathe fast. And I get jumpy."

"Thanks for mentioning it. And I think we'll be fine. From the pictures I've seen, the quarries below Paris tend to be pretty large caverns."

"Easy for you to say," I heard him mumble under his breath. "Pull out your flashlight. From here on out, it'll be dark."

"How do we lock the door behind us?" I asked.

Robert shrugged. "We don't. This building's security guy or janitor will relock it when they find it open."

Dark didn't quite capture the utter blackness that pressed in around me. Robert's tiny beam of light pierced only eight feet or so of the curtain of eternal night that wrapped itself around us the moment I pulled the heavy door shut. Paris might be the City of Lights, but this was its polar opposite.

We descended an interminable staircase that was starting to give me the heebie-jeebies as it went down, down into the earth. It must be making Robert's skin crawl. Without warning, his flashlight beam was swallowed up by a much larger space that glowed dimly. I looked around an open cavern where I couldn't feel the walls pressing in on us any longer.

And abruptly I realized we weren't alone. Perhaps a hundred people ranged around the room, tucked here and there in clusters or lounging alone. As we advanced across the space, head-banging rock music became audible. I didn't see a band. Maybe a boom box. The crowd was dressed mostly in vampire chic.

"It's the middle of the afternoon," I muttered, my sense of propriety offended by this Saturday night rave scene.

"It's always night down here," Robert replied.

"Who are they?"

He shrugged. "The cataphiles. The people who live and play here."

"People *live* here?"

He glanced over his shoulder at me. "Of course. An entire order of monks lived down here at the time of the French Revolution, and quarry workers used to stay down here for weeks at a time. The French Resistance had its headquarters here during World War Two, and nowadays this bunch inhabits the joint."

"Are you going to ask them about René?"

Robert shook his head. "This isn't the crowd he'd hang out with. Besides, if I were René, I'd be avoiding people right now."

"Shouldn't we be avoiding them, too?"

"Yeah, we should. Unfortunately, this is the way he brought me down here. If we entered some other way I'm afraid I wouldn't find his nest."

Robert stepped through a beautifully carved gothic arch of limestone into another chamber, this one low and wide. Its walls were covered with bright grafitti that shocked my senses. The violent cartoons looked to have been done by some sort of skinhead artist. A half-dozen candles burned low, lighting the space. Perhaps twenty people sprawled on the floor. They all looked stoned out of their heads.

"Why don't the police arrest these people?" I asked.

Robert threw me a wry look. "You're the police. You tell me."

"I told you, I'm not a cop. I'm an art historian."

We waded over and around the people sprawled on the floor, who were too busy engaging in every sort of lurid sin to notice us. I turned my gaze away from the drugs, sex and perversion and held my breath as we passed through the smell of feces and vomit. The hollow expressions in the eyes of the denizens of the dark were a hundred times more haunting than any pile of empty-socketed skulls we might have run into down here.

Robert startled me by stepping right up to one of the graffiti pictures and disappearing. I took another step and saw how he'd done it—a passageway whose shadowed opening was cleverly concealed by the painting around it. He all but ran down the low, dank tunnel, which was soon pitch-black again. The air stank of decay and was moist and cool upon my skin.

"Hurry," Robert murmured back at me urgently.

That sounded like more than claustrophobia vibrating urgently in his voice. I forced my deprived senses past the wall of darkness and silence now smothering us. And immediately, I was overcome by certainty that we were being followed. Crud. Our jaunt through that orgy hadn't gone unnoticed.

I thought I heard a footstep scuff behind us, but sound was distorted so weirdly down here it was hard to tell. Robert motioned me to cut off my flashlight and did the same with his. The dark descended upon us, surreal in its completeness. Who in the world could possibly have followed us out of that motley assortment of humanity back there, and why would they?

I bumped into him. He'd stopped in front of me. His hand touched my elbow, then slid down to grasp mine. He moved off gingerly, stepping lightly. I assumed he must be following the wall with his other hand, because he led me forward unerringly. My arm about came out of the socket when he wrenched me off to the side a minute or so later. We jerked to a halt.

"We're at a major intersection," he breathed in my ear. "I

need to read the runes, but I can't turn on my flashlight. We'll wait here in this side tunnel until our tail passes us."

We crouched there, huddled together, until my legs screamed for release. All I can say is, my compliments to baseball catchers everywhere. But then a faint light pierced the dark. I made out the tunnel around us and the wider chamber beyond us. We *were* being followed! Another flashlight joined the first. Two pursuers!

And then they walked past our tunnel. They had dark hair, black leather jackets and broad shoulders, but I didn't see their faces. Not that I needed to. It was our Italian friends again. It was so quiet I could hear them breathing. I froze, not moving a muscle, carefully holding my breath.

One of them murmured in Italian, "Can you see their lights?"

The other one grunted what sounded like a negative.

Go away. Go away. Go away.

Thankfully, after a few seconds their lights moved on and disappeared. I released my breath slowly.

Robert stood up and helped me to my feet. My legs shouted their indignation as blood flow returned to them. I followed him cautiously out into the intersection. In the glow of his flashlight, eight tunnels stretched away in a rough compass rose.

Robert peered from tunnel to tunnel, examining the runes beside each one. "I have no idea which one to take," he admitted.

Nor did we have any exact idea which tunnel those two men had taken. As Robert moved around the room, peering at the runes, a faint puff of air moved past me. At first I didn't pay any attention to it. But when it wafted past me a second time, it dawned on me. We were underground. There should be no wind down here! I turned in a circle, trying to ascertain the source of that wisp of a breeze.

"Come," a voice whispered so lightly my ears barely registered it. "Away."

"Did you hear that?" I blurted.

"Hear what?"

"That voice."

We froze, listening for several seconds.

Robert frowned. "I don't hear anything. We're alone."

He was right. It couldn't have been a voice I heard. "I felt a puff of air moving by. I could swear it sounded like it said, 'Come away.'"

"No air moves down here. Not unless someone is stirring it up with movement."

I was *not* losing my mind. I'd definitely felt that air! "Maybe those two guys made it."

"If so, they're too damned close for our good," Robert mumbled. We turned off our flashlights and stood in the middle of the round chamber, continuing to listen.

"Come." A pause and then the disembodied whisper sighed again. "Away."

Robert turned on his flashlight, his eyes wide. Thank God. He'd heard it, too. Insanity loves company, apparently, because I was profoundly relieved by his startled expression.

But then I noticed something else over Robert's shoulder. The faintest fog hovered at the opening to one of the tunnels. The fog roiled slowly upon itself, but was stationary in that spot.

"Do you see that?" I gasped.

Robert whipped around, staring hard at where I pointed. "I don't see anything."

Before my eyes, the fog resolved itself into a vaguely human shape about my height and slender. It had the curves of a female body and long wisps that flowed around its head like hair, but no face. A tendril of the fog detached itself from its side and reached forward about chest high. The tendril folded, like an arm gesturing me to come.

"You see *that,* don't you?" I said indignantly.

"Honey, I don't see anything but rock where you're pointing."

I closed my eyes. Squeezed them tightly shut. Opened them again. The lady was still there. And I could swear she was nodding encouragement at me. I *so* don't do ghosts. But there was no denying what was right before my eyes. Merciful God. *I was seeing a ghost.*

The apparition breathed, "Come." And then, "Runnn. They come."

I lurched in surprise. "Okay, Robert, I don't mean to sound like a whacko, but I definitely see a ghost, and it's gesturing me to go that way. It just said to run. They're coming."

Maybe he was so distracted by his claustrophobia that it didn't really register on him that I was claiming to see and hear a ghost. But he merely shrugged. "It's as good a reason to head down that tunnel as any other."

We headed toward the lady, and as I drew closer I made out a face. It looked faintly familiar…I put the thought aside. No time to think about it now. The poltergeist continued to hover there in front of us. We were going to have to walk right through her to get into the tunnel.

I reached out, grasping Robert's hand as we stepped forward into the white mist.

It was as if time stopped and reality fell away from us. The solid warmth of Robert's strong fingers entwined with mine, his warm palm pressed to mine, were all that remained. His head turned very slowly toward me, and he blinked so gradually I could see every individual lash as his eyelids slowly shuttered the storm-tossed gray of his eyes and then lifted once more. His gaze pierced my soul, seeing all I was, all my secret dreams, all my hidden thoughts of him.

Through our joined hands, I felt Robert's heart beat once, his pulse throbbing with life as my pulse rose to meet his. Heat built between our palms, and it was as if our entire bodies melded together, mine a part of him and his a part of me.

Another heartbeat.

And then something else surged from Robert into me. It was a driving sexual need, so powerful and overwhelming that it nearly drove me to my knees with wanting. My breath caught. Held. Then released on an infinitely slow sigh that parted my lips. His gaze shifted down to my mouth, and my eyes widened. I swayed toward him, and he toward me. And the fog was all around us, in us and on us. Alive. Carnal.

Something very close to an orgasm shuddered through me, making my whole body tingle from the roots of my hair to the tips of my toes. Robert shuddered, as well, his beautiful eyes glazing over for a moment.

And then the fog was gone.

Robert shook himself slightly. He cocked his head, listening for a moment, and swore under his breath. "Your ghost is right. I hear someone coming."

The spell the ghost had cast upon us shattered, leaving behind only stark, cold fear. My nerves were raw and I felt naked as I raced down the tunnel behind Robert. What the hell had just happened?

And more to the point, how did I get it to happen again— when we weren't buried beneath untold tons of rock and running for our lives?

First things first. We had to lose our tails. And it wasn't as if we had a whole lot of choices. The tunnel the ghost had guided us to was arrow-straight, running gently downhill, and went on forever. Speed was our only ally. We ran headlong into the eight-foot circles of light cast in front of us by our flashlights. If a cliff had opened up under our feet we wouldn't have stood any chance of seeing it in time to stop before we plunged off it.

I don't know how long we ran, but after an eternity, we began to see signs of humanity again. Splashes of graffiti began to decorate the walls. The occasional puddle of melted candle wax littered a niche. And finally, side tunnels began to open off the main tunnel. Robert slowed, examining the openings and their chicken scratch markings.

He ducked down one of them, and I didn't break the silence to ask why. I was completely lost down here and wouldn't have a chance in hell of finding my way out on my own. In a few minutes, we came upon a group of people sitting around in a living-room-sized chamber, complete with sofas, armchairs and coffee tables straight out of the 1950s. It reminded me of a strangely twisted version of Ozzie and Harriet's home. The people lounging around drinking weren't so far gone that they weren't startled by our popping out among them.

"Sorry," Robert announced cheerfully. "We're just looking for a friend. The Mouse. Any of you seen him?"

Negative head shakes all around. One of them pointed across the room and murmured that we should try the Coffin Bar. Robert nodded as if he knew what the heck that was. I wasn't at all sure I wanted to find out.

We walked quickly toward the tunnel the drinker had pointed at. "Who's the Mouse?" I whispered.

Robert muttered back, "It's an old nickname of René's."

Appropriate for an art thief, I supposed. We must have spent the next hour moving from chamber to chamber, asking around about the Mouse. A few people seemed to recognize the name, but no one had seen him. The act of asking after someone we knew down here seemed to make us okay, however. The bizarre collection of people were generally friendly and helpful to us, which was odd, given the general unfriendliness and formality of Parisians topside, as the city above was referred to down here.

Eventually, Robert stopped in a makeshift pub and had a seat. The place had little bistro tables and chairs, and a fully stocked bar complete with a bartender behind it. The guy's hair stood straight up in four-inch long spikes all over his head and his eyebrows were pierced, but he had a tip jar and a towel at his waist, by golly.

"Now what?" I asked.

"Now, we wait. This is a public place and the guys who were following us won't do anything in here even if they find us. And, if René gets wind of the fact that we've been asking around about him, he'll send someone here to give us a message."

We sipped at a couple beers in longneck bottles. They were cool but not refrigerated.

"About what happened back at that intersection," I started.

Robert propped his elbows on the table. "Did you really see a ghost? You called it a she. Was it a woman?"

"You don't think I'm crazy for saying that I saw one?"

"Of course not. It's no secret that such things exist. I just wish I could've seen her."

I peered at him closely, but he didn't seem to be teasing me. He really accepted that I'd seen a ghost. I wasn't sure I accepted it, however. I mean, I know what I saw. But maybe it was a hallucination or a trick of our flashlights on the walls.

And maybe it wasn't. What if that ghost *had* been real? My world tilted on its axis at the thought. It challenged everything I believed about logic and reason and reality.

"What did she look like?"

I recalled the vague features and suddenly I knew where I'd seen them before. In my bathroom mirror, the morning after my first dream about Queen Elizabeth. I frowned, trying to picture my vivid mental images of the queen from my dreams. Nope, the ghost wasn't her. Thank God. It was bad enough to see ghosts, but to see the ghost of a dead queen? Nobody would ever believe that. I almost laughed aloud. It wasn't as if they'd believe me if I told them I'd seen some commoner ghost, either.

"You *really* believe in ghosts?" I asked Robert.

"Sure. There are all kinds of things in this world that no one can explain. Why not ghosts? I don't know about you, but when I walked past the spot she was standing—" He broke off.

I *so* shared his loss for words. What did a person say about that incredible moment of connection we'd shared? Cautiously, I commented, "Maybe it was just the ghost messing with our minds."

Robert shook his head immediately in the negative. "No, I was having those sorts of feelings already. The ghost just…amplified them. I apologize."

Ohmigosh. That desire burning the two of us alive was *real?* My brain froze up. Completely. I stared at him openmouthed and couldn't for the life of me summon up a thing to say in response. It was almost more incredible to me than the idea of seeing a ghost!

"Yo, dude. Are you Chop?"

I started. It was the bartender, standing beside our table. When had he walked up?

"Yeah," Robert answered. "Who wants to know?"

"There's a guy over there, says he knows the gent you're looking for. Might have an inkling where to find 'im. Says your pal might be in a spot of trouble. He wasn't real clear on it. Maybe the Mouse is hurt. I dunno." The bartender rubbed his fingers and thumb together in the universal gesture for cash. "Just needs his memory jogged. Bit of a looney tunes, that one. But his information is usually good."

René was hurt? After seeing the state of the guy in René's clothes, I was highly alarmed at this bit of news.

Robert and I both jumped to our feet. I pulled a ten-euro bill out of my rucksack to cover our drinks and shoved it into the bartender's hand.

The messenger turned out to be a drunk old reprobate like René himself. But, after Robert forked over an obscene number of euros to the wizened little man with unnaturally pale skin, he was abruptly sober enough to lead us through a maze of passageways with unerring confidence. Each chamber we passed through became rougher, with fewer signs of human habitation. If I were the suspicious sort—and at the moment I was—I'd wonder if I were being led into a trap of some kind.

I held my hands away from my body at the ready, and my muscles hovered on high alert. I noticed that Robert was twitching at the slightest sound, too. Our guide stopped in a small chamber, little more than a widening of the tunnel. The rock walls were jagged and shined black with moisture. Of everywhere we'd been so far, this place smelled the most like a cave, with a pungent, earthy odor.

"Wait here," our guide mumbled.

And then the little jerk disappeared!

Robert and I both jumped toward the wall into which he'd melted. We took a few steps down the concealed tunnel he'd entered, but it forked immediately, and there was no sign of which passage he'd taken. The guy was gone.

And so, we waited.

And waited.

We finally scoped out a dry spot in one corner and sat down.

"Lean against me," Robert offered, holding out an arm and offering me his right side.

I certainly wasn't dumb enough to turn down that offer! We turned off the flashlights to preserve the batteries and sat there in the dark. With a certain amount of trepidation, I waited for a repeat of that time-stoppage moment of total sexual awareness. It didn't happen. But something else did. I got comfortable snuggled up against Robert. I began to register little details, like how muscular the arm draped across my shoulders was. And how little fat lay over the slabs of ribs and muscle beneath my arm. And how nice he smelled. I can't say that I was usually attracted to the sweat and body odor that marked most European men. But he smelled like the outdoors. And it was nice.

I was such a goner if I even lusted after the scent of this guy's perspiration.

"What time is it?" I finally murmured.

Robert removed his arm from around my shoulders and flashed his light at his left wrist. "A little after eight."

"Eight p.m.?" I echoed, shocked. We'd been down here nearly six hours? I'd had no sense whatsoever of time passing in this perpetual night.

"I'm hungry," he announced. "What have you got in that rucksack of yours?"

I laid out a picnic of the snacks I'd grabbed earlier, while Robert broke out a bottle of water for us. I lit one of the candles, and we ate in its flickering glow.

"Nothing like a vampire picnic to whet the appetite," he murmured, grinning.

"How long do you want to sit here and wait for René to show up?"

He shrugged. "Could you get us out of here if you had to?"

I shook my head. *Crud.* I thought he knew where we were going!

"Well, that answers that, then. We wait until René shows up."

I leaned back against the rocks, which were dry in this corner. "Where did you come by the name Chop? Is it because of your motorcycle?"

"No. I have a collection of knives and swords."

"What do you do with them?"

I suppose I expected him to say he looked at them or maybe collected them as an investment.

"I fight with them."

I reared back in alarm. "Who do you get into knife fights with?"

He laughed. "I train at a martial arts studio with them. I don't run around getting into brawls. Well, not often, at any rate."

We talked about our various interests and hobbies for a long time. We even ventured into discussions of politics and religion. I was surprised to discover how much I actually had in common with this leather-clad rebel. Either he wasn't nearly as wild a child as he appeared, or maybe I wasn't quite as straitlaced at heart as I thought I was. It was an encouraging realization. Maybe I wasn't sinking fast into old fogeydom after all.

"Why don't you take a nap?" Robert suggested awhile later. "I'll keep an eye out for René."

"You'll be all right?" I asked.

He smiled down at me. "You've done a remarkable job distracting me from my fear of enclosed spaces. I've actually been relaxed for the past hour or so. Now get a spot of rest. We still have to walk out of here."

The prospect was daunting. Enough so that I grasped the chance to close my eyes and escape our predicament, if only for a little while.

I awoke some time later in the dark to a hand pressing over my mouth. Panic lurched me to full consciousness and sent my hands up to the wrist in front of my face. But then my brain caught up with my fear and I recognized the strong, lean bones of Robert's wrist.

I felt him lean close and his lips grazed my ear. My usual response to him stirred in my belly until his whispered words chilled my blood.

"Someone's coming."

Chapter 10

We climbed to our feet as quietly as we could, and Robert pinched out the candle with a tiny sizzle that sounded like fireworks going off to my hypersensitive ears. I listened closely to the darkness and heard only the faintest scuffle before a figure suddenly loomed in front of us, pointing a flashlight into our eyes. I squinted painfully, blinded by the brilliant glare of light.

"Chop?"

I sagged in relief. Thank God. René.

"How are you, old man?" Robert asked warmly.

The two men embraced. Then René looked over at me in surprise and chided, "What are you doing tangled up with a rascal like this, Anabelle? He'll ruin your reputation."

How exactly did he mean? Professionally? Personally? Both? I opened my mouth to ask when Robert interrupted. Somewhat hastily, in fact.

"I have something for you, Mouse." Robert held out René's billfold.

René stared at his wallet in consternation. "Where did you get that?"

Robert answered grimly. "At the morgue. Ives Fouchard turned up there last night as a guest—wearing your clothes."

René's eyes were huge with fear, but not surprise. And then it hit me. Robert had known the guy in the morgue. He'd never let on for a second to the coroner or to me that he knew the dead man's identity. The idea of him keeping secrets like that suddenly made me more than a little uncomfortable.

"Who killed him?" I asked.

René shrugged. "Two men were chasing Ives. He came to me for help. We traded clothes and he ran. The men tried to strangle me but realized I was the wrong man before they killed me. They thought I was unconscious, but I was faking it. I heard them talk. They were under orders to kill Ives. They decided they'd better get him first and leave me. When they left, I crawled down here."

"Why did they want to kill this Ives guy?" I asked, aghast.

René set down the rucksack he was carrying and perched on an outcropping of stone that was about chair height. "I've been asking around about your theft like I said I would, Anabelle. Turns out Ives pulled your job. He told me it was a statue of a lady. Not all that valuable, but the client who paid him to acquire the piece was nuts to have it. Was willing to pay millions for it. Ives decided to squeeze the client for a little extra, apparently, and the man was not amused. Sent thugs after Ives to take the statue back."

Robert leaned forward, his forehead creased in alarm. "Did Ives tell you anything about the client?"

"Said he was some rich Italian guy."

Robert swore quietly under his breath. What was that all about? I turned my attention back to René. "Did you get a look at the men who jumped you?"

"Yeah. Two big, beefy, Italian guys. Middle-aged. Wearing

black leather jackets. Dark hair and dark eyes, but then that describes a lot of Italian men."

I glanced at Robert, and he nodded back at me. Sounded like the same guys. That description might, indeed, fit lots of Italians, but what were the odds that two unrelated pairs of Italian thugs were attacking everyone who'd come into contact with Elise's stolen statue? My hunch had been right. The attacks on René and me—and the murder of Ives—were all linked.

Lovely.

René was talking again. "I think the same guys are down here. A couple of my contacts spotted them earlier tonight. Why in the world they came underground to poke around, I have no idea. There's no way they should know my hidey-hole is down here."

"They didn't," Robert replied. "We must've led them down here. Straight to you, dammit. I'm sorry, Mouse. I thought we were clean when we came down."

So did I. We'd zigzagged all over Paris before we'd ventured below. How had those men found us? Did they know where I lived? It made sense. After they'd run away from us in the park, they must have gone to my place and picked us up from there. Were they responsible for ransacking my apartment, too? It made sense.

René shrugged. "What is done is done."

"Although it probably goes without saying," I piped up, "you're in danger, my friend. If they were after me, they'd have jumped me in my apartment. It's you they want. Come up top with us and let me put you in custody of Interpol. They'll take you away from here and tuck you someplace safe until this all blows over."

René snorted. "No place is safe from the likes of those men. Their employer is grotesquely powerful."

"More so than Interpol?" I scoffed.

René nodded solemnly. "Much more."

A chill clattered down my spine. "And who might such a person be?"

The wizened little man shrugged. "There are people in this world greater than the police, greater than any law. Greater than any government."

Robert added grimly, "And they wear Armani suits and refuse to give their names and carry fat bank books."

The roll of a pebble off to our right was my only warning before a man burst into sight, startling me violently. A nasty surge of adrenaline made my heart hurt, it pounded so hard. The drunk from the bar who'd led us here.

"They're coming!" he gasped.

No need to ask who he meant.

René snatched the rucksack off the floor and tossed it over his shoulder. He pointed at a tunnel to Robert and blurted, "Take the fourth right and run! And for God's sake, be quiet. I'll draw them after me."

"No—" Robert and I both blurted. But then he was gone, darting down another tunnel. Loudly. The sound of running footsteps echoed around us, those of René and his lookout retreating…and those of someone else approaching. Fast.

I snatched up my rucksack and threw it over my shoulder as Robert grabbed my hand and we took off, running pell-mell on our toes into the black void. Again.

I don't know how long we ran. But I was completely winded and had a ferocious stitch in my side before Robert finally slowed to a walk. Whether or not we had blasted past the fourth tunnel to the right, I had no idea. And frankly, I didn't care. I was good and ready to get out of this endless warren of tunnels. Clearly, I was not cut out to be a rat.

We walked until I was beyond fatigue. Beyond sore. Beyond exhausted. And then we walked some more. But finally, Robert shined his flashlight on a set of runes marking a passage and gave a satisfied little, "Ah."

"This way, Ana," he murmured.

He led me down a side tunnel. Past a stack of bones. And I was too tired to be grossed out. The old catacombs. We'd made it back to the mapped portion of the tunnels. And then there were more bones. And more bones still. We walked past floor-to-ceiling stacks of skeletal remains, most of them arranged into clever and even artful geometric layouts. The workers who'd deposited these remains must have either been complete sickos, or resorted to humor to save their sanity while they performed their gruesome job.

I have to say, I've never seen anything quite as macabre as a heart made of grinning skulls in the middle of a six-foot tall pile of femurs.

"Here we are," Robert murmured. He made an abrupt turn, and for the first time in forever, I saw a sign of topside civilization. A door.

"What if it's padlocked from the outside?" I asked.

"It won't be." The runes on this door indicate it's locked from this side. He tested the knob, and it was locked, however. My stomach fell. I so didn't need to get trapped down here indefinitely.

Robert pulled something out of an interior pocket of his jacket. A thin leather pouch, which he unzipped quickly. "Hold the flashlight for me." He thrust the black metal cylinder into my hands.

I watched as he expertly picked the lock. "An Art Theft 101 skill, I gather?" I asked dryly.

He grinned up at me. "Nah. Bored kid with the wrong friends skill. Art thefts these days involve defeating far more sophisticated electronic and computer systems than any simple lock."

I watched his clever fingers work at the lock, and it happened again. That slow, sensual burn low in my gut began to build as I imagined his fingers playing upon my flesh in that way. This man made an absolute panting fool out of me, even if he was in the middle of breaking and entering—or exiting, as the case might be.

It took him several minutes, but eventually, the lock turned beneath his hands. He pushed the door open and we stepped into a dim basement. He wound across it to another door, unlocked this time. Bright light seeped underneath it. Turned out it led to a hallway in what looked like a hospital—tiled walls, fluorescent lighting and a couple spare gurneys parked along the walls. We found an elevator and pushed the up button.

In a few seconds the heavy door slid open and we stepped inside. I frowned. Looked around. I knew this elevator! We were in Val de Grace Hospital! For a moment I was tempted to go up to the third floor and peek in on Elise. But then I remembered it was after midnight. No way would we get past the nurses and the armed guard outside her door at this hour, Interpol badge or not.

"At least we won't have any trouble getting out of this building," I murmured. "This is a hospital. It'll be open all night."

Robert shrugged, his expression grim. "Don't count on it. Have you looked at yourself?"

I glanced down and realized that I was covered in mud. And so was Robert. Why this should pose a problem in our leaving the building, I failed to see. But then the elevator door opened and we stepped out right into the lobby of the hospital. Wide glass exit doors stood right in front of us.

"You! Stop!" a voice barked behind us.

I lurched, fearing big Italian men. But instead, it was a security guard, already coming around from behind his desk.

"Run for it," Robert muttered to me.

We bolted for the door.

"You, cataphiles! Come back here. You're under arrest—"

I tried to stop to explain to the guy that (a) he had no authority to arrest anyone as a mere security guard, and (b) I had an Interpol badge in my pocket and had been in the catacombs on official business, but Robert grabbed me by the upper arm and bodily dragged me out of there. And truth be told, any time the guy laid a hand on me, half my brains fell out my left ear. He grabbed; I ran.

We burst out into the street, and Robert took off running to his right with me still in tow. We stopped a couple blocks later, which was just as well. I was beat after all the hiking we'd already done. The night wrapped itself around us, a living thing. Or maybe another ghost was just hanging around waiting for us to walk through it. Our surroundings were brightly lit relative to the total blackness of the catacombs, and while the tunnels had felt heavy and dead, out here, the night felt positively vibrant. Vibrant with threats maybe, but still better than below.

"Now where?" I panted. "We can't go back to my place. The Italians obviously know where I live. That must be how they picked up our trail earlier."

"I know a place. At least I used to. Let's see if it's still there."

Thankfully, his destination wasn't far away. But it wasn't the most savory of places, either. It was a Catholic mission serving homeless men, tucked in the shadow of a good-sized church. Not the same dimensions as Notre Dame, but a hulking pile of stone, nonetheless.

"Uhh, Robert, the sign says no women allowed. Not to mention I'm not Catholic."

He chuckled. "We've got to work on this tendency of yours to follow rules."

While I opened my mouth to protest, he dragged me inside, anyway, effectively silencing me before I could speak. The mission looked like a shabby apartment building at first glance. But then Robert led me off to the right, through a set of heavy double doors and into the main sanctuary of the church itself.

The cavernous space was lined with carved wood and stone statuary that spoke of great age. Candles flickered ineffectually against the darkness, lending it a distinctly medieval air. But it felt safe. Blessedly removed from the night we'd just stepped out of, with its thefts and ghosts and Italian thugs. This was an eternal haven out of place and time.

I jumped as sound abruptly burst forth around us. A giant bell rang once overhead, deep and gonglike. It had barely stopped echoing through the space above us when another sound rolled forth—a deep, nasal, haunting song of men singing. In Latin.

"Gregorian chant," Robert murmured.

The prayer rose and fell as I spotted the row of hoods kneeling up front. It felt to me like an invasion of privacy to be standing there in the wee hours of the morning listening to their worship. It struck me that for a thousand years or more, monks just like these had been getting up at this ungodly hour of the night to pray. That same sense of displacement out of time exploded in me again, making me want to ask not where was I, but when was I? I felt like a bridge between the past and present, one foot planted in each of two far-apart times and the rest of me stretched out thin between them.

It was that damned ghost and her wild dreams. For surely she was responsible for those, too.

The chant reached deep inside me, echoing of dark centuries past, of mystery and pain and ecstasy, of a time when faith was the only rock society rested upon, when kingdoms rose and fell in the name of religion, and men died by the thousands trying to force each other to worship their respective gods. I guess in that respect, times haven't changed so much after all.

The silence was as sudden as the bell that had called for the nocturn prayers. Their late-night prayer over, the row of monks rose without sound and turned to file out of the church. They seemed to ignore our bedraggled presence at the back of the nave, although it was hard to tell with their faces completely hidden by those deep hoods.

But then one of them broke off from the others. He gestured toward a wall of doors with carved wooden grills, his oversized sackcloth sleeve hanging from a pale, bony arm. For a moment I reared back in alarm at the skeletal apparition of that white hand protruding from the walking, faceless robe. I guess the overall horror of the catacombs still lingered with me a bit.

"Come on," Robert whispered, tugging at my sleeve.

The row of monks turned away from us and headed for a side door, and we headed to the opposite wall and those wooden, phone-booth doors. Robert pulled me inside one of the tiny booths with him. And I mean tiny. We barely had room to stand side by side, and there was nowhere to put our elbows that didn't involve poking each other. Not that I was complaining, mind you. I mean, who wouldn't want to be crammed into a tiny space with a hunky guy you have the hots for and are trying to figure out ways to get your hands on?

I whispered, because it seemed the right thing to do inside a confessional cohabited by a man and a woman with gigantic sexual energy flares zinging between them— "Now what?"

He grinned, and I about nibbled his ear because it was six inches from my mouth. "Now, we wait."

Great. More waiting. "Who are we waiting for this time?"

"An old friend. He usually takes the night shift here. At least he did the last time I was here. Let's just hope he's still alive."

"He who?"

"Father Bertrand. He took me on as a project a few years back. He's actually the guy who convinced me to turn myself in to the police."

"You turned yourself in?" Wow. That put quite a good-guy

spin on his cooperation with the authorities over the past few years. It had been voluntary. My disquiet over his felonious past subsided significantly.

"Yeah," he muttered, "but don't tell anyone. I wouldn't want to wreck my street rep."

"Shucks. Who'd have guessed such a do-gooder lurked under all that black leather?"

That earned me an adorable scowl that I suddenly found myself not taking the least bit seriously.

"Doin' good now, are we?" a voice said from behind me in a thick Irish brogue. "Then how might ye be explainin' bringin' a person of a female persuasion with ye into my confessional?"

While a door closed beside us, Robert sat down on the wooden bench and startled me by pulling me down into his lap. As I absorbed the sensation of his hard thighs beneath mine, his arm wrapped around my waist, his lovely scent filling my nostrils, Robert's eyes lit up with genuine pleasure. "Father Bertrand. How are you, you old fart?"

"Still preachin' the word of God to shameful sinners like you."

"It's good to hear your voice again."

And indeed the priest was mostly just a voice in here. I could barely make out the fellow's bald, liver-spotted pate through the carved grillwork between us. But then, I supposed that was the point of it being a confessional. People were more likely to spill their guts to an impersonal wall than to a frowning priest.

"The way I hear it, you're back in the soup," the priest said sternly. "Am I going to have to drag ye by the ear to the police again?"

"Nope. I brought the police with me this time. Father Bertrand, meet Ana Reisner." He paused for dramatic effect. "Of Interpol."

"Ye don't say!" the little man exclaimed. "Why hasn't she arrested yer sorry arse, then?"

Robert gave me a perplexed look. "Why would she do that?"

"Why because of the statue ye stole."

"What do you mean, they got away?"

"They slipped away from us in the catacombs, sir. They had help. Several of the men in Fraser's old gang laid false trails for him and the girl."

"I don't want to hear your excuses. I want that statue, dammit!"

"We got one of Fraser's buddies. He should be able to tell us where it is and what they plan to do with it."

That gave the client pause. Eventually he said more calmly, "Make him sing. Do whatever it takes. I want to know everything about Fraser and the woman."

"What do you want us to do with him after we're done?"

"Kill him."

"Yes, sir."

"And then capture the pesky old bastard who caused this whole mess in the first place!"

Chapter 11

"What statue? I didn't steal any statue!" Robert exclaimed.

"Why sure you did. I got a phone call just this afternoon asking after ye."

"Who was it?" I demanded, as offended as Robert that someone would wrongly accuse him of theft. My brain registered vaguely that the protective ire in my breast hinted at deeper feelings than mere lust for my companion. But at the moment, I was more interested in knowing who was flinging around false accusations about Robert. "What did they say?"

The priest peered in my direction. "Well now, lassie, it t'were a higher-up official in the Church if ye must know. Said he'd received word from the Papal Seat itself that an old and valuable relic had been stolen by an acquaintance of mine. Asked me if I'd seen ye recently. And good thing I hadn't, or I'd have turned ye in, young man!"

Robert leaned forward, gripping the grill until his knuckles turned white. "As God is my witness, Bertrand, I didn't steal anything. I swear. It's a lie."

"Now why would someone lie about something like that?"

"I have no idea," Robert bit out. "I'm being framed. But then, that's easy to do since I'm a criminal already."

I piped up, "He's telling the truth. The statue was stolen on Saturday here in Paris, and he didn't enter France until Sunday afternoon."

"So ye know which statue the man was referring to, do ye? Then the two of ye are involved in the theft in some way? Shame on ye, young lady, being an Interpol agent and all. Here I was, hopin' ye'd rehabilitated the lad."

I rolled my eyes at Robert, who said, "What was the name of the man who called you about me?"

"Now that you mention it, I don't think he ever said."

"Where was he calling from?"

"Italy, for sure. My caller ID said it were an unknown caller from Vatican City."

I frowned as alarm bells clanged wildly in my head. Someone had called from the Vatican to frame Robert? What in the world for? The statue he was researching wasn't even Christian, according to Catrina Dauvergne. The Black Madonna cult was a goddess worship group that rejected the male centered doctrine of the Catholic Church.

This development just *so* couldn't be good. Particularly given where we were slated to head tomorrow. Did we dare continue with the trip or should we cancel it? I desperately needed to research ley lines and try to figure out their connection to the French power outages. And the only lead I had was the directive from Elise to go to the Vatican archives. But I also had no desire whatsoever to walk into a trap. Certainty broke over me that on this one, I was damned if I did and damned if I didn't.

"Did you tell anyone else about this phone call?" I asked in sudden alarm.

"Of course, lassie. I would never disobey an order from the Holy See itself." He crossed himself as he said the words.

Robert closed his eyes for a frustrated second. I'm sure I was having the exact same thought he was. The priest was delaying us while one of his colleagues called the Vatican contact to let them know we were here. Or worse, the monks might have even called the police.

I had confidence we'd be able to talk our way out of criminal charges without any trouble, but we seriously didn't need the hassle right now. Time was of the essence in my investigation, not only to stop the power outages, but also to save Elise's life. The deeper I got into this insane situation, the more convinced I became that it was entirely possible that an ancient statue with supernatural powers had been keeping her alive. And Robert had possibly even more reason than I to want to avoid the police, particularly under circumstances where he was accused of an art theft.

I stood up as Robert opened the door beside us and said, "Thank you for everything, Father Bertrand. You've been more helpful than you could possibly imagine."

"Wait, son. What about your confession? Ye've yet to give it me."

Yup, stalling us.

Robert replied gently, "You should know by now that I'm neither Catholic nor the repentant type."

Surprisingly enough, the old man's tone of voice changed to one of true regret. "I'm sorry, my boy. But orders are orders. I'm bound by oath to obey them." Then he added sotto voce, "Go out through the sanctuary. Just as you reach the altar, you'll see a small door on your left. It takes you out the west side of the building. The others won't be looking for you in that direction."

Robert and I tumbled out of the tiny booth. Did we dare follow the priest's directions, or was he leading us straight into the arms of the police? Robert made the decision for us, grabbing my hand and racing with me through the sanctuary and toward the altar.

We burst outside into the cold and darkness once more. And were alone. Father Bertrand hadn't betrayed us after all.

And again, we were thrust out into the night and all its dangers. I was getting really tired of this. Actually, I was just getting really tired. We'd been walking forever, my feet were sore, my eyes gritty, and I wanted nothing more than to lay my head down and pass out for a few hours.

"We've got two choices," Robert murmured. "We can go so grungy no one will find us, or we can go so high-class we can buy our anonymity."

"Given the way we look right now, we'd better opt for grunge."

Robert grinned ruefully at me and we took off running. Again.

This time we stopped at what could marginally be called a hotel. Flophouse would be a more accurate description. The North African–looking proprietor spoke barely a word of French and was grumpy at being woken up by our banging continuously on the little bell on the counter until he came out of the back. When Robert argued over the cost of the room, I elbowed him. I was too damned tired for such shenanigans.

Under his breath in English, Robert murmured, "He'll remember us more if we *don't* try to stiff him."

I subsided. He was the thief after all. He knew this Paris a lot better than I did.

The door closed behind us into a bare but thankfully reasonably clean room. Uh-oh. With one narrow bed in it. "You did ask for a double bed, didn't you?" I asked.

Robert rolled his eyes at the iron bed that had a mattress I could see sagging in the middle from here. "Yeah, I did. You take it. I'll sleep on the floor."

"If I couldn't see that line of ants marching across the floor from here, I might let you do that," I replied, "but no way are you sleeping with those critters. We're adults. We can sleep in the same bed."

Robert's mouth tilted up wryly. "I'm in no condition to threaten your virtue right now, anyway. I don't know about you, but I'm beat."

We used washcloths and the room's sink to scrub off the worst of the grime, then crawled into the bed back-to-back, both set our wristwatch alarms for 6:30 a.m., only a scant few hours away, and crashed. After all, we still had a plane to catch.

The sound of a door closing woke Elise not long after sunrise if the fresh, bright light streaming in her window was any indication. Someone had just slipped out of her room. Who? Nobody'd woken her up to take any more infernal vital signs. A nurse maybe, peeking in to check on her? Except they knew to leave her alone and let her sleep until a decent hour, which this most certainly didn't qualify as yet.

"Charles?" she called out.

The night bodyguard stepped into the room immediately. "Madame?"

"Who was just in here?"

"That would be me. I was delivering those flowers for you. A man brought them by and said they were for you." He gestured at a tall vase filled with a stunning display of several dozen lilies.

Madonna lilies to be precise. Elise lurched upright. "Who was he?"

"He did not give his name, Madame. He merely said he's an old admirer of yours."

"How long ago did he leave?"

"Three minutes or so, I guess."

She swore under her breath and threw the covers back.

"Help me over to the window." Thankfully, she wore her own nightgown and not one of those open-backed, naked-rear things. Heaven only knew the state of her posterior right now. She winced to think what the sudden old age had done to it.

The guard supported her elbow and steadied her solicitously as she made her way over to the window. It looked down over the front entrance of the hospital. If she were lucky, maybe she might catch a glimpse of her secret admirer. "Point out the man who brought me the flowers if you see him," she told the guard.

He looked around below. "I don't see him—wait. There he is. Just coming outside."

Elise craned her head to look down on the main entrance and the gray-haired man just emerging from the building. He looked vaguely familiar, but she couldn't place the face. She had the feeling she'd known him as a much younger man, and age had smeared his features until they were unrecognizable to her now. Of course, it didn't help that her own memory was failing at an alarming rate. Perhaps her least favorite side effect of the rapid aging her body was undergoing.

He was a handsome gentleman. Patrician. Tall, trim. Expensively dressed. Gray hair and aquiline nose. Carried himself like a European. He stepped toward the curb, and then all of a sudden, another man stepped up beside her admirer. This man was a good thirty years younger, big and burly. He took the older man by the arm and all but lifted him over to a black sedan that was just pulling up. The vehicle was big and plush, with blacked-out windows, the kind of car exclusive limousine services use for their clients who don't wish to be conspicuous.

The gray-haired man tried to struggle, but another man jumped out of the front seat of the car and took him by the other arm almost immediately. The two much larger, much younger men bodily lifted the man into the car. Both men were dark-haired, olive-skinned and wearing black leather—very sinister. They leaped into the vehicle, as well. The black car sped away. From this angle, she couldn't see the license plate. And even if she could've, her abruptly eighty-year-old vision wouldn't have been able to make out the letters and numbers. Damn.

Elise looked over at her guard in consternation. "Did we just witness a kidnapping?"

He looked alarmed, but said soothingly, "I'm sure nothing is wrong. That gentleman is probably a high-risk client and those other men were merely his bodyguards, taking every precaution to minimize his exposure on the street."

Except the street was practically deserted at this early hour. And nobody out there had tried to approach the older man or shoot him or in any way harm him. She frowned as the guard took her elbow to lead her away from the window.

Who could she tell that she thought she'd just seen a man abducted? They all thought she was crazy already. And it didn't help that she'd just aged thirty years in under a week.

She climbed back into bed and let her guard tuck the blankets in around her. He left the room, but sleep refused to come to her. She looked over at the elegant white flowers. Who *was* that man?

What a plane it turned out to be. Plush didn't quite describe the inlaid rare woods, the glove leather upholstery, and even what looked like a small, honest-to-God Renoir painting. The full bathroom was even better, with its hot shower and closet full of women's clothes. Elise's clothing was immeasurably more elegant than anything I'd ever dreamed of wearing, but it fit as if it were made for me. Like I said before, we were nearly identical in height and build.

I went first, scraping off the filth of the past day with relish. I used the hair dryer and a brush to dry my hair in soft waves around my face, and I even indulged in some of the cosmetics I found in the medicine cabinet. Finally human once more, I stepped out and relinquished the hot water to Robert.

He was gentleman enough to pause for a moment, taking in my changed appearance with an appreciative head-to-foot sweep of his eyes. Ah, a bold Scotsman was good for a girl's ego.

While he was in the shower, the copilot came back and laid the table with bone china, Waterford crystal and sterling silver. And then, from the refrigerator, he produced a cold breakfast fit for a king. I dug in, famished, and Robert joined me shortly. There must've been a razor in there, because he was clean-shaven. And looked excellent, if I do say so myself.

We finished the spread of fruits, cheeses, cold cuts, pastries and coffee with gusto, then Robert pushed the plates aside.

"Okay, Ana. Time for some straight talking. What's so important about this statue you're tracking down that someone's trying to frame me for stealing it?"

"I don't know. The owner told me it wasn't especially valuable in and of itself as a work of art but that the…sentimental value…was very high." I hoped he didn't notice my momentary hesitation over my choice of words, but I expected he did. Robert Fraser was a sharp cookie.

"What exactly is this statue?"

"I don't know. You tell me," I retorted. "You're the one tracing its provenance, after all."

He frowned. "You think we're working on the same piece?"

"How can we not be? Two mysterious private citizens approach us at the exact same time over apparently identical statues? I've been sent to work from its last known location, and you've been sent to work from its first known locations."

Robert shrugged in acquiescence to her logic. "I know it fell briefly in the hands of Adolf Hitler at the beginning of World War Two. He held it until a few months before his death. I don't know where it went after that."

I leaned forward, very interested. I had a decent idea of how it came to be in Elise's hands, given that she worked as a double agent within the Nazi government during the war. Next time I saw her I'd have to ask if the Führer gave it to her personally or someone else had it first. "What about its history prior to Hitler?"

"It was a gift to him from a British nobleman before the war when England was still trying to make nice with the bastard and avoid bloodshed."

"And that nobleman got it where?"

"The guy was a cousin of Queen Victoria's. Apparently she owned it for most of her life. Didn't pay much attention to it if my sources are accurate, but it sat in a bookcase in her bed-chambers, apparently."

That was interesting. Hitler didn't die until he lost the statue—and according to what I'd heard about his drug addiction and the assassination attempts on him, his survival up to that point was considered to be something of a miracle. Then, Queen Victoria lived to eighty-one and safely bore nine children, all while in glowing health. Jeez Louise…that statue really packed a punch!

"Where did Victoria get it?"

"That part's a little fuzzy. Apparently it was passed down through a family known for acting as men- and ladies-in-waiting to the British royal family until it was given to her. They were only minor nobles themselves."

A shiver rattled through me. "And the name of this family?"

"The Norvilles."

Lady Jane Norville. My ghost.

"And how did they get the statue?" I choked out.

"I have no idea. I've found no record whatsoever of it prior to the early 1600s. That's what I'm hoping to research at the Vatican. The Norville family apparently thought it had something to do with the Catholic Church in England. They, themselves, were Protestant, however. I can't figure out how or why they'd have ended up with a relic like this, especially if they thought it was a Virgin Mary image."

The answer was right there on the tip of my tongue. I could taste it. It was as if something inside my head already had the answer and I couldn't quite pull it up to conscious memory. Maybe this was why Lady Jane's ghost had been pestering me.

Hello.

Did I just acknowledge that I thought my ghost was real?

Ghosts. Do. Not. Exist.

Period.

Except of course, the one inhabiting my head.

Which was starting to ache ferociously right about now.

"I need a nap," I announced. "We've still got a little time before we get to Rome."

"Good idea," Robert replied mildly. He propped his feet up on the chair beside mine, laced his fingers across his flat stomach and closed his eyes.

I followed suit.

I should've known better than to fall asleep with Jane on my mind.

I was there again, in Liz's bedroom. Jane was arranging a fingertip-length purple velvet cape over the queen's shoulders. The dress was high-waisted and several layers thick, more medieval in cut than Elizabethan. If you looked really closely, you could see the swell of her belly. Her pregnancy was probably a good seven months along. But, if you didn't know to look for it, you probably wouldn't notice the distinctive bump, especially when that cloak was pulled forward around her.

Jane commented, "The ladies of the Court complain when you are out of earshot that they do not like this new style of dress. They say it makes them all look pregnant."

Elizabeth snorted. "Better that they should all look pregnant than I be the only one. Jesus, I cannot wait to be rid of this babe."

"You do not mean that, Your Highness. Do you not long for the sweet smile of your babe nestled in your arms?"

"I do not," Elizabeth answered tartly. "This bastard will do nothing but complicate my life. How shall I ever find a suitable husband from among the kings of Europe with this child hanging around my neck like a millstone? The greedy fools may want England, but not at the cost of being saddled with an impure wife and her bastard offspring."

"What will you do, my lady?"

"I will kill it."

Jane hissed in her breath along with me. Although Elizabeth said the words with great conviction, the pain in her eyes when she uttered the words gave me hope that she was not sincere.

"You must not, Your Highness! You will damn your eternal soul to the deepest circles of Hell!"

"Well, at the least, I shall get rid of it. Foist it on some baker's mistress to raise."

"Nay, you cannot. This will be a child of royal blood. Of your flesh."

Elizabeth rounded sharply on her servant, yanking the hem of the velvet cape out of Jane's fingers. "You presume too much!" she snapped.

Jane, to her everlasting credit in my book, did not bow and scrape before this display of wrath as I expected her to. Instead, she stuck her chin up—albeit trembling—and replied gamely, "I cannot let you forfeit your immortal soul, for I love you like my own sister. If that is a crime, then take my head and hoist it on London Bridge for all to see, for I shall not repent of caring for you."

Surprisingly, Elizabeth stepped forward and wrapped her arms around Jane. "Dear Jane. Then you shall take this baby and raise it as your own."

Lady Jane pulled back, staring in shock. "I am not married! It is not mete that I should do so!"

"This child will be a fatherless bastard one way or another, for I have forbidden Winchester upon pain of death from ever uttering a single syllable about the parentage of this child. You shall take the babe home to your family and raise it as your child. Here. We will stuff a pillow under your dress and let all the Court know you have taken a lover and met a most unfortunate fate."

Jane spluttered, "But my family—my father—he will be crushed—he hoped for me to make a good settlement here at Court—to increase our family's purse—"

Elizabeth whirled away and went to her desk. "And so you shall. I shall provide all the coin you ever need to raise this child. Gold aplenty to buy off your disgrace. If no man is intelligent enough to see your true nature beyond the shame of your bastard babe, then he does not deserve you."

Jane looked about ready to throw up. Couldn't say as I blamed her. Nothing like having your boss's indiscretion turn into a scarlet A on your chest. And the poor girl was only trying to look out for an innocent baby. It hardly seemed fair. Jane opened her mouth a couple of times, no doubt to protest this arrangement, but no sound came out. Eventually she turned away, shaking her head and fiddling with the objects sitting on the writing desk....

And someone was shaking me, as well.

"Ana. We're there. Time to wake up."

I swam groggily to consciousness, my brain unwilling to relinquish the vestiges of the dream. Yet again, I had that feeling of an answer dangling just out of my reach.

But Robert was insistent. The airplane's engines shut down just then, and I realized the plane had come to a complete stop. The copilot came back to tell us to stay put and customs would be out momentarily to clear us. Wow. Personalized customs service. All kinds of perks came with this jet, apparently.

While we waited for the customs agent, I went into the bathroom to grab a toothbrush, some makeup and a couple outfits from Elise's stash. I was sure she wouldn't mind. I would have them cleaned and return them when we got back to Paris. I folded several garments carefully and opened my rucksack to put them in.

And frowned. I hadn't packed a brown paper bag in here last night before we went into the catacombs. And my flashlight, candles and chalk were gone. I opened the bag more fully and peered inside. Then I had a look at the manufacturer's tag. No doubt about it. This wasn't my rucksack! Thank goodness I always zipped my passport and Interpol badge into one of my coat pockets.

When in the world had I lost my backpack? I thought back to the catacombs. The last time I'd gotten in it was when we stopped to wait for René and had a picnic by candlelight. I tried to remember back. Then René and his drunken buddy showed up. We talked briefly and my rucksack had been sitting near my feet. And then the Italians had shown up. René had bent down to grab his bag and I'd bent down to grab—

We'd switched bags. This was René's pack. And, as I focused my memory in on the inadvertent switch of our bags, I came to another startling conclusion. The switch had been deliberate. René had leaned over in front of me and taken my bag on purpose, leaving this one behind for me.

I reached down for the rumpled paper bag and opened it. And my jaw dropped. Literally. As in hit my chest.

"Ana!" Robert called through the door. "The customs agent is here."

Oh, shit.

I stared down at the beautiful little statue nestled in the plain paper, her motherly eyes and those of her chubby little baby smiling up at me.

The Black Madonna.

Chapter 12

Now what was I supposed to do? I couldn't very well pass through customs with a stolen piece of art in my bag. But I dared not leave the statue lying around somewhere. Should I hide it here in the plane? Take it with me?

I had no way of knowing how long we'd be in Rome and whether or not this plane would sit here the whole time waiting for us. I decided to brazen it out and take her with me. After all, I had my Interpol badge with me and I had a legal right to have the statue. I'd been charged with finding and returning it to its rightful owner, after all. I just didn't want Robert to get into trouble for being near it.

I stuffed Elise's clothes in and around the statue and put on my best innocent face. I never could lie worth a darn. But this time it was Important. Capital I. I hadn't done anything wrong. I owed nobody any explanations. I was—technically—a cop. I took a deep breath and stepped out into the salon.

A pinched-looking man in a black wool suit stood there,

looking impatient. We handed over our customs declarations. I'd filled mine out before we landed and hadn't declared anything of value in my possession on it. Oops.

The guy asked about our luggage and Robert answered that we had none.

Casually, I mentioned, "I have a rucksack that I use like a purse. It has my wallet, a few personal items, a change of clothes and my Interpol badge in it."

The guy's eyebrows about shot over his hairline. "I see. We weren't informed. Welcome to Rome, Agent Reisner. If there is anything the local authorities can do for you while you are here, by all means let us know."

I smiled as pleasantly as a bald-faced liar could and wished him a good day.

The guy left the plane and we were free to go.

I let out a long, relieved breath. And caught Robert's questioning gaze on me. Ten to one, he'd sensed that I was lying to the guy. "That badge sure is a handy little sucker," he commented dryly.

"And how. Let's go visit some archives and see what we can find."

The copilot cleared his throat. "The plane will be refueled in an hour. Do you have any idea when you plan to return to Paris?"

"I honestly haven't the slightest," I answered. "We need to get back there as quickly as possible, however. Our work here should take at least several hours."

"We will be standing by and ready to go as soon as you return."

I turned to Robert. "Let's get rolling. I really need to get back to Paris right away."

He gave me another significant look. Man, he was good at reading me. He definitely knew something was up. We walked through the small flight operations center and grabbed

a taxi that was conveniently sitting right out front. "Where
to?" the driver asked.

I answered in my somewhat shaky Italian, "Vatican City,
please. The archives."

The guy nodded and floored the taxi, bolting out into
traffic like a suicidal maniac. Between brake squealing stops
and neck jarring accelerations, it was a supremely uncomfortable ride. Welcome to Italy.

I murmured, "Last night, my rucksack got switched with
our friend's."

He glanced down at the navy blue nylon pack and back
up at me. His eyes widened. "Is what I think is in there
actually in there?"

I nodded solemnly.

"Well, then."

I was at a bit of a loss for words myself.

"Do you mind if I look?" he asked.

I reached for the sack and unzipped it. I fished around in
the clothes, peeling them back to reveal the Black Madonna,
nestled within a cream silk Chanel blouse. He reached out a
single finger to touch her cheek. "She's beautiful," he breathed.

I took a closer look at her. She really was. Unlike most statues
of her time, her features were not elongated and dour. Her face
was full and cheerful, and her eyes almost twinkled up at me.
And the chubby, smiling toddler in her arms practically
squirmed to get down and run free. While the sheer happiness
of the pair made the statue of little worth as a Christian-style religious relic, the quality of the workmanship was extraordinary.

I touched the Madonna's dress with my fingertip and it was
almost warm to the touch. An odd—and definite—tingle shot
through me. I looked up at Robert in surprise. "Do you…feel
anything…when you touch it?"

"Like what?"

"A vibration. Almost like an electric current."

"Where did you touch her?"

I showed him and he laid his fingertip on the exact spot on the lady's robe that I had just touched. He concentrated for several seconds.

"Nope. Nada."

Damn. First I saw ghosts, and now this. I was turning into a certifiable lunatic. In despair I glanced up and noticed the taxi driver looking at me intently in the rearview mirror. Even he must think I was nuts. Sheesh. I tucked the Black Madonna back into her nest and zipped up my pack.

The driver stopped on the far side of St. Peter's Square, from where I knew the archives to be. "From here, you must walk," he announced.

Robert paid the driver from the obscene stack of euros in his pocket, and we got out. The morning was chilly, and we walked across the giant St. Peter's Square and the hulking, yet graceful, curving colonnades surrounding the square, which was actually an oval. We headed east a few hundred feet, past the Leonine Wall, built as a defense against Saracens, and through St. Anne's Gate into Vatican City proper.

No surprise, we were immediately directed to the left into the Swiss Guard's headquarters just inside the gate. Fortunately, their computer system was nowhere near as antiquated as their garish mustard-yellow and cobalt-blue striped uniforms, complete with conquistador-cut jackets over starched white shirts with stand-up collars that propped up their cheeks. Their puffy knickers stopped just below their knees, and mustard- and cobalt-striped spats covered their shins and shoes. They'd look like clowns if it weren't for their stern visages and their honest-to-goodness pikes, which stood taller than they did.

Also fortunate, they took after their Swiss namesakes and, after verifying my passport and Interpol credentials, issued me a new pass to proceed to the Secret Archives. My old one was at home, lost somewhere in the wreckage. Even if I'd managed to get home last night to retrieve it, I don't know if I'd have been able to find it. My place was pretty trashed.

We walked north and east to the beautiful Court of the Belvedere, which houses the Secret Archives. A pair of Swiss Guards stopped us as we entered the main courtyard, and again at the base of the staircase leading up to the Vatican Library and Archives. Each time someone ordered us to halt and produce identification, it was a toss-up whether Robert or I flinched harder. The guilt I felt at having the Black Madonna was even heavier than the statue itself in the bag slung over my shoulder. I guess I'm just a law-and-order kind of gal. How Robert had stolen art for a living and not had a nervous breakdown, I couldn't fathom.

But then, finally, we were inside.

The prefect, Monsignor Perretti, met us just inside the door and welcomed us to the archives. And made sure we weren't planning to just wander around poking into things, no doubt. "What brings you here to see us, today?" he asked me in perfect English as soon as he ascertained that I was American and Robert was Scottish.

"I'm here to research ley lines."

"An atypical subject for a religious archive of this nature, don't you think?" he said smoothly.

"Perhaps. But I have reason to believe that the archives contain pertinent documents. Could a librarian look it up for us?"

One does not just go to the card catalogue and browse through what this library holds. There was an entire room of indexes and inventories holding giant, handwritten volumes that listed the contents of the archives and their locations. Finding anything in this place was an art form.

Monsignor Perretti replied, "Your search may be an obscure one. Perhaps if you come back in a few days, we can tell you if the archives contain any documents pertaining to these lines of yours."

A few *days?* Impossible! I had to get the Black Madonna back to Elise right away so she wouldn't die! Time to cash in on that handy badge of mine again. "I'm sorry, Monsignor. That won't do. You see, I must get back to Paris right away. Interpol business, you understand. Madame Villécourt was absolutely clear that the archives do contain information on ley lines. I'm confident that if you look, you will find something."

"Ah! Madame Villecourt!" The man's' face lit up. "Why did you not say so earlier? I will summon Father Romile right away. He always helps her when she is here. He will know which documents she is referring to."

Now we were talking. The prefect moved over to one of the many telephones scattered throughout the place and spoke into it quietly.

A small, bald man who was as wrinkled as a raisin hobbled up to us almost immediately. His accent was heavy and Slavic, but his faded blue eyes lit up, as well, at the mention of Elise.

"Please, Father. Madame Villecourt sent me here to research ley lines."

He nodded right away. "The Papal Registers and the Miscellanea. Which would you like to see first?"

I had no idea. All I had to go on was Elise's last whisper before she conked out in the hospital. "If I said 'into the wind,' would that mean anything to you?"

His face creased even more into an oversized, denture-filled smile. "The Tower of the Winds. The Papal Registers, then. Come with me."

He led us down a corridor lined with steel bookshelves two stories tall with impossibly narrow staircases built into the second level. It was windowless and nearly dark, and we made our way down the first floor gallery past the treasure trove of documents.

"Would you like to see a rare document or two?" he offered. "They're really quite extraordinary."

"Sure," I answered. "What have you got?"

Father Romile chuckled. "You would be amazed at the variety. Name a great personage out of history, and I will show you something from him."

Without hesitating, I said, "Queen Elizabeth the First."

Father Romile's ceramic grin grew even wider. "Trying to trip me up by naming a Protestant, are you? Hah. Come with me." He detoured into a small passageway that wound back into the steel rows of shelves. "This section contains all correspondence with the popes in the sixteenth century."

On a hunch, I said, "How about something from—" I calculated fast. Elizabeth was born in 1533 and crowned queen at age twenty-six. In my dreams, I would place her at around age thirty if I had to guess "—1563 or so?"

Father Romile nodded and dived into the stacks of leather books with almost childlike enthusiasm. He emerged a few minutes later, covered with dust that laid in the creases of his skin like day-old makeup. "Let's have a look."

It took him several minutes of browsing the volume he'd retrieved, but then he gave a satisfied, "Aha!" Then, "My eyes are too old to read in here. What does it say?"

I leaned over the tome in the dim light and skimmed the letter, my gut churning more and more with every word. It looked authentic all right, written in the impeccable secretary-Italic hand Elizabeth was known for. I translated the Latin in my head.

…I entreat you most humbly to consider my offer. Immunity from insult or prosecution within my Realm to all who practice the faith of Catholicism. I ask only that you recognize the legitimacy of my reign and that of any child who should issue from my loins and whom I should name as my heir…

I was reading the very letter I'd watched Elizabeth pen in her own hand in my dream. To say that it spooked me was an understatement. I looked up from the document. "Do you, by any chance, keep copies of the replies the popes sent to these missives in the archives somewhere?"

"Often, a draft or a copy of the final reply is the next document in the register. Turn the page, child, and see what comes after your letter."

And there it was. A short, succinct note from Pope Pius IV to Queen Elizabeth.

Neither my predecessors nor I see fit to recognize you as anything other than a bastard born out of wedlock to your adulterous father and his mistress, the sorceress Anne Boleyn. We do not now, nor shall we ever, accede to your request. We do, however, insist that you extend full protection of the law and God to those practitioners of the true and Catholic faith living within your domain...

Yikes. Not long on diplomacy, was ol' Pius. I could just imagine Elizabeth's reaction to such a letter. I wouldn't want to have been anything breakable in the same room with her! I hoped poor, long suffering Jane hadn't been around when Liz read this particular note.

Father Romile replaced the volume on the shelf and led us onward through miles of shelves—he told us that, stretched end-to-end, there were nearly thirty miles of book-shelves in the archives—to a small, twisting, circular stair that led upward into the Tower of the Winds.

As we climbed the difficult steps, Father Romile told us a bit of its history. The tower was built as an observatory, and on its top floor, the Gregorian calendar had been worked out in 1582.

I frowned. 1582? "Wasn't the Catholic Church still espous-ing the theory that the sun revolved around the earth at that time? What were they doing with fancy observatories like this?"

Father Romile chuckled. "Many of the greatest astrono-mers of the ages were devout men—Copernicus, Kepler, Galileo and Newton, to name a few. Contrary to popular perception, the Church has always embraced mathematics and the sciences, seeing their elegance as a manifestation of God's perfection."

I blinked as I took all that in. "Then why did the Church reject the theory of Earth circling the sun for nearly two hundred years after it was proposed and proven?"

"Ah. Now we come to the heart of the matter," the priest announced. "This is the Room of the Meridian."

We stepped into a beautifully frescoed room, surprisingly not crammed with books as every other corner of this place had been so far. On the floor was a zodiacal diagram oriented to the sun's rays, which streamed into the room through a slit high in the walls.

While we looked around in wonder, Father Romile looked over his shoulder furtively, as if he was about to reveal a great secret that he shouldn't. His voice dropped into an old man's papery whisper. "That which the Church declares publicly and that which it knows to be true have not always been one and the same."

My jaw dropped. "Are you saying that the Catholic Church believed Copernicus when he proposed that the earth circled the sun?"

The old man scoffed, "Of course it did. We were not stupid. The greatest mathematicians and scholars of the day were priests. We grasped right away that he was correct. If you have time, I can show you the letters wherein our scholars informed the pope that it was so. And let me tell you, young lady, they are dated within a few *weeks* of the publication of Copernicus's great treatise."

"Then why was Galileo tried by the Inquisition? Why the rejection of the truth?"

The priest nodded sagely. "Why indeed? Why would the existence of powerful and potentially dangerous knowledge be suppressed, and suppressed brutally in some cases?"

And suddenly, I had the feeling we weren't talking about Copernican theory anymore. Father Romile stared at me intently, silently demanding that I answer his question. Except I didn't know how to answer it.

I'd almost forgotten his presence in the intensity of my conversation with the priest, but Robert said from behind me, "The Church has always done what it thought best for its followers. I imagine the Church decided that this new, scientific knowledge of the universe would weaken the faith of its believers."

As soon as Robert spoke the words, the answer was so obvious it had to be correct.

The priest nodded and said, his voice barely above a whisper, "The Church was willing to go to any lengths to suppress information it believed to be damaging to the Faith. *It still is.*"

And then something strange happened. A question came out of my mouth that I didn't ask. I mean, I said the words aloud, but I swear, I didn't think up the question or form the words in my mind. It just came out.

"What other great knowledge has the Church suppressed in the name of protecting the Faith?"

Father Romile clapped his hands together in glee. "You are a sharp one, you are!" he crowed. "I see why Madame Elise sent you to read about the leys."

And that strange, unconscious part of my mind that I was not in control of suddenly made another connection. "The Church has suppressed knowledge of ley lines, too, hasn't it?"

"Of course!" he exclaimed. "And magic and witchcraft and old cults, and any other number of mysteries that contradict Church dogma."

Excuse me. Magic? This guy was telling me the Catholic Church believed in magic at some point? And witchcraft? What about witchcraft? My already out of kilter world tilted even more on its axis. Either this guy was a little bit heretical or a whole lot batty.

A heavy thump startled me, and Father Romile dropped a huge, leather-bound tome on the room's lone table and opened it. A faded parchment, its ink faded to a warm yellow, lay before us. Thankfully, the priest translated the Latin for us. "Look here. This letter, from 1158, suggests the site for a great cathedral to be built in Paris over—" he ran his finger across a line of text "—an intersection of ley lines of exceptional power. It has the additional benefit of lying on an island in the Seine River, which will aid in making the citadel safe against sackers and marauders."

"Who is this letter to?" I asked.

"The pope, of course. From the chief architect. His Holiness approved the site selection—" the priest flipped to a page of text later in the volume "—here. 'I am pleased that the confluence of so many great energy lines has provided us with such a fortuitous site upon which to build. You are ordered to proceed with construction with all due haste'…" He closed the volume. "Construction on Notre Dame Cathedral was started in 1163 on the exact spot the architect recommended."

"Did ancient Church scholars ever study ley lines in a scientific manner?"

"Of course. Those documents are in the next register. It's heavy, though. Perhaps you would help me lift it down, my son?"

Robert stepped forward and lent a hand to the elderly man. This volume was even larger than the last, taking up almost the whole table when it was opened. And then I saw why. Its contents were entirely made up of maps.

Father Romile turned the pages carefully until he arrived at the one he sought. "Here it is. A map of all the great ley lines of Europe."

I gaped down at the spiderweb of crisscrossing lines. I'd seen that pattern before. I frowned, casting back in my memory for where it could have been. As an art historian, I tend to have excellent visual recall, particularly for details. It took me a minute, but then I had it. *The globe in Elise's library.* It was covered with an inlaid networking of crisscrossing lines that exactly matched this map. Then another salient detail clobbered me between the eyes. The globe stood right next to the pedestal where the Black Madonna usually was displayed. Surely that was no coincidence. I decided to take a flyer.

I lifted my rucksack to the edge of the table and unzipped it. I reached inside and pulled out the Black Madonna. "Do you know anything about this?" I held it out toward Father Romile.

He gasped and went white as a sheet before my very eyes. "How dare you bring that blasphemy into the House of God!" he rasped. He backed away, frantically making the sign of the cross over and over in the air in front of him. He reached the stairs, turned and ran, his robes flapping behind him like crow's wings.

"What the hell was that all about?" Robert demanded.

I looked at my companion, my eyes as big as saucers. "I haven't the foggiest idea."

"Well, I know one thing for sure. That old geezer is going to yell for help. If we're lucky we'll just get thrown out of here. And if we're not…"

Right.

I jumped as Robert grabbed the edge of the ley line map, still lying on the table in front of us. He gave a yank and ripped the centuries-old document out of the book.

"Robert!"

"Yell at me about it later. Right now, we've got to go."

He took me by the arm.

And we ran.

Chapter 13

Robert raced downward with the agility of a mountain lion and I was hard-pressed to keep up with him. Around and around we went, down out of the Tower of the Winds. Instead of turning right, back toward the main archives, he turned the other way. We ran down yet another long, windowless corridor-stuffed floor to second-story ceiling with books. I couldn't believe I was fleeing like a common criminal from the scene of a *crime*. Me. Miss Law-and-Order. I didn't even speed when I drove. And here I was.

We raced down a narrow hall of tall stacks, fear making my feet fast. And then I happened to glance over at Robert. I swear to God he was smiling. He was actually enjoying this! A sick feeling overcame my terror. I'd just helped a known felon gain entrance to one of the world's greatest treasure troves. And on my watch, he'd stolen a priceless map. I began to slow down, to tug against his hand. I couldn't do this. I had to turn him in. Give back the map.

Hell, resign from Interpol—assuming I didn't end up in jail alongside Robert.

Robert had just looked over at me, a questioning look on his face as he registered my resistance to him, when the lights went out. All of them.

Good grief! It was just like being back in the catacombs! Robert tugged on my hand, and I really had no choice. He was stronger than me and showed no sign of letting go of me. And short of letting him pull me off my feet and onto my face, I had to keep going.

Once I had resigned myself to continuing on, we actually had a pretty good system worked out for running in the dark. I guess twelve hours spent in the Paris catacombs can do that for a soul. The fear was the same, too. The pounding heart, the pulse throbbing in my head, the second-to-second certainty that someone was going to reach out of the dark and grab me. I was beyond skittish. Beyond scared. This raw terror was unlike anything I'd ever experienced.

And then I ran smack-dab into something warm and solid and resilient, slamming blindly into what I realized was Robert's solid back. "Oof. Sorry," I muttered.

"No prob."

"What's the hold up?"

"Door. Locked."

Locked? We were trapped? Oh, God. I *was* capable of dumping more adrenaline into my bloodstream, after all. My body shook from head to toe. I was hot and cold at once and my stomach felt so light it could float out of my throat if I opened my mouth. Something hard and tubular was thrust into my hands, which were so clumsy I could barely grasp the object.

"Hold this for me," Robert ordered.

I recognized the cold, steel cylinder of a flashlight.

"And while you're at it, take the map, will you? Stuff it in your rucksack so my hands will be free to open this lock."

He sounded like this whole fiasco was just another walk in the park for him! How did he do it?

He instructed quietly, "When I tell you to, put your hand over the light and turn it on. Then I'll want you to let out a tiny amount of light pointed at the lock. The last little bit of this lock will require me seeing it. And I left my night-vision goggles at home."

I didn't know whether he was kidding or not. At the moment I didn't care. I just wanted desperately to get out of here without getting caught. While he picked the first part of the lock by feel, I put the map in my rucksack. I didn't exactly stuff it in my bag as he'd suggested. I'm too much of an art historian for that. But I did roll it up carefully and ease it diagonally across the back of my pack so as to cause it·a minimum of crumpling. A pang of guilt that felt like a hot knife straight to the gut stabbed me. I am such a wimp.

I started hearing excited voices faintly behind us. Oh, God. "They're coming," I breathed, trying to sound calm but failing miserably. The remnants of my breakfast threatened to join us in the hallway any moment.

"The light. Now."

I opened my fingers slightly to let a thin beam of white light illuminate his work. Four thin metal rods stuck out of the lock like pins torturing a voodoo doll. They might as well be stuck in me, I was in such an agony of horror.

"Almost got it," he mumbled, peering into the lock. He stuck another pick in the lock and rattled a couple of the ones already there. "Okay, light off."

I felt him stand up beside me. The agitated voices behind us were getting close, and the bright beams of flashlights slashed the darkness not far behind us. My bladder threatened to empty itself. And the potential humiliation of that was about the only thing that could distract me from my panic. I all but jumped up and down in my agitation.

Robert opened the door, and thankfully, darkness met us on the other side, as well. No spill of light gave away our escape. We slipped through the opening into the Vatican Museum. Robert locked the door behind us, and we made our way through what turned out to be an exhibit of life-sized statues in front of a room full of gorgeous tapestries.

A voice in front of us called out in English, "Ladies and gentleman, please proceed to the nearest illuminated exit sign." The instruction was repeated in several other languages.

We joined in with the crowd. My relief was such that I felt light-headed. It wasn't the best cover ever, but it was better than nothing. As we filed outside, I heard a couple of the docents murmuring that there was some kind of general power failure Vatican-wide. Another power outage? Were these things following me from France to Italy? Actually, the idle thought gave me pause. Was this power outage part of the same series of failures that had swept across France? What if more countries than just France were experiencing these? It wasn't impossible to believe that the various European governments were quietly suppressing the occurrences in the name of economic stability.

We stepped outside into bright sunlight, squinting along with all the other tourists. I started as someone approached me quickly from the left, and with purpose. Crud. Blind as a baby mouse, I turned to the silhouetted figure, defensive words rising to my lips.

"Ana!" a female voice exclaimed. "I thought that was you!"

My eyes adjusted to the light just enough to be nearly blinded again by a head of shockingly red hair that Mother Nature never dreamed of producing. "Scarlet? Scarlet Rubashka?" I responded, "What are you doing here?"

I'd met her last month at the Black Madonna exhibit. She was a photographer and one of those infectiously bubbly people whom it was impossible to dislike.

"I'm in town for a party—"she leaned in, smiling conspiratorially "—actually for the man who invited me to the party." She straightened back up. "To pay my way, I'm doing a photo spread on the treasures of the Vatican Museum for *Le Monde*."

I nodded, appropriately impressed. *Le Monde* was Paris's largest daily newspaper.

Scarlet replied with the predictable and crashingly awkward question, "And what brings you to Rome?"

"Research," I said evasively. As seemingly bubbleheaded as she might be, Scarlet was still a journalist.

"And who's this yummy specimen hovering protectively over you?"

I glanced over at Robert in surprise. Hovering, was he? Protectively? "This is my colleague, Robert Fraser. He's an art history professor at Edinburgh University, and we're collaborating on our research."

Collaboration. Now there was a nice word for theft of Vatican documents, possession of stolen art and smuggling. Robert's gray eyes twinkled at me.

"So, where are you staying?" Scarlet linked her arm casually in mine, European-style.

"We only came in for the day. We're heading back to Paris later this afternoon."

She rolled her eyes. "I wouldn't count on that. These power outages have been lasting for hours. And once the electricity's back on, Rome takes forever to unsnarl. All that Italian machismo means no one's willing to let anyone else go first."

"How widespread is the failure?" I asked, surprised.

"I dunno about this one. The one that happened last week wiped out all of Rome and lasted nearly twenty-four hours."

"Wow. That stinks." Robert and I really didn't need to get stuck in Italy with both the statue and the ley line map. "How many blackouts have there been?"

"The way I hear it, they've had about five major ones over

the summer. That last one was really bad. Nearly collapsed the whole country's grid before they got it fixed."

I stared at her. "How come that never made the news?"

She shrugged. "Politics. I heard about it from an inside source in the Italian government who wouldn't let me quote him on it."

"Too bad," I commented. "It would make a heck of a story."

Scarlet grinned and shrugged. "I don't do real news. I specialize in shallow, but pretty, thank you very much. Fluff pieces."

I couldn't help grinning back. "And you do both shallow and pretty very well, I might add."

She pretended to punch my upper arm. "Ha ha. Very funny. Hey, if you do get stranded in town, you should come to the party tonight. It's a private art exhibition of medieval pieces like the one in Paris last month where we met. More Black Madonnas."

That snagged my undivided attention. "Who's sponsoring it?"

"The same family who did the one at the Cluny, remember? The Adrianos. They're an old Italian family and really rich. Black Madonnas are a hobby of theirs. Have been for generations, apparently."

A hobby, huh? The kind that involved stealing the Black Madonnas their millions couldn't buy? Had we, perhaps, stumbled across the rich Italian client René said was behind Elise's theft? "Where is this exhibition?" I asked.

"It's at the Palazzo del Furiano. Eight o'clock."

"You're sure the Adrianos won't mind if we crash it?"

Scarlet laughed gaily. "They won't mind a bit. Caleb Adriano himself invited me. I'm sure he won't mind putting a couple more names on the guest list. Frankly, I don't think he'll even notice you. At least not if I have anything to say about it!"

Her good cheer was contagious. We strolled past a pair of Swiss Guards, and it occurred to me that Robert was acting as if he didn't know us. Of course. The guards would be looking for a man and a woman together. Right now, Scarlet and I were a pair and Robert was solo.

Fortunately, with the power out, the Swiss Guards were plenty busy emptying museums and directing the tour buses through intersections now devoid of traffic signals. We were able to walk out through the same gate we came in without anyone attempting to stop us. And then we were clear of Vatican City. I breathed a huge sigh of relief. I turned around to congratulate Robert…

…and he was gone.

I looked around frantically. He wasn't anywhere in sight outside St. Anne's Gate. Which could only mean one thing. He was still inside the Vatican. Someone must have spotted him and stopped him on the way out. Oh, God. Not good.

I had to do something. Fast. Before he got hauled away and tossed into the erratic Italian justice system. Unfortunately, it wasn't like I had a lot of options at the moment. *What the heck.* I shoved my rucksack into Scarlet's arms. "Hang on to this for a sec, will you? Robert's gone and gotten himself lost again. I swear, that man couldn't find his way out of a paper bag by himself."

Scarlet blinked in surprise but took the backpack. "I bet he refuses to look at maps, too, doesn't he?" she called at my retreating back.

Little did she know.

Going back into the Vatican was an exercise in swimming upstream like a dying salmon against the crowds of people flowing out. I shoved and dodged and flat out elbowed my way back inside. I headed left for the Swiss Guard's Court. And sure enough, I spotted Robert right away. A guard was in his face, pulling a drill sergeant routine on Robert and screaming his head off, demanding to know who Robert was and what mischief he was up to in the Vatican.

To his credit, Robert's face was completely impassive,

and he wasn't flinching, wasn't moving a single muscle under the withering attack. Prison probably taught a man how to do that. He might be able to set aside his emotions in the face of such fury, to bottle them up and control them completely, but I, on the other hand, could not. Rage at the way the guard was tearing into Robert roared through me. It was white-hot and burned me clean through, consuming every cell of my being. I rode the wave forward.

Reaching into my jacket pocket for my badge, I strode forward, beyond irate. "What is the meaning of this?" I demanded in a furious tone of voice that would have given even my German grandfather pause.

The Swiss Guard and his two buddies rounded on me. "Who the hell are you?" one of them snarled back at me.

I noticed then that they had Robert's hands yanked behind his back and wired together with narrow, plastic handcuffs. My anger escalated even more. "Release this man immediately. This is an outrage! Professor Fraser, I am so sorry."

I shoved my Interpol badge in the face of the guard who'd been chewing out Robert. "This man is an internationally known art expert, and he's helping Interpol on a high-profile investigation for President Dupont of France. Personally."

The guards eyed my badge with a modicum of alarm. Ruthlessly, I pressed my advantage. I pulled out my cell phone and began to dial. "I am calling Carl Montrose right now. He's the personal assistant to President Pierre Dupont. And in about three minutes, President Dupont is going to be on the phone to the pope." I finished punching in the number and slammed the phone to my ear.

A female secretary answered the other end of the call.

I growled, "I need to speak to Carl Montrose. And if he's not available, I want Pierre Dupont. Now. Tell them this is Agent Ana Reisner of Interpol and this is a matter a national security. They will know who I am."

That shot up not only the Swiss Guards' eyebrows, but Robert's, too. I was going to have some explaining to do to him later. The secretary stuttered that both Montrose and the president were in a press conference and couldn't be reached for another half hour, even if it was an emergency.

"Then do me a favor. Tell the Vatican policeman I'm about to put on the phone who you are."

"Uh, all right."

I shoved my phone into one of the guards' hands. The guy spoke to Montrose's secretary for a little under a minute. I have no idea what she told him, but she convinced him she was for real, because when he hung up, he looked noticeably rattled. I glared at him and his companions, and looked down pointedly at the handcuffs. The guy with my phone barked at the yelling guard in Italian, and the latter leaped forward to cut the cuffs off Robert's wrists.

"I want your names, ranks and serial numbers," I demanded. "And the names of your commanding officers."

That put some starch in their spines. "Uh, yes, ma'am," Phone Guy said. "If you would come with me, I'm sure my superiors will make time to speak with you."

I glared down my nose at him. "The professor's and my research is of a time-sensitive nature and I do not have time to fool around with listening to apologies from your boss. If you will kindly write down the information I asked for, President Dupont's office and Interpol officials will contact them later."

Better to let these poor schmucks sweat for a few days than take the time to stage a tantrum for their bosses' benefit now.

The head guard wrote down the information on a note pad he pulled out of a pocket. He tore off the piece of paper and passed it to me along with my cell phone. The yelling guard mumbled a not particularly sincere apology to Robert—who had the good sense to put on a silent, fuming act throughout my tirade. And then we actually got escorted to St. Anne's gate by two of the guards, whose pikes and clown suits did a marvelous job of clearing the way for us.

The whole incident must have taken under two minutes. But as we stepped through the gate and safely into Italy once more, my heart pounded as if I'd just finished a marathon. A niggling little voice in the back of my head wondered why they'd let us go so easily. But I wasn't about to look that gift horse in the mouth.

Scarlet rushed up to us and thrust my rucksack back into my arms. I have to admit my legs went a little weak at the knees at having the two treasures tucked inside the bag safely back in my possession.

"There you two are! I was beginning to wonder if you'd been arrested or something!"

Robert and I both forced laughs at her quip, and for her part, she didn't seem to pick up on the shaky quality to our laughter or the relieved glances we traded. But you never knew with Scarlet. While she was irrepressibly Scarlet, she was also no dummy. It was hard to tell what she was observing and taking note of underneath that carefree, happy-go-lucky exterior.

We walked with her for several blocks, entertained by the horn-honking, fist-shaking mess the Rome streets had become in a matter of minutes. No wonder Scarlet said it would take hours to unravel this mess.

We stopped at a café and sipped espressos, and Scarlet repeated her invitation to the exhibition that evening. We promised to try to make it if we were still stuck in Rome. Finally, Scarlet got up to head for an appointment with a hairdresser to "brighten up" her hair color. It was hard to imagine the brilliant red hue getting any redder, but apparently, she was going to give it a go.

And then we were alone.

Robert took a long, careful look around us in every direction, and then he leaned across the suddenly tiny bistro table toward me, the expression in his eyes thunderous. "What in the *bloody hell* was that phone call to Dupont's office all about? What aren't you telling me?"

Chapter 14

Robert's gaze pinned me to my wrought iron seat. Crud. Carl Montrose had been clear. I was to tell no one about the power problem and its possible relations to the ley lines. But I couldn't very well lie to Robert. He could smell my being dishonest from a mile away. Maybe I could distract him with a piece of the truth.

"The owner of the lady in my bag is named Elise Villecourt. She's an old friend of Pierre Dupont's. They go all the way back to World War Two. She's also an old friend of my grandmother's. When her statue was stolen, she called Dupont and asked him to arrange for Interpol to put me on the case."

"What about the bit where you told Dupont's secretary that it was a matter of national security?"

I shrugged. "I...exaggerated...a bit. But when I saw that guard screaming at you, I was pretty furious."

His mouth quirked up into a grin. "I noticed. You came

roaring in there like a mother bear." He reached across the table and squeezed my hand. "It was quite a sight to see, I must say."

Heat began to climb my face, and Robert laughed quietly. "I already told you, Ana, there's no need to blush—yet. I'll let you know when it's time."

And all of a sudden it was back. Every last electron of that incredible sexual electricity snapping and crackling between us. The noises of cars and horns and frustrated drivers faded away, leaving behind only silence and the North Sea–gray of his eyes burning like a beacon, calling me to him.

The waitress came over to ask if we wanted more coffee, temporarily breaking the spell. The real world took shape around me once more. Robert paid the tab, and while we waited for change, something disturbing occurred to me. "You do realize, of course, that you've put me in an incredibly awkward position by swiping that map from the archives. Whatever possessed you to take it like that?"

Robert stopped in the act of putting the returned euros in his wallet. "You told me to take it."

I blinked. "I beg your pardon?"

He blinked back at me. "You told me to take it."

"I did not."

He half laughed incredulously. "You most certainly did. You said, 'Take the map, Robert.' You murmured it just after that priest disappeared down the stairs. It startled the hell of me when you said it."

I looked him square in the eye. "I swear, Robert. I said no such thing. I didn't even think it. There's no way those words came out of my mouth."

He frowned sharply. "I'm telling you. I know what I heard. I'm not crazy."

And as soon as he said that, I knew exactly what had happened. Or more precisely, who.

Jane.

"It was the ghost," I announced.

Now he did stare at me like I was crazy. But after a few seconds, he nodded slowly. "It could have been. The voice was too quiet for me to be certain it was yours. I just know it was a female voice. That makes sense."

I laughed shortly. "Well, maybe in your world it makes sense. In mine, it's nuts. But I'd lay odds she's the one who spoke to you. It's definitely her style." And before he could say anything in response to that, I added, "And I can't believe I just said that. I'm actually talking like this Jane person exists."

"She has a name?"

I grinned ruefully. "Lady Jane Norville. I've been dreaming about her for the past several nights. She was a lady-in-waiting to Queen Elizabeth the First."

"Why is she haunting us?"

"I'm not sure. I think Elise sicced her on me."

"Oooo-kaay," Robert said skeptically.

"Hey, you're the one who claimed to believe in ghosts before I did."

"Well, maybe in theory. I never expected to be tricked into committing a *theft* by one."

And therein lay the root of my latest dilemma. Should I believe his story about hearing the voice or was he borrowing an excuse from my earlier claim of hearing Jane speak? Had Jane tricked him into taking the map? It sent a deep sense of disquiet vibrating through me that he'd stolen something. Again. Was he still a thief at heart? Was he reformed as he claimed at all? Or was I aiding and abetting a felon in working his way back into the art theft community? He'd certainly seemed to enjoy the whole business of fleeing through the Vatican. As for me, I'd been just plain scared. Did I dare continue to work with him?

Robert stood and held my chair for me as I got up. "We need to get moving. And we need to find a telephone and call your pilots. See if the airport has power or not."

"I've got my cell phone," I offered.

"I'm betting all the circuits will be busy, assuming the cell phone towers still have power, but you can give it a try."

He was right. I dialed the number on the card the pilot had given me a good twenty times, and all I got was a busy signal or a message I half understood in Italian that I thought said something about all the circuits being busy. We walked down the street, moving significantly faster on foot than the cars beside us, who were caught in what looked like a city-wide gridlock.

A few blocks later, Robert exclaimed, "Tally ho!" We crossed the street in the middle of block, winding our way between a veritable parking lot of cars and their fuming drivers. And then I saw what he'd spotted. A public telephone. I tried the phone number again on the landline. The first time the call didn't go through, but the second time I tried, it did.

"Hello, this is Ana Reisner. I was calling to see if there's electricity at the airport and whether or not we can leave now."

The copilot replied ruefully, "No, we're hit, too. The airport's completely shut down. All the radar over and around Rome is down. No air traffic is moving over central Italy."

"Can we take off without radar and get back to Paris today?"

"It would be exceedingly dangerous to try it, and the captain and I would rather not."

"Are you simply expressing a preference with that statement, or are you saying we can't fly at all during this blackout?" I asked.

The guy answered apologetically, "I'm telling you it's unsafe and that we won't do it as a matter of safety of flight. It's for your own good, Mademoiselle. I know it's frustrating, but we have no choice. We can't take off until power is restored."

I sighed. "All right."

"If you'll call us when you get ready to leave the city to head for the airport, we'll have the jet preflighted and ready to go before you get here. We'll do everything in our power to get you back to Paris as quickly as possible."

"Thanks." I hung up the phone and relayed what the pilot had said to Robert.

He nodded. "I thought as much." Then he added, "And we're in such an all-fired hurry to get back to Paris why?"

I sighed. "How crazy do you want to think I am?"

He grinned at that one. "Why do you ask?"

"It will determine how close to the actual truth I tell you."

"Lay it on me."

I sighed again. "Elise Villecourt believes this statue is keeping her alive. When it was stolen, she was convinced that the theft was an attempt to murder her."

He absorbed that one in silence. I did see a faint frown cross his face, though. Yup, he thought I was loony tunes.

He said slowly, "That would explain why so many people seem to want this statue so bad."

I blinked. "You believe the statue has magical life-giving properties?"

He grinned. "That's no weirder than hearing a ghost tell me to steal a map."

I had to laugh. Whether it was out of humor or sheer relief, I couldn't say. Maybe it was both. "Now what?" I asked.

"Now, we get off the street. We've told any number of people that we're only here for the day and that we're heading back to Paris right away. Therefore, we need to do the exact opposite."

"What would that be?"

"Let's go find ourselves a swanky hotel and check in. With this power outage, they shouldn't be able to run any credit cards. We ought to be able to pay cash and get a room in complete anonymity. With the exception of not being able to fly out of here, this blackout has been a real boon for us."

"Nothing like making lemonade out of lemons," I retorted.

We took off walking again and went for what felt like miles. And eventually, Robert found what he was looking for. It was a very old, very elegant hotel just off via Manara in the ancient Trastevere neighborhood.

And when I say old, I mean *old*. The place looked as if it had been built pretty darn close to Roman times. The inside was a mix of ancient and modern as only Italy can do. Stone walls bearing ancient tapestries were shown off by subtle halogen spotlights. The front counter was a beautifully carved wood piece that looked as if it had come out of a cathedral, but a state of the art computer system sat behind it.

Fortunately, that system was, indeed, down. We checked in using cash. I was startled when Robert gave the guy false names—Mr. and Mrs. McManus. Then he slipped the manager roughly a hundred dollars U.S. in euros and murmured something about wishing for complete privacy. He hinted that I was a celebrity of some kind, and the manager seemed to buy the line of bull. Robert definitely knew all kinds of things about being sneaky that I was clueless about.

We went up to our room, which was breathtaking. The high ceiling boasted dark wood beams and the walls were plaster and stone. A large fireplace dominated one wall, but was balanced by the glass doors leading out to a balcony and an incredible view of red tiled roofs and the hills of Rome. The bed was a baroque canopy affair draped with satin and piled high with pillows. It was a room made for lovers. I almost hoped the power didn't come back on any time soon. I could definitely envision myself spending a month or two ensconced here with a gorgeous, sexy guy like Robert.

Since we had no luggage, settling in to the room took about thirty seconds. Robert went downstairs to see if he could scare up any sandwiches or something that didn't need cooking to eat, and I stretched out on the luxurious bed and closed my eyes.

It was late afternoon when I opened them again. Golden light flooded the room, turning the walls the color of a wheat field ready for harvest. The oil painting of a Tuscan landscape on the wall glowed so real, I felt as if I could step through the picture and into the place. Dust motes floated in the shafts of sunlight streaming past me, and I watched them lazily as sleep retreated slowly from my brain.

The balcony doors stood open and a breath of air moved through, stirring the white gauze curtains faintly. The air was cool against my skin where the sun had warmed it.

Robert lounged in a chair that looked more like a throne than anything else, his elbow propped on an armrest, his chin resting on his hand, reading. Bathed in the golden light, he looked like a mythic god, so achingly beautiful he was almost painful to look at.

He and I were so different I almost couldn't comprehend his presence in this room—in my life. He loved excitement. Craved adventure. Lived on the edge. I was cautious. Pragmatic. Boring. He was a thief and I worked for the law. We were doomed.

But what a ride it could be.

Did I dare jump on that runaway train with him? So far we'd limited ourselves to mutual attraction and the unspoken promise of more. I could think of a dozen reasons why I shouldn't step across the line with him. Not only could he destroy my career and all I had worked for, but I wasn't at all sure I trusted him. Ah, but he was such a charming rogue. And the sexual pull between us—I seriously doubted I had the will to withstand it. Or maybe more accurately, I lacked the desire to withstand it.

It struck me in that instant that my self-esteem had taken more of a bruising than I had realized when Jean-Michel rejected me because of my infertility. It was an attack on my womanhood. And I had yet to recover from it. Maybe I needed a man's man like Robert to make me feel whole again.

And maybe he was just the most attractive man I'd ever met.

He turned a page and glanced up. Seeing that I was awake, he put aside the book and stretched in his seat. "Sleep well?" he asked.

"I did," I smiled. "Do we have power back yet?"

"No. Can't you hear the silence? No air-conditioning, no traffic to speak of, nothing beeping at us."

I listened for a moment, and all I heard was a faint murmur of voices outside from below, pedestrians or maybe shopkeepers exchanging a few words. This must be what Rome had sounded like two thousand years ago. It was peaceful. Unhurried.

I yawned and stretched, feeling supremely lazy. "I could get used to this."

"Me, too. Looks like we may be able to make that party tonight, assuming it's still on. I talked to the concierge, and rumor has it the Italian authorities don't expect to have full power restored until tomorrow morning."

"Do we have running water at least?" I asked.

He grinned. "Yup, the modern convenience of flush toilets, just not a whole lot of hot water. The concierge said if you'd give him about an hour's notice, he'll have the kitchen prepare some hot water and send it up. Apparently, they have some sort of wood burning oven they bake in and they've filled it with pots to heat water for the guests."

I spent the next couple of hours fiddling around, ordering and taking a bath, toweling my hair dry, and putting on my make up before it got completely dark. We took turns dressing in the bathroom. While I was sleeping, Robert had gone shopping and purchased a black silk turtleneck shirt and gray cashmere sweater that exactly matched his eyes—gray tinged with silver. Paired with his black jeans and black leather jacket, he looked sophisticated and sexier than ever. But then, maybe I was a teensy bit prejudiced.

I put on the ivory Chanel blouse and a slim wool skirt in a pale aqua color that made my eyes positively glow. Or maybe it was the prospect of spending an evening on a real, live date with Robert that put that sparkle in my eyes. Fortunately, Elise only had low-heeled pumps on her plane, so I was set up to walk to the Palazzo del Furiano, where the exhibition was. It turned out not to be too far from the hotel in the same general area we were already staying in, which was a good thing. If possible, the streets were even more snarled than they'd been this morning. The transportation chaos was complete. What little order there usually was to the Italian roadways had completely broken down.

When we arrived at the palazzo it was full dark. The entrance glowed eerily, lit by a pair of enormous, no-kidding torches. Valets took our coats and ushered us inside, and time fell away with each step, peeling back the centuries until we'd been transported straight into the fourteenth century. A gathering hall opened up before us, its great Gothic ribs arching up into the gloom. Torches guttered and smoked around the margins of the room, their dusky glow augmented by literally thousands of candles in wrought iron sconces hanging overhead from chains as thick as my wrist. Firelight danced on the giant tapestries covering the stone walls, turning them into living, moving pictures. The effect of the candles and spotlights combined was magnificent.

Electric spotlights illuminated the numerous and breathtaking Madonna images. They must have a generator running somewhere nearby to power the lights.

At least two hundred people strolled around the room, but it didn't look or feel particularly crowded. They were looking at the various art pieces on display around the space, some hanging from the walls, and some displayed on pedestals.

Robert and I descended the long, shallow staircase into the hall. Pleasure lit his face as he looked around the room. I could only pray it was his appreciation of the art and not its potential value on the black market that brought such a gleam to his eyes.

A handsome, dark-haired, olive-complexioned man met us at the foot of the stairs. I'd put his age in his midthirties, but he was one of those casually elegant men who will look irritatingly gorgeous at seventy-five. "Good evening and welcome. I am Caleb Adriano. I don't believe we've had the pleasure of meeting."

I managed to control my eyebrows and not let them shoot up. One of the Adrianos in person? From everything I'd heard, this family was more than a little reclusive. They rarely made public appearances. And while this wasn't a tabloid-newspaper-headlines sort of appearance by any stretch, I was still startled. But then, lots of ultrarich people live fairly low-key lives. Probably trying to avoid robbery or kidnapping or worse.

Robert spoke in surprisingly good Italian as Caleb bent over my hand, kissing it as only an Italian in full flirt mode can. "We're friends of Scarlet Rubashka's. She invited us to come this evening. I do hope we are not intruding."

"Ah, yes. Her French and English friends. She mentioned that you might be coming. No, no. No intrusion at all. I'm so glad that this unfortunate power outage didn't prevent you from joining us."

I didn't correct him and explain that I was American and Robert was Scottish. My French usually was taken for native Parisian. I did, however, politely extricate my hand, which he still held long after he'd finished smooching it. "Actually, it's because of the blackout that we were able to come tonight. We'd planned to leave this afternoon, but the airport is closed."

He nodded in commiseration and captured my hand once more, tucking it into the crook of his arm. Sheesh. How pushy was that? Then he said, "Let us go see if we can find *bella* Scarlet. She asked me to let her know when you arrived."

I was startled when Caleb abandoned his post by the door and dived into the crowd with me, leaving Robert to trail along behind. I glanced over my shoulder at him, and he rolled his eyes, looking irritated. I couldn't blame him. I had definitely been absconded with. And while I might not be all that accustomed to alpha males like Robert, there was no doubt in my mind that having his date swiped this blatantly would not amuse him.

Fortunately, we found Scarlet quickly—not that it was hard to spot her flaming hair from the other end of the long room, even in the semidarkness. She wore a tight knit dress almost as brilliantly red as her hair and starkly avant-garde in design. She looked like a time traveler from the twenty-fifth century displaced into this gathering. But then, that was Scarlet. She was one of those people who would decorate her Christmas tree in lime and fuchsia and somehow make it work. I always felt as boring and bland as a bowl of oatmeal beside her, but I couldn't help loving her joie de vivre.

"Annie! Robbie! I'm so glad you could make it! Some collection, huh?"

Caleb didn't let go of me until Scarlet had spotted him hanging on to me. I'm sure he did it on purpose. Trying to make her jealous, was he? I smiled to myself. I was all about advancing the cause of romance between the two of them. Scarlet was a great girl. She deserved a rich, sexy guy like Caleb, who'd pamper her forever. Had I met him a few days ago, I might have been interested in him myself. But she could have him.

Yeah, I know. I was feeling extremely generous now that I had a gorgeous, sexy guy of my own to flirt with. Belatedly, I answered her. "We've only just arrived. We haven't really had a chance to look at the collection."

Scarlet reached out casually and snagged Caleb's cashmere suited arm. Staking her claim on him, was she? Good for her.

"Then come on!" Scarlet exclaimed.

For his part, Robert wasted no time moving in and resting his hand in the small of my back, laying claim to me in no uncertain terms, either. My bones liquified as heat radiated outward from his palm, through the thin silk of my blouse and straight to my core. And then that weird time-stop thing happened again.

The centuries fell away from around us, and the hall was new, echoing with the sounds of a lute and a young male troubadour singing in a clear tenor voice. Ladies flirted over their hands with lords posturing for them in their medieval finery.

Robert's head turned in super slow motion and he gazed at me, surprise dawning in his expression. His fingers tightened on my waist, and I felt an overwhelming need to turn, to lean into him, to lay my body against his. My hands came up, resting on his chest. I felt the softness of his sweater, the hardness of the man beneath. His heart beat once beneath my palm. It resonated through me like Notre Dame Cathedral's thirteen-ton bell ringing under my hand.

The vibration rolled through me and over me, grandiose and yet intensely personal. As personal as the sexual vibrations this man would send crashing through me if I but took that last step into a relationship with him.

It was almost as if an invisible hand between my shoulder blades was shoving me toward him. But it wasn't as if I resisted it. He leaned toward me at the same time I leaned toward him, and our entire bodies came into contact. The effect was incendiary. Wildfire rushed through me. And I burned for this man.

"Whoo! Get out a bucket of cold water and toss it on you two!" Scarlet laughed, effectively breaking the spell.

Robert blinked down at me and I up at him. He murmured, "Did Jane do that, or was that just us this time?"

"Does it matter?" I managed to say, as blown away as him. His grin nearly knocked me over. "I will admit I'd like to take credit for all of that, but no. I don't give a damn where it comes from if you don't."

"Nope, no complaints from me."

His arm tightened around my waist and he steered me toward the nearest exhibit. I stared at it, registering only that it was a wooden triptych painted with an image of a black-skinned woman holding a baby. They both had golden halos above their heads and looked like fairly traditional Virgin Mary images. My eyes passed across the placard at the bottom and saw the words describing several variations of the depiction of Black Madonnas, ranging from nearly identical to the Virgin Mary as in this painting, to images including swords, keys and urns of water, which were perhaps a holdover from earlier pagan forms of worship.

Urns of—Elise's tapestry in her front hall! That was a Black Madonna image like this card described. I recalled wondering about that urn.

We moved on to a tall, narrow statue. It looked very similar to the one Catrina Dauvergne had displayed from her personal collection at the Cluny last month, but this one looked older, less detailed in its execution.

I was relieved to let the art suck me in and distract me from the man plastered against my side. Otherwise, I surely would have embarrassed myself and him in public by throwing him down and ravaging him right there on the spot.

Caleb Adriano was similarly plastered to Scarlet and strolled around with us, adding the occasional comment beyond what the placards said. He seemed to know a fair bit about the history of the medieval Madonna cult and told us it was thought to have been centered in southern France.

I did notice that Scarlet went very quiet and still when he brought up the subject. But then, maybe Caleb's hand roaming up and down her mostly naked spine was distracting her.

After a few minutes, a petite, striking brunette walked up

to us, limping slightly. She had shoulder length dark hair, and was maybe in her early thirties. Hard to tell in this light, though. What really captured my attention was her long velvet gown, laced in the medieval style across her midriff to show off a trim figure. She wore this room almost as if it had been built for her. Then I spied the tall glass of bright red liquid in her hand. Good grief! In the torchlight, it looked just like blood. I was relieved when she smiled politely at our host and no vampiric fangs protruded.

"Pardon me, but you wanted to know when the Cardinal del Vecchio arrived, Caleb."

Our host dropped Scarlet like a hot potato and hurried off in the direction the woman pointed. She stared after him, dismayed.

The brunette said under her breath, her lips barely moving, "I'm telling you, Scarlet. Stay away from him. He is *not* what he seems."

The redhead rounded on the slightly older woman. "You keep telling me that, but you won't give a single, specific example of what you're talking about! He's polite, smart, funny, handsome, sexy, single and rich. What else matters?"

The brunette shook her head. "Just be *careful* around him."

Scarlet rolled her eyes as the brunette huffed in exasperation. Robert went rigid against my side. Shocked stiff. "Ginny?" he asked incredulously. His arm fell away from my waist.

The woman turned sharply and stared at him. For just an instant, similar shock showed in her gaze. "Robert! It has been a long time. How *are* you?" And then she stood on tiptoe and kissed him. On the mouth.

My stomach plummeted past my feet and right down into the solid stone floor. *Oh, crap.*

Chapter 15

The brunette *had* to be a former lover. Or, given that kiss, maybe not so former. I thought I was going to throw up.

And then Robert did something that made me fall a little bit in love with him right there on the spot, although in retrospect, perhaps I was already head over heels for the guy. He stepped back from the beautiful brunette, wrapped his arm around my waist and said, "Ana, this is Ginny. A former colleague of mine from a long time ago. Ginny, remember how you used to say you'd love to meet the kind of woman who could capture my heart? Well, here she is. This is Ana. She works for Interpol."

My jaw dropped. *Could capture his heart?* My own heart skipped and jumped like a carefree foal frolicking in my chest. And then the rest of the introduction sunk in. He'd called her a colleague. Not a lover, not even a friend. From a long time ago? Like when he used to steal stuff for a living? Was she a thief, too? I eyed the woman speculatively. Lithe and petite, she exactly fit my conception of what a cat burglar must look like.

Scarlet said, "Caleb's waving for us to join him over there."

The four of us strolled around an illustrated manuscript resting on a tall lectern, its pages open to display a magnificent illumination of a Black Madonna, and we joined Caleb Adriano and his newest guest. The man was mostly bald, and what hair he had was cropped into a silver fuzz near his scalp. He wore a dark suit, but with a clerical collar in place of a tie. A priest, then.

A faint movement caught my eye. Ginny had glided around to our right, placing Robert and me between her and Caleb. No love lost there, apparently.

Caleb looked…sulky. Not in the least thrilled to find himself babysitting this ecclesiastical gentleman. Then he did something odd. He draped his arm around Scarlet in an even more blatant display of affection than I'd seen from him so far. Frankly, it looked forced. And, based on the knock-me-over-with-a-feather look on Scarlet's face, was a whole new level of public familiarity between them. It was almost as if Caleb was trying to insult the priest.

Then he drawled, "Cardinal del Vecchio, this luscious specimen is Scarlet. These are her friends Ana and Robert from France and England." Apparently the priest already knew Ginny, for they nodded at one another and Caleb didn't introduce her.

We made uncomfortable small talk for a few moments, chatting mostly of the power outage and the mess it had caused. And then I happened to ask, "Where do you work, cardinal?"

"I am curator of the Vatican Museum."

I about swallowed my tongue as Caleb remarked almost, but not quite, snidely, "I hear you had a theft over there today. I thought your security was better than that. What did they get?"

The cardinal replied gravely, "A map. Torn right out of a fourteenth-century codex. Shocking bit of vandalism."

Ginny frowned and her gaze flickered over toward Robert. Oh, yeah. She knew Robert had been a thief. Was she one, too? Or maybe a fence for stolen art? Or someone with inside knowledge she sold to thieves? A colleague, indeed.

Her dark gaze fixed on Robert, Ginny asked the Church official, "Why would anyone steal a single map like that?"

I glanced up at Robert with as much innocent interest as I could muster. For his part, he didn't betray with even the slightest hint in his expression that he knew a thing about what they were talking about. Note to self: never play poker against this man.

The cardinal answered Ginny. "That's the odd thing. It was an ancient map of ley lines in Western Europe. At the time it was made, architects used it to choose building sites for important religious structures. I can't fathom what a thief would want with it now."

This time it was Caleb, who'd been starting to look a little bored, who about spewed his drink all over the rest of us. He, too, had been sipping the bloodred stuff Ginny had been drinking earlier.

Frantic to divert the conversation into less dangerous waters, I asked him, "By the way, what's that you're drinking? I hesitate to tell you what it looks like in this dim light."

Caleb laughed and slid a sly gaze in Ginny's direction. "Pomegranate juice. She swears by it. Makes us all drink it."

Ginny rolled her eyes back at him, scowling. "And you're in glowing health, aren't you?" she snapped.

The persistent, and I might add pesky, cardinal piped up with, "Did I tell you we got descriptions of the thieves?"

Caleb turned back to del Vecchio, and I felt myself edging toward the nearest door. Robert's arm tightened around my waist, holding me firmly in place.

"Do tell," Caleb responded.

"It was an American woman and an Scotsman. She had

fake police credentials and said she was there to research a police matter,"

Scarlet glanced over at me, startled, while Ginny shot Robert a very nearly suspicious look. But I just looked back at my friend blandly, and Robert did the same to Ginny. *Fake credentials?* My badge was as real as they came! How come I hadn't shown up in the Interpol personnel database as a legitimate employee of the agency? That was odd.

Still curious over Caleb's violent reaction to the mention of ley lines, I asked into the settling silence, "Your Eminence, what is the Church's interest in ley lines, anyway? A map of them seems a strange item to house in your museum."

"Oh, the map wasn't in the museum. It was in the archives. No, no. *Our* security is far too good for even the most minor theft to succeed." This was delivered with an arch look in Caleb's direction. No great love lost between those two.

"So you consider this a minor theft?" Scarlet piped up, wiggling just enough against Caleb to hold his full attention.

The cardinal turned to my photographer friend, whom I could hug for diving in to the conversation. "No theft is a minor thing, not in the eyes of the Vatican or of God."

"I gather then that God takes an interest in ley lines, since you collect maps of them?" I replied dryly. I can't help it. People who get on their moral high horses have always bugged me. The way I was taught, no one's perfect. We all have flaws and mistakes aplenty—enough to keep us all humble.

The cardinal paused just a fraction of a second, obviously trying to decide whether or not to be amused or offended. He chose to laugh. "No, young lady, we do not concern ourselves with such things. The Church emphatically denies the existence of ley lines or any such fertility-goddess, earth-magic mumbo jumbo."

Hmm. Then how did he know they were traditionally linked with fertility goddesses and earth magic? Was this one of those cases of a Catholic hard-liner trying to suppress factual knowledge he felt was dangerous? Or perhaps this guy still thought the Earth was flat, too. There was something…off…about this cardinal. I couldn't lay my finger on it exactly, but he gave off a dodgy vibe.

A week ago, I'd have scoffed at the idea of ley lines causing power outages all over France, and apparently Italy, too. But now—now I wasn't so sure. If I could have visions and see ghosts, why not ley lines?

Robert commented lightly, "Too bad the power's been out all day. That must have really hampered the police response to the theft."

The cardinal nodded. "The Swiss Guard is having to do things the old-fashioned way. They're going to every police precinct in Rome on foot to give a description to the Italian police."

"Good for them," Robert replied bracingly. "So. What brings you to this exhibition tonight, Your Eminence?"

"The Church has a long and close relationship to the Adriano family. They are great friends of the Faith and great friends of mine. During this change of the ages, it is important to stand by one's oldest and closest friends, is it not?"

Strangely, he seemed to be aiming that question as much at Caleb as at us.

Color me a little slow, but I was confused. According to what I'd read on the placards all around me in this room, the Virgin Mary cult—of which this Black Madonna cult was a possible offshoot—had all but eclipsed worship of Jesus Christ at one point in the Middle Ages, particularly in southern France. Not to mention historians theorized that perhaps its roots lay in ancient goddess worship. Hence, its brutal and complete suppression by the Catholic Church by the end of the fifteenth century. Yet, here was a cardinal, choosing to attend a display of possibly pagan-rooted images of women to show his support of the Adriano clan—a gesture which Caleb Adriano seemed ambivalent about at best. It made no sense. Unless the Church and rest of the Adrianos were very good friends, indeed.

And what was up with that change of ages comment? My understanding, admittedly limited on the subject, was that astrological "ages" changed approximately every two thousand years, and were doing so now. We were passing from the Age of Pisces, which began right at the time of Christ, into the Age of Aquarius. Since when did the Catholic Church embrace astrology, too? This guy was just a barrel of surprises.

I addressed Caleb. "How long has the Adriano family been associated so closely with the Church?"

He shrugged. "You would have to ask my father. He pays more attention to that sort of thing. Speaking of *Il Duce*, here he comes now."

As the senior Adriano moved toward us with alacrity, I got the distinct impression he was alarmed at the prospect of Caleb being alone with the cardinal for any period of time. The familial resemblance could not be denied, from the aquiline nose to the intensely intelligent hazel eyes. Simon's brown hair was slightly darker than his son's, and his shoulders weren't as broad, but this man wore an air of command that equaled or even surpassed that of the cardinal.

"Simon, my son!" del Vecchio exclaimed warmly.

The Adriano patriarch paused to kiss the cardinal's ring, then embraced the priest in a traditional Italian hug. Old friends, then…or putting on a good show of it, if they were not. I also noted that we pointedly did *not* get an introduction to Simon from Caleb. Ah, the nuances of life among the upper crust. All of a sudden, I felt like a terrible interloper at this party.

Even Scarlet, who to all appearances was about to be sleeping with his son, barely merited a condescending glance from Simon

Adriano. No wonder I'd glimpsed a touch of conceit in young Caleb now and again, if he'd been raised by this guy.

As an awkward silence fell among the mismatched group of us, Caleb dived in. "Father, these people were just asking how long the Adriano family has been associated with the Catholic Church."

Simon, a tall man already, drew himself up even taller. "As long as there has been a pope, there has been an Adriano by his side."

"Literally?" I blurted. There had been popes since shortly after Christ's death.

Simon rolled an offended look down his nose at me, but Cardinal del Vecchio chuckled. "Ever faithful, the Clan Adriano. For nearly two thousand years they've given us their sons in service. One of these days, we may yet see an Adriano on the throne of St. Peter."

That threw a look of real alarm into Simon's eyes. "I should hope not! We prefer to move quietly behind the scenes. It has been our role to assist the Holy Father in whatever ways we can, not to bask in the limelight ourselves."

So why did I detect an edge of disapproval in the cardinal's eyes? Definitely deep currents flowing between these Adrianos and their Church. I was struck by the incongruity of Simon's statement about preferring to work quietly. He and his son both struck me as more than a little arrogant. Why would they choose to serve in humble anonymity behind the popes? Although come to think of it, that's where all the power was.

Caleb turned to his father. "The cardinal was just telling me about the theft at the Vatican today. You'll never believe what they lost—"

The cardinal cleared his throat uncomfortably, and Simon interrupted, "I've already heard. We beefed up security tonight because of it. He glanced around the room. I've got enough muscle in here to take on a small army. What did you say the thieves looked like, Your Eminence?"

Bile rose into my throat. It tasted like spoiled seafood. The cardinal was going to describe both of us and someone would put two and two together. We weren't French and English at all, but an American and a Scot, standing right there in front of them!

I was relieved almost to the point of nausea when Robert chose that moment to nod a farewell and excuse us to the younger and older Adrianos and lead me away into the shadows. In another minute or two, the army of security guards discreetly ringing the room was going to close in on us, and the jig would be up. Legitimate Interpol badge or no, we would be so hosed then.

We stopped in front of a crude painting, maybe twelfth century, done in some sort of tempura-like medium. I stared at it, trying my best not to look all around me in panic and give away my guilt before I absolutely had to.

"We've got to get out of here. Any suggestions?" Robert muttered under his breath.

"The back door?" I muttered back.

"Smile. Look like you're enjoying yourself. I have a really bad feeling about this Simon guy. He's too smart for our own good. He'll match us with our descriptions from the cardinal in a second."

If I was allowed to see ghosts, he was entitled to his gut feelings.

"This way," he murmured.

I pretended to be pleased that he'd directed my attention to the painting on the wall beside us and absently studied the rather mediocre piece, whose only real merit was being very old, while he scoped out the room. He took off walking—more like gliding actually—and led me through the crowd. We moved, then paused, moved some more. Made a moment's conversation with some stranger standing beside us. Moved again. I was amazed at how quickly we traversed the cavernous hall without ever appearing to be in any sort of a hurry.

The shadows were darker at this end of the great hall, the pervading gloom heavier. I got the feeling we were being watched, but then that was probably just my guilt and paranoia working on me. Except didn't I hear someone say once that it's not paranoia if someone really is following you?

Robert startled me by walking right up to a guard by a closed doorway. *"Toletta?"* he asked in terrible Italian unlike his usual fluent ease with the language. *Bathrooms?*

The guard nodded and pointed at a door not far from us. Robert nodded and we headed for it. I took one last glance around the hall. No one seemed to be looking for us. Yet.

We slipped into a hallway nearly as dark as any tunnel in the catacombs. I swear, in the past few days, I'd spent more time wandering around in the dark than I had in my whole life! Robert moved past the bathrooms confidently as if he knew where he was going. But then, maybe he did. These medieval places tended to be laid out fairly logically. Seen one, you'd seen 'em all.

We took a sharp right-hand turn, passed through a vaulted wood door with iron-banded hinges, and found ourselves in a modern kitchen that gleamed in the faint torchlight seeping through its windows. Not a soul was in there. "Where are the caterers?" I whispered.

"Probably down in the old kitchens using the wood-burning ovens and fireplaces to cook." He headed for another door on the opposite side of the room and reached for the handle. I sighed in relief as it opened under his hand. No need to stand here fretting while he picked the lock.

We stepped outside into a high-walled garden. It wasn't all that large, but was cunningly laid out to look much more expansive than it was. My eyes adjusted to the dim moonlight filtering through a thin layer of cloud cover. I began to pick out plants here and there. A pair of climbing roses were glossy and black on the trellis beyond a sage bush glowing silver beside me. And the tall wall of a box hedge towered straight ahead. Robert groaned under his breath and we headed for it.

Then I saw the telltale opening in the hedge. A maze. No wonder Robert had groaned. We didn't have time for this foolishness.

"How big do you suppose the property is around this place?" he asked.

"Not very. We're smack-dab in the middle of the city."

"Let's see if we can find another way out of the maze. Maybe if we're lucky there's a gate at the other side of this thing."

We started off, and I did my best to keep my directions straight. But as soon as the paths started branching off at forty-five degree angles and even curving, I was done for.

Robert stopped, looking around in frustration. "Jeez. Where's a ghost when you need her?"

I laughed quietly. "Maybe we don't need her, yet. Her absence probably means nobody's chasing us with the intent to do bodily harm to us."

"Good point."

Most garden mazes I'd seen were relatively simple affairs that, if you kept your wits even slightly about you, could be solved in a few minutes. Not so, this one. It was purely evil, more like a castle defense than an entertaining garden curiosity. The paths were narrow, the hedges dense and tall, and while I suppose we could've just pushed through them, we saved ourselves some serious scratching by walking the paths. And walking. This maze was huge. Either that, or we were retracing our steps. A lot.

Then, without warning, a hand clapped over my mouth and I was yanked back against something—someone—hard and hostile. Panic slammed into me. I tried to scream, but I could barely breathe, let alone make noise.

Horrified, I watched Robert take several steps forward. He hadn't heard my silent attacker. Wasn't aware I was in huge trouble back here. He was walking away from me!

I squealed then under the big, hard palm and fought like a maniac. My first impulse was to grab for the fingers over my mouth, but I belatedly remembered from my self-defense training that my strength would be useless against my attacker's in that way.

So, I elbowed the guy's ribs with all my might. He was wearing some kind of thick jacket if the dull, painless *whump* of my elbow against his side was any indication. I mule-kicked his knee next. That got his attention. He let out a grunt and cursed in Italian. But more to the point, he let go of me.

I whirled to face him, but something big and dark flashed by me. Robert barreled into my attacker and knocked him to the ground in the prettiest rugby tackle you ever saw. His shoulder drove straight into the guy's solar plexus, and wool coat or no, the guy went down like an oak tree. Robert rolled off the attacker and scrambled to his knees, his fist drawn back. But the jerk didn't move. Must've knocked himself out hitting his head on the ground, or something. We didn't stick around long enough to find out.

We took off running, and now we did start crashing through hedges. It only took me about two painful, scary shoves to get the technique. You turn so your back takes the worst of it, and you try to fold yourself into the narrowest possible shape. Then, you slide around the big branches that get in the way and push through the twiggy stuff. Lots of scratches but fewer bruises.

Someone shouted behind us. They'd found my attacker. Crud. Now it sounded as if a whole bunch of men were in here with us. I sincerely hoped they were running around in circles, too. But odds were our pursuers knew their way through this insanity. And we did not. Sprinting for your life is one thing, but sprinting for your life in circles is quite another. Helplessness threatened to paralyze me as the voices behind us got closer and closer, and Robert just kept crashing through hedges and dragging me along behind him. I had no idea where we were or where we were going, and that scared me almost more than the fury tinging the shouting voices now all but surrounding us.

We ran even faster, the green walls leaning in on us, hemming us in on all sides. It seemed no matter which way we turned more hedges always loomed, determined to snare us in their leafy arms.

Footsteps pounded very close behind us, but where they were exactly, I couldn't tell. My head was spinning. I had no idea which way was forward or back. I was barely keeping up and down straight.

And then I heard someone breathing heavily in the next row over. Robert froze instantly, one foot suspended in the air in the act of taking a step. I did the same behind him. He gestured me to come up beside him, and he began to creep forward, placing each foot down with exquisite care. We approached the next intersection, and he moved ahead to peer carefully around the corner. Then he waved his hand at me and we darted forward.

I have to say, I wasn't aware of just how much ambient light there is in a city, even if all the lights directly near you are turned off. But I noticed its loss acutely in this power outage. A band of thicker clouds had drifted in front of the moon, and at the moment it was pitch-dark out here. I had to squint to make out Robert's back, and he was only a few feet ahead of me. Thankfully, the dark seemed to sharpen up our hearing considerably. When the heavy breathing came again, from our right this time, Robert and I darted to the left down the intersection. And hit a dead end.

"Push through," I whispered frantically.

"Can't. Stone wall behind it."

Oh, God. Well, at least we'd found a wall. I prayed it wasn't a wall back into the palazzo. It would be ironic, indeed, if we ended up right back where we'd begun.

Robert leaned over and breathed in my ear, "If there's a gate at the edge of the property, it has to be to our right and behind us."

That was no help. We would still have to move back toward our pursuers to get to it. At that moment, I experienced rare regret that I didn't have my Interpol-issued firearm with me tonight. We crept along the wall of bushes to our right, keeping to the thickest, darkest shadows we could find.

And then with a tremendous crash of noise something—someone—exploded out of the bushes behind us, grabbing Robert around the throat from behind. I watched in horror as the two men struggled. I looked for an opening to dive in and clobber the guy now wrestling with Robert. The attacker rolled to the top, his hands wrapping around Robert's throat. I made a fist and swung it backhanded as hard as I could at the side of the guy's head.

It knocked the guy a little silly, at least enough for Robert to rip the guy's hands off his neck, give a heave and toss the attacker off him. Both men jumped to their feet. And then I saw it. A long, wicked-looking knife slid down out of the attacker's right sleeve and into his hand.

I screamed then. I'm not usually a screamer, but the shock of seeing a deadly weapon aimed at Robert was tremendous, and my terror over the idea of him being killed overwhelmed me. The attacker's eyes flickered in my direction, and Robert leaped, wrapping his hands around the wrist holding the knife. So maybe screaming wasn't such a bad thing after all.

The two men locked arms overhead, the bad guy trying to stab Robert for all he was worth, and Robert holding the blade at bay for all he was worth. It looked just like a fight scene in the movies. Except in the movies, the helpless heroine doesn't step in and kick the snot out of the bad guy's nearest knee.

I did.

I'm sorry, but I wasn't about to fight fair when Robert's life was at stake. The bad guy's leg collapsed and he went down to the ground hard. The knife skittered away in the dark and the guy rolled on to his belly to scramble after it. Robert chopped the guy across the back of the neck with the side of his hand, and the jerk went limp on the ground.

"Let's go," Robert bit out.

My attention suddenly expanded beyond the life or death struggle I'd just witnessed to the maze and the pursuers around us. My God, they were practically on top of us now!

We ran then. Like the wind. We ran straight ahead until we hit a wall of green, and Robert shoved straight through it. I threw my arm up in front of my face and charged after him. I had effectively destroyed Elise's silk shirt by now, but that was the least of my worries. We ran again, and shoved through again, silence be damned.

Shouts erupted all around us. How they hadn't caught us yet, I couldn't imagine. Maybe the darkness and the featureless walls of green all around had disoriented them, too. I felt like a fox trapped by a pack of braying hounds with nowhere to run. Nowhere to hide. I looked around frantically.

"Jane!" I screamed in a bare whisper. "Help!"

"This way," Robert bit out, no longer bothering to be quiet.

We ran to our left this time, into a section of the maze I was sure we'd traversed before. The voices were getting closer. Quickly. And they sounded as if they were converging on our position with confidence now. We crashed through a couple more hedgerows, and then, all of a sudden, a stone wall loomed in front of us. A really big one with extremely unfriendly looking spikes at the top. We were trapped!

I felt her before I saw her. A wisp of air moving past where there should be no breeze. And then the faintest shimmer of gray off to the right. About sixty feet away. I opened my mouth to tell Robert, but apparently he saw her, too, for he took off running right for her.

We reached the spot where she'd been and screeched to a halt. Now what? She'd disappeared. I thought I'd seen her drift to our left, which would have taken her into the bushes. Except a stone wall rose on the other side of the shrubs.

Robert threw me a questioning look and I shrugged. His guess was as good as mine as to why Jane had brought us down here. He plunged into the leaves and I stared after him for a second. He had more faith than I to blindly follow Jane like that into a corner where we would be not only trapped but immobilized.

And in that millisecond I learned something startling about myself. I trusted Robert. Completely. Much more so than a figment of my imagination that occasionally took the form of a ghostly woman.

What the heck. I took a deep breath and plunged in after him.

Chapter 16

We stood there, pressed against the cold wall, the hedges thick in front of us, and didn't breathe. At least, I didn't. Only seconds later, three men ran past where we stood, frozen. After they'd disappeared, Robert eased off to his left, slipping between the hedge and the wall. I followed as quietly as I could.

We'd only gone about ten feet when Robert stopped. He turned around so his face was to the wall. And then, very carefully, he crouched down. What in the world was he doing?

Two more men passed our hiding spot, this time moving more slowly. The clouds thinned a bit just then, and I saw the distinctive shape of a pistol in one of the men's hands through a tiny gap in the leaves. And given the way the other guy was walking with his right forearm extended in front of him, they must both be armed.

I held my breath again. And again, these two guys walked right past us without seeing us. How they weren't spotting my light colored clothing, I couldn't fathom. But I wasn't complaining.

After those two goons passed out of hearing range, I risked turning my head to see what in the world Robert was up to. And was stunned to see him picking a lock. What in heaven's name was a lock doing set into the middle of a stone wall covered by bushes? I noticed the wall looked slightly different where he stood. I reached out to touch it, and instead of the cold roughness of stone, my fingers brushed against smooth wood. Hallelujah. A forgotten—or at least old and overgrown—gate. We'd found the back door, and not a moment too soon. Or rather, Jane had. God bless friendly ghosts.

We froze while three more pairs of guards passed our position, each team looking more frustrated than the last one. The guards were shouting back and forth, trying to figure out where we'd disappeared to. They'd just started shouting about looking in the bushes themselves when Robert eased to his feet beside me. We started hearing the sounds of leaves rustling as the guards literally shook the bushes.

Robert gave a pull and a blindingly loud, rusty squeak split the night. He yanked the gate then, managing to open it about six inches against the force of the hedge blocking it. As more shouts erupted behind us, I squeezed through that tiny gap without the slightest difficulty. Funny how running for your life makes such things possible. Suddenly, the ability of rats to squeeze through impossibly narrow spaces made sense. I popped out onto a street with Robert right behind me. A regular, boring, city street lined with shops and apartments. It was a total shock to my system after the green purgatory we'd just spent the last half hour racing around in.

Robert yanked the gate shut behind us, then jammed a stick into the lock and broke it off.

And we ran again.

But this time no feet pounded after us. No shouts echoed

behind us. No armed men chased us with the intent to arrest or kill us. We'd made it. Sort of.

It was a pretty good bet we were fugitives now. Obviously, someone back at the palazzo had put two and two together and figured out we were the thieves from the Vatican archives. Arrest warrants would no doubt be issued for us, and we'd have a whole lot of explaining to do if and when they caught us.

We must have run a mile before Robert finally slowed down to a walk. I panted, "One thing I can say for hanging out with you. You're good for my health. All this running will whip me back into shape in no time."

He grinned at me, and I nearly swooned as his dimples caught the moonlight.

"Come on," he said. "I see a phone over there."

"And who are we calling?"

"Your pilots. We need to get out of town. Fast."

Right. Before the authorities traced us back to Elise's private jet and put surveillance around it or impounded it.

I made the call. The first thing I noticed when the pilot answered his cell phone was he didn't sound as if I'd woken him up. It was after midnight, and I'd assumed he'd be asleep in preparation for tomorrow's flight home. And then he called me "sir." That's when I knew something was terribly wrong.

"Ah, hello, sir. Thanks for returning my call," he said.

"I beg your pardon?" I replied. "Is everything okay?"

"Not exactly. The police are here and they just searched the plane."

Thank goodness I didn't leave the Black Madonna on the jet!

"Seems the passengers we flew down here yesterday have gotten into some sort of scrape with the law."

Oh, crap.

The pilot continued, "The authorities are with us now. They're asking us to leave the country as soon as power is restored, which they think should happen by around noon tomorrow."

Noon? Wow. This power outage must have completely collapsed the power grid in this area.

The pilot spoke again, startling me mightily with his next question. "Where do you need us to position the jet to pick up our next clients, sir?"

"Uh, just a second." I covered the mouthpiece of the phone and relayed what the guy had said so far to Robert.

"Tell him Algiers," Robert said after a moment of thought.

"Algiers?"

"Yeah. There's a big underground railroad into France from there for illegal aliens. If we miss the jet, we can still catch a freighter and sneak in that way. Besides, the authorities will be looking for us to return to France, not head for Africa."

I pulled the phone back down to my mouth. "How about Algiers?"

"Right away, sir," the pilot answered crisply. "I'll tell the police we're headed back to Paris first thing in the morning."

"You're the best," I replied. "We owe you huge. We're not criminals, by the way, at least not usually, and the reason we need to get home fast is to save Madame Villecourt's life."

"Then by all means, we'll do our best to help the authorities," the pilot replied.

I got his meaning.

When I hung up, Robert said, "We've got to get off the street. I would suggest we leave Rome right now, but we'll have a whole lot more camouflage in the morning when everyone's trying to get to work. Let's go back to the hotel and get some rest. We'll head for Algeria tomorrow."

We walked the rest of the way back to the hotel. Thank goodness Robert had such an unerring sense of direction, because in the winding medieval streets of Trastevere, I was totally turned around. I might have been okay if there had been street lights and landmarks I could reference, but every building looked the same in the heavy night, just another ancient pile of stone squatting beside its neighbor.

The front door of the hotel was locked when we got there, and there was no sign of either the doorman or a night manager. Robert tried our room key, and thankfully, it opened the lock. We passed through the deserted lobby and up the great stone staircase to the second floor—or as Europeans would call it, the first floor.

We tiptoed down the long, dark hallway to our room and slipped inside. I was startled to see a red glow around the edges of the door as Robert opened it. He was cautious, too, spinning into our room fast and low. But no one was there. The glow came from a dying fire in the fireplace that someone had laid several hours ago if the pile of glowing embers was any indication. A basket of firewood stood on the hearth, and Robert laid a couple more logs from it on the fire.

I looked down at my clothes and abruptly realized why nobody had spotted me hiding in the bushes. The skirt and blouse were covered with mud and green stains—juice from the leaves we'd crushed as we slammed through the bushes. My clothes were nearly as dark as the night outside.

The fire flared up, giving off a rush of heat that felt wonderful. Now that I stopped to notice, there was a certain chill in the air tonight, and the warmth from the fire was just right to take the edge off of it. I went to my rucksack to pull out my cell phone—

—and started violently as I realized the Black Madonna statue wasn't in my bag!

"Robert! She's—"

He cut me off gently. "Not gone. I hid her before we left."

I watched in suspended panic as he pulled a chair over to the draperies and climbed up on it. He fished around near the curtain rod and emerged in a moment with the beautiful little statue in hand. He set her on the table beside the bed and she smiled up at me, as motherly and cheerful as always.

I sagged in relief.

Then I remembered. My cell phone. I dug it out of the bottom of my rucksack and dialed the phone number for my office at Interpol headquarters. Even though I worked in the lowly Cultural Properties department, even we never slept. There was someone on duty around the clock.

While I waited for the international call to go through, Robert asked, "Who are you calling?"

"My office. I want them to straighten out the glitch in my Interpol identification in case we get picked up by the police."

He nodded as the phone started to ring in Lyon, France.

"Cultural Property Division," a harried voice said in my ear.

"François?" I said in surprise. What in the world was François Littmann doing at the office at this hour? He *never* pulled night shifts. Said it was the boss's privilege.

"Ana? Is that you? Thank God. Where are you?"

I don't know what it was, but something in the way he blurted out that last question sent up a warning flag in my head. Normally, I'd have told him I was in Rome right away. But that was before I'd stolen an ancient map. Before men had chased me through a maze and tried to kill me. Before a ghost started looking over my shoulder and giving me strange, but unerringly accurate, intuitions about things.

"Why do you ask?" I replied. "What's happened?"

"It's terrible. Just terrible. Armande St. Germain is dead. And they're saying you did it. I keep telling them it's not possible. But your badge was found at the scene, and ballistics has matched the ballistic markings of your pistol that we keep on file to the bullets that killed him."

"What?" I gasped, "That's impossible! When did this happen?" Sick heat flooded through me followed by an icy chill of pure fear that closed in on me from all sides. St.

Germain dead? He was a decent man, a competent manager.
A husband, father and grandfather. And there wasn't the
slightest doubt in my mind that his shooting was related to
my investigation. Everyone who even got near the Lady was
dying. Some life-giving magic she was turning out to have.
More like a curse of death.

"He was murdered last night."

"I wasn't anywhere near Lyon yesterday!" I exclaimed.

"He was in Paris. He went up to oversee your investigation for Madame Villecourt. They say you sneaked through
the catacombs to his hotel, went up top and shot him, then
escaped yesterday morning on a private jet."

"They who?" I demanded.

While he rattled on about all the various Interpol and
French police officials who had questioned him already, I
rifled through my coat pocket. Sure enough, I pulled out
my Interpol ID badge. It was in its usual black leather case,
and still had the same dent in the upper right-hand corner
it had had ever since I dropped it getting out of a cab and
stepped on it two years ago. It was definitely my badge.
And police officers were only issued one badge for this
very reason.

"Look, François. I'm staring at my ID badge right now.
My badge couldn't possibly be with St. Germain. The one
they found has to be a fake."

"But I saw it," François retorted. "It was definitely a legitimate Interpol badge."

"Then someone made a duplicate with my ID number on
it." And didn't *that* make the mind spin off in alarming directions! Who had the connections—the raw power—to get
a real Interpol badge made and put into the hands of a killer?

"My apartment was ransacked day before yesterday," I explained with a certain desperation. "I reported it to the Paris
police. That's when my gun must have been stolen."

"They told me that. They think you staged the break-in to give yourself an alibi for using your own gun to murder St. Germain."

"They're working awfully hard to come up with reasons to find me guilty. And you know as well as I do that I would never murder anyone. Who's pushing this thing?"

Littmann's voice dropped into a whisper. "Rumor has it the investigation is being run at the very highest levels of Interpol. They got a tip."

"From where?" For once in my life, I was abjectly grateful that François was an inveterate gossip.

His whispered answer sent icy chills down my spine. "The Vatican."

The Church was willing to go to any lengths to suppress information it believed to be damaging to the Faith.

Surely not.

Maybe not the Church as a whole, but perhaps certain extremists within the Church. Elise Villecourt was an expert in the history of the Catholic Church. What if she had stumbled onto something? Some knowledge—some Truth—that elements within the Church wanted suppressed? Could they be responsible for the theft of her statue in an attempt to kill her, thereby silencing her permanently? At least her enemies hadn't succeeded in blocking us from entering the archives. They weren't all powerful, then.

She'd specifically told me to research ley lines and their relationship to the power outages in France. Was that the big secret? The existence of ley lines? No, wait. Not their existence...

Their power.

If they were knocking out an entire country's power grid, these ley lines were powerful, indeed. No wonder the folks at the Vatican archives were going nuts over the theft of the map. It was a map of the very thing they were trying to suppress knowledge of!

I realized the phone was still plastered to my ear. François was shouting into it, "Ana? Are you still there? Ana? Where are you?"

I hung up on him. And felt as if I'd just been drop-kicked in the stomach.

I turned around and Robert was there, his arms folding me into a big, warm, cashmere wrapped hug. For a moment, I gave in to despair and buried my face against his chest. I did manage not to cry like a baby, but it was a close thing.

"I gather you're not having a good day at the office?" he asked quietly.

"My boss's boss has been murdered. My gun shot him and an Interpol badge with my ID number on it was found at the scene."

Robert's body went rigid against mine. He swore quietly under his breath. We stood there in silence for several moments. A log popped in the fireplace, but otherwise, the entire world was quiet around us, as if it held its breath.

Finally he said, "What can I do for you?"

I half laughed, half sobbed, and answered, "Take my mind off all this madness."

He looked down at me solemnly. "I think I can do that. For a little while at least. I'll give it a try, anyway. Stay here."

He let go of me, and I stood there watching him as he piled even more logs on the fire. In a few minutes, that was going to be a roaring blaze. He turned back the coverlet on the bed, and then he lit every candle in the room. And there were dozens of them. By the time he was done, the entire space was filled with a golden glow that seemed to emanate from the very walls, filling the space completely.

And then he came back to me. Standing in front of me, he reached behind my head and released the clip holding my hair up in a loose French twist. It tumbled down about my shoulders, and he ran his fingers through it, smoothing it against the torn remains of the silk blouse. And the magical heat that always hovered close to the surface between us began to bubble up once more. It shimmered through me like a dream I never wanted to waken from.

He reached for the buttons running down my front, and one by one, slipped them free. With each little tug of silk across my breasts, my body ached a little more for him, burned a little brighter. He pulled the shirt free of my skirt and slipped it off my shoulders. Then he took a step closer. My breasts just barely rubbed his sweater and I gasped with the exquisite pleasure of it. But then his arms were behind me and my bra gave a soft pop. And sagged loosely. I shook it down my arms, and Robert pulled it the rest of the way off.

It felt sinful to stand here in shoes, hose and skirt, but completely topless. Robert's dark head bent to my chest. I expected him to zero in on the obvious targets, but instead, he merely pressed a gentle kiss to the spot right over my heart.

Then, he stood up and continued disrobing me. My skirt unzipped with a quiet slide of plastic teeth and Robert smoothed it down over my hips. Then he hooked his fingers in the top of my panty hose and expertly slid those down, as well. I started when I realized his clever fingers had hooked my panties on the way down, too. Balancing with my hand on his shoulder, I stepped out of my shoes and he finished peeling off my stockings. And then I was naked in front of him. He took my fingertips in his hands and stepped back from me. And just looked at me. At first, I was shy, but the longer he studied me, and the warmer the expression in his eyes grew, the bolder I felt.

By the time he finally led me over to the bed and laid me down upon it, I was perfectly content to lounge against the piled down pillows in all my glory and watch him undress in front of the fire. He didn't dawdle about it, but neither did he rush. His movements seemed to say we had all night, and he planned to take every moment of it to enjoy this. To enjoy me.

And as I lay there watching him, something happened. The entire universe shrank down to hug the margins of that golden glow filling the room. All without was the blackest of night, and all within was warmth and gentle light. The air around us vibrated with life, bathing us in tangible, but not quite visible, energy. The sexual pull between us became a presence in its own right, a hand on each of our backs, pressing us inexorably toward one another, consecrating the moment with its blessing.

Robert walked toward me, naked and glorious. The fire silhouetted him, outlining his muscular physique and the blending of grace and power that was uniquely male. And something inside me shifted. My heart expanded and opened, and I realized my arms had done the same, welcoming him. He put one knee on the bed beside me and paused, half kneeling as if in reverence to the moment.

His skin was light brown with the exception of a bathing suit line—he must swim for exercise. Outdoors. In a skimpy racing suit. A line of sparse, straight black hair ran down from his navel into that paler flesh, leading the eye toward the secret pleasures to come. Awed at the unfolding power of the moment, I looked up into his eyes.

And I realized that time had stopped again.

His long, dark lashes slid downward with exaggerated languor. The night, the magic, the smiling statue wrapped around us, shrouding us in something more powerful, more fundamental than simple desire. Man and woman. Heaven and Earth. Darkness and light. Our wondering gazes locked together.

And then we were one.

Making love didn't capture the aching slowness of it. The endless, rocking slide of flesh on flesh. The eternity of each individual breath entering and leaving my body. Each slow motion blink of the eye. Each unfolding smile. Each trembling touch.

Making love didn't capture the wonder of it. The miracle

of two bodies, two hearts, entwining until neither had beginning nor end. The crescendoing straining toward an explosion of such majesty that words fail the moment. And all the while, we gazed directly into one another's naked souls.

Making love didn't begin to describe any of it. This was worship at an altar older than time itself. Of Man and Seed, Goddess and Earth Mother. It was a sacred act. Of the very creation of Life itself.

When we had finally collapsed in a tangled heap of exhausted limbs, the golden firelight licking lazily at our skin, we were silent for a long while, as befitted the moment.

And, then, all he said was, "Marry me."

Chapter 17

My gaze snapped to his, stunned. *Marry him?* Was he *serious?* Surely not. We'd known each other less than a week. We came from completely different worlds. If you could call tonight a date—at least, up till the part where people started trying to kill us—then we'd had a sum total of, let's see. That would be *one.* We'd only made love one time.

A wispy voice murmured from the general direction of the fireplace, *"Once can be enough to know."*

I mumbled, "If that's you, Jane, stay out of this."

Robert added, "Yeah, Jane. Butt out. This is between Ana and me."

But was it? Was this some magically induced fog of sexual desire that held us in its thrall, or was this the real thing? I had no way of knowing. And as much as my heart screamed for me to accept his surprising proposal, my head told me to wait and see if any of this remained once the pixie dust blew away.

Robert raised himself up on one elbow beside me, propping the side of his head in his hand. With his other hand, he stroked lazy shapes on my stomach. "If it makes you feel any better, I'm as shocked as you to hear myself say those words. But then, I never counted on meeting you, either. I'll not pressure you into answering before you're ready, but the offer stands."

I nodded, at a loss for words.

"Sleep now," he murmured. "I'll watch over you."

And there it was again. That swirling connection of two souls meant for one another. I was safe with him. He'd always look out for me. And I, in turn, couldn't help but love him back. Cradled in his arms and his protection, I slept....

It was a hellish scene. A roaring blaze poured out heat, turning the chamber into a veritable sauna and tinging the room infernal red. A woman thrashed on the bed, her hands tied to the headboard. A leather strap was clenched between her teeth, and her body, naked from the waist down, was drenched in sweat. She gave a strangled cry and the tendons in her neck bulged as she strained against some terrible agony.

Only one other person was there, bending over a huge kettle by the fire, dipping a bloody rag into the boiling water with a stick. Her dress was bloodstained, and her cheeks were tearstained.

Jane.

She wrung out the hot rag and carried it back over to the bed, pressing it between the woman's thighs. Good Lord, that was Elizabeth! In the throes of childbirth.

Another muffled cry from the bed.

"The babe. It comes now, m'lady. You must push it out of you."

The Queen spit out the piece of leather and snarled, "I want nothing more in this world than to do just tha—aagghh."

Hastily Jane shoved the leather strap back into the queen's mouth. "You must not scream, else I will not be able to keep

*out the members of the Court. If you wish for this birth to
remain a secret you must be quiet," she urged.*

*The contraction eventually passed. Elizabeth spit out the
strap once more and cursed in several languages. "Don't tell
me what I must do," she snapped. "You try being ripped in
two in silence. How much more of this must I endure?"*

*"I...I do not know, Your Highness. I have never attended
a birth. I have heard that the length of labor depends on the
purity of a woman's soul. This is God's punishment for your
sins, after all."*

*"I could not perpetrate enough evil in my entire lifetime
to merit this torture," Elizabeth groaned, obviously starting
into the next contraction.*

*"I can see the head!" Jane exclaimed. "The babe has red
hair just like you!"*

*My sympathies to the baby. Eliazbeth's hair was a
bright, carrot-orange that clashed horribly with her milky-
white complexion. Of course right now, the queen's face
was beet-red as she held her breath and pushed with all her
might. Clearly hadn't heard of breathing through the con-
tractions. Of course, Lamaze was still about four hundred
years off.*

"Oh, just one more push. The head is almost out," Jane cried.

*Elizabeth growled something unintelligible around the
leather strap, but it was undoubtedly not repeatable in polite
company. Jane reached between the queen's legs. I didn't
need to be right on top of the action to recognize by the way
Jane's arms were moving that she was catching as the child
was born.*

Elizabeth let out a triumphant cry.

"'Tis a girl!" Jane exclaimed.

*Elizabeth fell back against the mattress, panting. "Thank
God. A bastard son might fight for my throne from a legitimate heir. But a girl will pose no threat."*

Jane wiped off a small object covered in red and some white, sticky-looking substance, and the baby commenced squalling for all it was worth. "Do you want to see her?" she asked, in between making frantic shushing sounds.

"No. I want you to take her away from here as quickly as you can. Go to your family and raise her as your own."

"What do you want to name her?" Jane asked coaxingly as she wrapped a cloth around the child. I had to give Jane credit. She was doing her best to interest Elizabeth in the tiny bundle that was beginning to quiet as she rocked it in her arms.

"I care not. You pick something."

"I've always liked Marie," Jane cooed down at the infant.

"Not that!" Elizabeth snapped.

Jane and I both started at the sharpness in the queen's voice. I looked up at the not so motherly mother and saw her glaring over toward her desk. I glanced in that direction.

And I finally saw it.

The Black Madonna statue. The very same one that was sitting on the table beside my bed back in Rome. Why in the world had my mind inserted it into this dream?

"No name that sounds like Mary or Marian," Elizabeth ordered imperiously. "I've had more than enough trouble from women of those names. In fact, they are responsible for all of this!"

I got the distinct impression she wasn't talking about her Catholic half sister, Mary, from whom she'd inherited the throne. My mind wandered. Could she possibly be referring to the Marians? I thought they were all wiped out by Elizabeth's time! Had some of them survived? Carried on the cult? Somehow involved Elizabeth in it? That seemed far-fetched. Her religious beliefs were well-known and solidly Protestant. Then what was the connection, other than the statue of the Lady?

I tuned back in. Elizabeth was giving Jane a series of in-

structions regarding the raising and education of her baby. For wanting this child to just go away, she sure had a lot of opinions as to how the girl should be raised.

"...and of course, you shall raise this babe a Protestant."

"Of course, Your Highness."

"When I die, you must see to it that she receives my statue of the Lady. I have written a letter to that effect and placed it with my personal effects, but I charge you or your descendents with seeing it through."

"Do you wish for me to take the statue now and keep it with the babe?"

"No!" Elizabeth exclaimed. "I am queen! I have more need of its magical properties than some diapered brat. It is mete that I, as ruler of a nation, should reap the Lady's gift of long life and not my offcast bastard. When I die, 'twill be soon enough for the babe to receive the statue's gift."

Ah. There it was. The statue was the connection to the Marians—the cult of women in southern France who'd worshipped a goddess older than Christ. A goddess of Earth and Nature, of birth and love, of mothers and daughters and sisters. A goddess older than time. It was a Marian artifact that Elizabeth believed would give her a long life.

It worked, too. Elizabeth lived seventy robust years in a time when the average life span was more like half that. And now I knew why. And maybe I also knew why she ended up being called the Virgin Queen. She'd had to choose between long life without sex—else risk another statue-induced pregnancy—or a probably much shorter life span, but one where she could indulge in pleasures of the flesh with only normal fear of pregnancy.

Hmm. Tough choice.

I also knew now why Elise Villecourt looked a good thirty years younger than her actual age when I met her, and why she'd aged so rapidly after the statue was stolen. Elise was, indeed, correct. The loss of the statue was killing her—or at least aging her back to her correct biological condition.

Elizabeth was speaking again. "And unlike my grandmother, who bequeathed the statue to the next Tudor Queen of England without warning of its unusual properties, I entreat you to pass this warning along to my daughter. Not only does the Lady grant the gift of long life, she also grants the gift of Life. Literally. She is a fertility talisman. Tell my daughter to have a care for her affairs of the heart lest she find herself in the same kettle of fish that I have landed in."

Jane nodded her understanding.

"Off with you, then. The babe will want her wet nurse soon." This last was said with just a hint of human tenderness.

Jane smiled gratefully at her queen and turned to leave the room.

The door closed behind her, and I was shocked to hear a muffled sob of wrenching grief from the bed....

"Ana, wake up."

I blinked up at Robert, disoriented as I always was after one of *those* dreams.

"Are you all right, sweetheart? You started to cry. Was it a nightmare?"

I frowned. I didn't know what to call it. A vision? A hallucination, maybe? "I was dreaming about a woman giving away her baby to another person to raise."

He made a sympathetic sound.

I rolled into him, tucking my forehead in the bend of his neck. His arms wrapped around me, and he murmured into my hair, "Never fear. Our children will always be safe and loved."

Our—

"Uh, Robert. There's something I need to tell you. It may make you want to reconsider your earlier proposal, and I won't blame you if it does."

He rolled me on my back abruptly and loomed over me in alarm. "You're not a serial killer, are you?"

"Good heavens, no!" I exclaimed.

"Good. Because that's about the only thing I can think of that might change my mind."

We'd see about that. Jean-Michel had dumped me in two seconds flat over it. I took a deep breath. "I have a problem with my ovaries. If I'm to have children, it will have to be by in vitro fertilization."

"And?"

"And that's it."

His forehead knit in a perplexed frown. "What does that have to do with my wanting to marry you?"

"I can't have children naturally."

"So? That just means we don't have to mess around with birth control and can pick when we have kids. Where's the downside to that?"

I stared at him. "Are you serious?"

He shrugged. "Even if you can't have children at all, it's no big deal. We can always adopt. I want to marry *you*. Not your ovaries."

Okay, that did it. I was officially in love with this man.

"Have you got any more deep, dark secrets to reveal before we say I do?" he asked laughingly.

"No, that's it. How about you?"

That wiped the grin off his face. "You already know my deep, dark secret. I was an art thief. I went to jail for a year, and now I don't steal art anymore." A flustered look crossed his face. "Well, not unless Jane tricks me into it." He looked up at the ceiling. "And you'd better not do that again, ghostie girl!" he called out.

I could swear I heard a tinkle of laughter shimmer through the air. Or maybe it was just my heart, singing with joy.

"It's still several hours until sunrise. Go back to sleep.

I'll watch over your dreams, too." He kissed me gently on the forehead.

And somehow I believed he could. He was just that kind of guy.

I awoke the next morning to the sight of the red, digital face of the bedside clock blinking. *The power was back on.* Robert wasn't in bed beside me, and the water was running in the shower. I stretched lazily, so relaxed after last night I hardly recognized myself. Even when it all came crashing back—St. Germain's murder, my being framed for it, some extremist element in or near the Catholic Church trying to silence us permanently along with Elise—none of it touched my core happiness. Apparently, mind-blowing sex and a marriage proposal have that effect on a girl. They did on me, at any rate.

Robert emerged from the bathroom with a white towel slung low around his hips. Oh, my. Now there was a sight I could wake up to for the rest of my life.

I did a mental double take on that thought. Whoa. Was I actually considering saying yes?

I threw back the covers a little self-consciously and, naked, climbed out of the high bed. I turned around, and was immediately wrapped up in a warm, humid, shower-fresh embrace.

"Good morning, beautiful," he murmured into my hair.

"Hi, back atcha, handsome," I laughed.

"Ahh, lassie, ye fairly glow when ye smile like that."

"Scots rogue," I accused him with a poke in his ribs.

He flinched, laughing. "You've discovered my deepest, darkest secret of all. I'm devilishly ticklish." He swatted my bottom as I headed for the bathroom and a hot shower of my own. After yesterday's tepid and then cold bath, it felt heavenly. I turned off the water and heard him talking on the phone in the other room. Eventually I emerged, dried, dressed, and yes, primped—complete with a little makeup and my hair blow dried and round brushed. I was officially done with my man-repelling phase and had dived head first into be-attractive-for-my-hunky-guy mode.

Robert was off the phone and our meager possessions were all packed in my rucksack. "Ready to go?"

I nodded. He had it all arranged. A car and driver pulled up in front of the hotel and we climbed in with a word to the doorman about doing some sightseeing and shopping. The car drove southwest out of Rome to the seaside city of Anzio, and its large, industrial waterfront. We found the numbered berth at the docks that Robert gave the driver, and a rusty cargo ship a couple hundred feet long was moored there. I made out the name *Al Amar* in the faded paint chipping off the prow.

A truly scary-looking guy came down the gangplank when we walked up to it, a huge black man with shoulders like a bull.

It turned out the stack of euros in Robert's pocket was as effective, if not more so, than my Interpol badge at greasing skids. The two men dickered in French for a few minutes, and then a good chunk of that stack of euros changed hands. The surly sailor gestured us to follow him aboard.

The ship smelled like a truck stop—must be diesel fueled—overlaid with a smell of something foul and chemical in nature. We walked down a filthy, dark tunnel to a rusted steel door. We stepped over the ankle-high threshold and into some sort of equipment room. Round gauges and big steel, steering wheel–shaped valve handles filled the space. I tripped on a cable lying on the floor and righted myself against the sailor's broad back. He grunted and threw me an annoyed look as he opened what looked like an electrical access panel. The guy swung back an entire steel panel of circuit breakers and gestured to me to go in. Perplexed, I crouched down in front of the opening and realized a tiny room was tucked back there. A bare single mattress covered most of the floor and a naked lightbulb hung from the ceiling. It had no other openings in its steel walls. I crawled through the door and stood up inside. It smelled like bitter coffee grounds and urine. Robert followed me inside and the metal door clanged shut behind us.

"So how long are we going to be locked in this lovely suite?" I asked.

"The trip itself takes about six hours. But we don't sail until tonight."

"In other words, make myself comfortable."

He nodded, apologetic. "It's not pretty, but it's relatively safe. This crew has bought off the customs officials at both ends of its Italy-Algeria run."

We napped on and off through much of the day. At noon, the sailor let us out to make bathroom visits and brought us two big, steaming bowls of a delicious stew he called a terrine. Chunks of meat and squash floated in a creamy base that tasted of coconut milk and curry. Thankfully, the pungent fragrance of the stew masked the other, less pleasant odors of our accommodations.

The sailor paused in the doorway on his way out. "There's someone been hangin' round the dock most of the mornin'. Jus' one person. L'il guy. Me an' the boys, we try to see 'im, but he's sneaky. He's got a bit of a limp. You's got enemies, me thinks."

I closed my eyes in dismay as the sailor closed us in once more.

"It's not the police," Robert commented, "or they'd have gotten a warrant and searched the ship already."

Lovely. It was probably more of those Italian thugs who'd been so bent on catching up with and killing us for the last several days. But there wasn't a darned thing we could do about it at the moment.

Around suppertime, the sailor brought us roast beef sandwiches on crusty rolls spread thick with horseradish. And even better, he brought us a couple of newspapers. We dived into them with relish.

Not surprisingly, the headlines all shouted about the massive, simultaneous power outages in northern France and southern Italy yesterday. And best of all, one of the papers, the English version of the *Frankfurter Allgemeine,* had a map of France in it, pinpointing a whole series of recent power outages in France. Carl Montrose must be having a cow. This was the very story he'd been so frantic to keep out of the press.

"Pass me the rucksack," I said suddenly.

Robert did so, and I pulled out the ley line map that had gotten us in so much hot water. If I was right…holy mackerel!

"What's up?" He must have sensed my sudden intensity.

"Hold those corners down," I directed as I carefully unrolled the ancient parchment. I laid the German newspaper map and the ley line map side by side so the two images of France were only inches apart.

"Aha!" I exclaimed. "Look at where the big intersections on the ley line map fall, and then compare them with where the French power outages have occurred."

Down to the last outage, they were centered exactly over spots that contained intersections of three or more ley lines.

Robert leaned back on his heels, thinking hard. "This is the national security crisis you used in that phone call to get through to Dupont's office, isn't it? They've got you investigating the French blackouts and your research took you to the Vatican to read up on ley lines."

I didn't like the way his eyebrows came together. He was bothered that I hadn't told him about it. Since it was front page news all over Europe now, I probably could admit it to him without breaching any security agreements with the French government. I said quickly, "I'm sorry I couldn't tell you earlier. I do trust you, but I was sworn to secrecy."

Robert didn't say anything for a while. Then he looked up at me. "You seem to have gotten beyond my past. I certainly owe you the courtesy of getting beyond this minor omission on your part." He smiled and held his arms out to me.

I didn't hesitate to accept the invitation. Had the mattress not been so completely foul, we might have headed for an encore performance of last night. But as it was, we settled for snuggling close and continuing to study the two maps of the ley lines and the power outages.

Eventually, Robert commented, "It looks to me like whoever's causing the blackouts has blasted just about every major ley line nexus—or whatever you call these intersections—in France."

"Do you suppose a node can only be used once? Is that why the blackouts have been happening all over?"

Robert shrugged. "Could just be a clever criminal making sure he's staying several steps ahead of the law by moving around. Or maybe you've hit on something and each node can be used only once. Maybe after power surges through the nexus point the node is—burned up—for lack of a better word."

Good point. Except—

"If the nodes can only be used once, then eventually these folks are going to run out of major nodes to blast. If France just sits tight, maybe it can ride out these attacks."

Robert gestured at the stack of newspapers and their flashy headlines. "And maybe France can't afford to wait that long. Each blast seems to be getting stronger, and the last one nearly wiped out France and Italy."

"If we mark the nodes that have already been used on this map in the newspaper, maybe we can narrow down where the attackers are likely to strike next based on what nodes are left to be used."

"Then what?" Robert asked somewhat cynically. "We call in the French Foreign Legion and tell them to go have a look?"

I shrugged. "If it's a matter of French national security, why not?"

"There's the small problem of both of us being fugitives. Hell, the French police are doing everything in their power to frame you for St. Germain's murder. And you and I both know you went nowhere near that guy on the night of his death. You were with me in the catacombs the whole time."

I sighed. We both knew his word wasn't worth a plug nickel as an alibi, though.

He added, "Besides, who'd believe us if we said magic earth energy lines were being used to zap the French power grid."

"President Dupont would believe us. He's the one who told me to get the statue back and keep Elise Villecourt alive."

"And maybe she's just his dotty old friend he's humoring as a favor. I mean, no offense, Ana, but you're not exactly Interpol's most experienced or highly trained criminal investigator."

That gave me pause. He was right. If Dupont thought Elise was telling the truth about the ley lines, he'd have put real police on the job, wouldn't he? But instead, he'd assigned me, and only me, to the case. He probably figured Interpol could spare someone as generally useless as me to go play police with a crazy old lady who'd asked for me.

Like it or not, we were on our own to stop whoever was using the ley lines to destroy the power grids.

We compared the ancient ley line map and the newspaper map with great care, and finally came to a stunning conclusion. There was only one major ley line intersection left. A massive node with no fewer than twelve ley lines running smack-dab into it. The only mapped node any larger in France was centered in Paris under Notre Dame Cathedral. And my guess was that node had been used somehow to create those totally inexplicable earthquakes in Paris last month.

"When we get to Algiers, we'll have to have Elise's pilots

fly us in as close as they can to that spot. Where is it, anyway?" I asked.

"Looks to be in the Languedoc region in the south. Near a little town called Lys," Robert replied.

"Lys? Isn't that where Catrina Dauvergne has a country house?"

"I have no idea. I only met her that one time at the Cluny. She struck me as being firmly off the dating market, so I didn't make much small talk with her beyond asking about the Black Madonnas and the religious cult they stem from. Odd group, those Marians."

The word sent a tingle of...*power*...crashing through me. No doubt about it. Marian magic was tied up in these power failures and in the statue tucked in my backpack. And someone in or near the Catholic Church was out to stop that magic, or at least prevent anyone from finding out about it.

I wondered if the woman who'd willed the statue to Elizabeth was a Marian. She'd said her grandmother willed it to the next Tudor queen. That would be Henry VIII's mother, then.

I thought back through my rusty British history. Henry's mother was Elizabeth of York. She was the last York, in fact. Her husband, Henry Tudor, was a Lancastrian. And their marriage effectively ended the bloody and vicious War of the Roses between the houses of York and Lancaster. It would have been vital for Henry Tudor and Elizabeth of York to have heirs to ensure that the war over control of the English throne didn't flare up again. I could definitely see a woman like that being given a fertility statue to make sure she had plenty of children to keep the feud from resuming.

The Marians had been referred to briefly at the Adriano exhibition. They were described as a shadowy cult of women who worshipped a Virgin Mary–like figure. They supposedly died out late in the Medieval period, although the Adriano exhibit hadn't mentioned they were persecuted to extinction by the Roman Catholic Church. That I'd learned in Paris from Catrina.

I commented, "I thought the Marians disappeared before, say, Queen Elizabeth the First, came along."

Robert shrugged. "Weren't you listening the night Catrina and I talked about all this?"

My cheeks heated up. "Actually, I spent most of the time trying to avoid ogling your rear end. I wasn't paying much attention to the conversation."

"Now *that's* an appropriate reason to blush." Robert grinned and chucked my pink cheek. "Catrina intimated that small pockets of Marians might have survived in secret. She suggested that, if this was the case, they would have used nontraditional means to record their beliefs and pass them on to their daughters—codes in letters, pieces of art, songs or poetry perhaps."

An image of the Black Madonna in my backpack exploded across my brain. What had Elizabeth called it? A fertility talisman that also gave its owner a long, healthy life? The gift of Life, she'd said. That certainly jived with a cult of women mixing pagan and Christian images together.

"Are there still Marians today?" I asked eagerly.

Robert shrugged. "I dunno. Last time I checked, I don't have the right gender of equipment to find and join them."

"Aww, come on. But you like women! What better place to meet tons of chicks than at a goddess worship meeting?"

He leaned over the maps and kissed me thoroughly. Eventually he sighed, "Ah, lassie, but I've already got me hands full with a right-spirited filly. I canna' spare a thought for any other ladies."

"A *filly?*" I grinned back at him. "If you weren't such a good kisser, you could be mistaken for a male chauvinist."

His eyes twinkled, the silver flecks in them more prominent than usual. "Go ahead. Admit it. You love alpha males like me."

That did make me laugh aloud.

He treated me to several more delicious minutes of Me, Tarzan, You, Jane making out. Man, the guy could kiss. When every last hair on my body was standing straight up, my toes were tingling, and my entire being ached to make love to him, he was a complete cad and pulled away from me.

"This place is not fitting for making love to a lady like you. I'll wait until I can shower you with rose petals and surround you with sterling silver candlesticks and crystal champagne flutes."

I couldn't fault the man for the noble and romantic sentiment, but his restraint left me more than a little frustrated.

Our friend the taciturn sailor showed up soon afterward to let us out for another potty break. I was able to stretch my legs and move around a bit, as well. I needed to check my voice mail messages and see if there were any further developments in the St. Germain murder investigation. Or even more worrisome, in Elise's health. We were out in the middle of the Mediterranean, and all I could see around us was black water and nearly black sky. But these satellite cell phones advertised that they'd work anywhere. What the heck. I flipped the lid open. I had seventeen voice mails waiting for me, mostly from Littmann and few from the Paris police. I started when I saw Elise's home phone number in the list.

My heart leaped into my throat. Oh, Lord. Had something happened to her? My fingers fumbled as I returned that call. It took two endless minutes for the call to go through, and the connection was scratchy when it did finally start to ring. But I was too scared to care.

"Allô?"

"Madame Trucot? Is everything all right?"

"Analise. She has been waiting for your call. She wishes to ask the same of you."

"Elise is there? She's home?"

"Oui. She refused to stay in the hospital another day. But

when she heard about the murder they believe you did, perhaps it would have been better had she stayed at Val de Grace a few more days."

"I didn't do it, I swear."

"Child, I know you did not. I have looked into your eyes and there is no murder in them. Believe me, I have seen it before. I know what the soul of a killer looks like."

I had no answer for that other than abject gratitude that someone believed me. I waited while the housekeeper went to pass the telephone to Elise.

"Ana? Is that you?"

I closed my eyes in distress. Her voice was tissue-thin and weak. So…old. "It's me, all right. How are you feeling?"

She laughed. And while the sound of it was old, I still heard a spark of her charming effervescence in it. "I am fine, now. I have been so worried about you. What has been happening?"

I filled her in very briefly, glossing over the parts where we'd been in danger. She was elated when I told her we'd recovered the statue, and deeply concerned when I told her what few details I knew about St. Germain's murder and how I was being set up.

She said fiercely, "Do not worry about the police. You have friends who can pull just as powerful strings as your enemies can. I will make some phone calls and help the police see reason."

I thanked her, but I wondered just how seriously she would be taken.

"And in the meantime, young lady, if you and your handsome Scotsman can stop whoever's attacking the French power grid, you will go a long way toward clearing your names. I may be able to arrange some small amount of help for you in Languedoc, but I cannot promise much on such short notice."

I replied, "We should be back in Paris late tomorrow morning with your statue. After that, we'll head to Languedoc and see if we can track down whoever's trying to wreck the power grid."

Elise said gently, "You know, I am in fact an old lady. It is not a tragedy if I should happen to feel my age. I had a pretty good run of it, there. You needn't hurry back here on my account. The authorities are looking for you, and I expect they are staking out my home to that end. It could be dangerous for you to sashay right back into Paris at the moment."

I made an impatient sound. "I don't care about myself. I'm worried about *you*. I don't want you to die."

"Child, I'm not about to die. I've been in vigorous health my whole life. I have another ten or twenty years left in these old bones even without the Lady's help. It's more important that you stop those who would use the ley lines for their own ill-gotten ends. It is an offense against Mother Earth."

Spoken like a true Marian.

Abruptly, my mind completely vapor locked. Could it be? Was Elise Villecourt one of the elusive Marians?

"Elise," I asked slowly, "have you ever heard of a group of women called the Marians?"

Only static answered me for the longest time. And then she finally said, "More to the point, where did *you* hear about them?"

"Queen Elizabeth the First referred to them in my dreams. And then a family called the Adrianos had an art exhibit while we were in Rome that talked about them a little—"

Elise cut me off, ordering sharply, "Say no more. Not over the phone!"

Startled, I subsided.

She continued forcefully. "Go to Languedoc. Save the world. And then get yourself up here to Paris. We need to *talk*."

And with that, she hung up.

Well, then.

Night on the water was cold, and a damp chill soaked right through to my bones. It actually felt good to crawl back behind the electric panel and the abundant heat it put off.

"Sleep," Robert urged me. "Tomorrow could be a long day. We've got to get back into France undetected, and then we've got to find the exact location of this nexus of doom. And most of the features on this map are hundreds of years out of date. The cities and roads are mostly gone by now." Then he added grimly, "I have a bad feeling about this. I think whoever's blasting the French power grid is going to go for the big one sooner rather than later. Especially if they find out we've stolen the ley line map and can track them down."

I frowned at that implication. The only way anyone would know we had the map, besides happening to have access to the Italian police database, was to be closely connected to the Vatican and the Catholic Church itself. Was our attacker a random terrorist, or was he a religious zealot of some kind? Either way, we could be walking into serious danger by tomorrow evening.

But what really scared the living hell out of me was not any concern for myself. The thought of any harm befalling Robert sent me into a near panic. Oh, God. I really had fallen for the guy. Hard.

I was seeing ghosts. I'd become a thief. A nation's safety rested on my shoulders. And people were trying to kill me. What next?

Chapter 18

Elise's jet made a hair-raising descent into a steep-sided valley and landed at a deserted private airfield slightly after noon. It took me a moment to peel my white knuckles off the armrests and stand. But we'd made it. The pilots said we were east of a town called Limoux and roughly twenty miles south of Carcassonne. That put us in the heart of the Languedoc region.

The mountains around us were steep, but their tops were rounded with age and erosion. Their green flanks were just starting to show hints of gold for the fall to come. The valley floor was flat, and the strip of concrete we'd landed on sat in the middle of fields, whatever had grown in them this summer already harvested. The black dirt lay fallow around us.

"Any idea how we're going to get out of here?" I asked Robert.

"The copilot said it had been taken care of."

We turned around as the two pilots stepped out of the

plane to have a look around and stretch their legs. The co-pilot said on cue, "Your ride should be here momentarily. They knew when we were landing, and we're exactly on time."

Sure enough, just a few moments later, a plume of dust rose up from across the fields, headed our way.

A late model Land Rover pulled out onto the runway and drove toward us. It pulled to a stop and I was shocked when none other than Catrina Dauvergne stepped out of it.

"Welcome to Languedoc," she said with a laugh at our disbelieving expressions.

The two pilots wished us good luck and climbed back into their jet. They would continue on to Paris. Their flight plan had them proceeding there nonstop from Algiers. Funny how they hadn't put on quite enough fuel and had been forced to make this quick, unscheduled stop along the way.

"I'm sorry I'm late," Catrina was saying. "I had to borrow the neighbor's car. Our little Saxo won't get up the mountain to the house with three adults in it."

The Land Rover, however, cruised up the rough, winding road to her farmhouse without the slightest trouble. Catrina chatted easily about the countryside, sharing some of the history of the region and pointing out landmarks here and there. It wasn't a long drive. Maybe twenty minutes. But finally, I interrupted her.

"How did you know to come pick us up?"

Catrina threw me a guarded look. "A friend called and asked me to do a favor. I had to laugh when I found out I was to pick you up, since you are already a friend I would do such a favor for."

I took that as a great compliment. Catrina was not the sort of woman who made friends easily or lightly. But then, neither was I.

We turned off the paved road then, onto a rocky and very rough dirt road that commanded all of Catrina's attention. We rounded a last curve and then, before us laid the most wonderful French country home. It was a rectangular structure, golden stone with a red tile roof. Young roses grew under the ground floor windows and crisp, white cotton curtains fluttered in an open window.

As we drove up, a man walked out of a partially cleared and pruned orchard beside the house. He had an ax and a long-handled pruning saw slung over his shoulder. Rhys. The ex-priest who had so swept Catrina off her feet. He was a handsome man in a pure, boyish sort of way. Not at all like dangerous, brooding Robert. The two men were of similar height. And thank God, they didn't do any of that macho sizing-up crap that men so often do when they first meet. They just shook hands after Rhys wiped his hand on his jeans and nodded politely.

Introductions were made all around, and we went through the house, which was in full renovation mode with projects in progress everywhere, to the back porch. I laid out croissants and pastries on a tray while Catrina made tea for everyone. We all had a bite to eat and enjoyed the bucolic sound of birds singing and the smell of earth warming under the warm morning sun.

Catrina seemed totally at peace in this place and with this man. For that matter, Rhys looked pretty darned content, too. They made a powerful argument for saying yes to Robert and being done with it. I had a feeling he and I would be as good together as these two.

It came up in conversation that Rhys was an amateur Holy Grail hunter and took frequent outings in the area to track down leads in the quest. As soon as he said that, Robert and I traded significant glances. Robert nodded in subtle agreement with my unspoken question.

"Maybe you could help us, then, Rhys," I said.

"Of course. With what?"

"We have a very old map of France. We're trying to locate a spot on it to go visit. But because the map is so old, most of the landmarks on it have disappeared."

He leaned forward eagerly. "I have mapped a number of old village sites and roads onto current maps of the area."

I reached into my rucksack and pulled out the stolen ley line map. Rhys exclaimed in pleasure over the quality of the drawing. Thankfully, he didn't ask where it came from. I didn't relish the idea of telling a former priest we'd stolen it from the Vatican archives.

I helped Catrina carry the dishes into the kitchen while the two men began to study the map. There was no dishwasher, so I dried while Catrina washed.

Over my linen towel, I asked her, "I notice there's no ring upon your finger yet. Is he going to pop the question soon?"

Catrina looked up at me in horror. "I should hope not! If he does, then that would mean we've been having premarital sex, and that would be a sin. Better to stay unmarried and just be involved in a serious relationship." She smiled mischievously. "What about you and Robert? Are you becoming an item or does he look at every woman that way?"

I laughed. "He's already proposed."

Catrina stared. "But you've only known each other what? A week?"

"About that."

She shook her head in disbelief. "Scotsmen. So impulsive. You, too. Who'd have guessed?"

Me? Impulsive? Hah. But then, I was actually contemplating his proposal, so maybe the shoe fit. I shrugged and picked up a teacup to dry it. "There's something between us. Almost…magic. It's as if I already know everything about him and he knows everything about me. Like we're meant to be."

Catrina nodded wisely. "I know exactly what you mean." She broke off as Rhys walked through just then. He came back in under a minute, striding enthusiastically through the room with several rolled maps tucked under his arm. Catrina and I rolled our eyes at each other, smiling. Men could be such overgrown kids sometimes.

We'd just finished putting the cups and saucers away in the cupboard, which was minus its door at the moment, when Robert called from outside. "We've got it, Ana. The location of the nexus."

As soon as he said this, Catrina gave a startled lurch and looked over at me closely. "Nexus?"

I nodded. "Our map shows all the major ley lines in France—at least, the ones people knew about in the four-teenth century."

"Ley lines?" she asked cautiously.

If I didn't know better, I'd say she'd heard of them before. I sighed. Time to make someone else think I was crazy. "They're naturally occurring lines of energy—of power—running all over the earth in a sort of grid. People from old, pagan religions first mapped them a long time ago. They believed the power of those lines could be harnessed for healing and other magical effects."

Catrina hurried outside to look at the map, her brow furrowed. The mention of ley lines seemed to strike a big chord with her, that was for sure. I joined the rest, poring over the map. Rhys had his finger on a spot on a modern map.

"There's a large cave complex right here. I'd bet your nexus point is in one of them. Maybe marked by an old altar or monument of some kind. The pre-Christian religions tended to mark places of power with piles of stones or statues, maybe a basin for ritual washing or a flat stone for making sacrifices."

Robert nodded. "How far from here is this cave complex?"

Rhys put another finger down on the map. "We're here. I'd guess it's no more than two hours' drive. Although if the roads are bad, it could take several hours to get back that far into the mountains."

Robert looked up at the sun. "Then we'd better get going if Ana and I want to get there with any daylight left."

Rhys laughed. "Daylight won't matter once you head down into those caves. It'll be pitch-black inside."

Robert grimaced. "We got stuck in the catacombs overnight a few nights back. I know what you mean about it being pitch-black."

Rhys and Catrina exchanged almost embarrassed looks with each other and Rhys said uncomfortably to Robert, "Yeah, we got stuck in the catacombs once, too. It was…interesting…to say the least."

Catrina laughed. "Good thing you and I did get lost in there, or we might never have gotten together."

Rhys smiled at her, and it looked as if it came all the way from his heart, through his eyes to his mouth. Her return smile was just as sappy. Oh, yeah. Those two were head over heels for each other.

Robert stood up. "Mind if we borrow this map?"

Rhys replied, "Not at all. I've got a fair bit of spelunking gear if you need it, too."

"That would be great," I replied. After fun with catacombs, I did not need to head anywhere underground ever again without absolutely everything I needed to make sure I made it back out again safely.

Rhys led us down into an earthen cellar through old-fashioned folding doors outside the house. The steps were new, though, the wood still fresh and gold.

Robert and I armed ourselves with ropes, flashlights, gloves, cleats that strapped onto the bottoms of our shoes, emergency blankets—silver plastic affairs that folded up into a palm-sized bundle—a first-aid kit, canteens, protein bars and even a small pickax. We looked more like gold prospec-

tors in the Klondike than we did tourists out for a day hike
to explore a few caves.

Rhys and Catrina walked us over to one of the outbuild-
ings behind the main house, and the two of them wrestled
open a squeaky garage door on rollers. Inside was a tiny,
aging Citroën Saxo.

Rhys dug a set of keys out of his pocket and handed them
to Robert. "It's not much to look at, but it'll get you there
and back." He added with a grin, "And I think it'll hold all
that gear."

It did, indeed, take all our equipment in the backseat.
Barely. We climbed in and, armed with Rhys's map, set out.
The little Saxo was a gutless wonder that labored up every
steep hill. But it was better than walking. And it proved sturdier
on the horrendously bad dirt roads the map took us over than
I'd have expected. We had to stop once at a farmhouse to ask
directions, but the farmer knew right where the caves were and
gave us exact directions to go the rest of the way.

We parked at the base of the mountain where he'd told us
to and looked up in trepidation. The farmer said all we had
to do was walk about halfway up the hill and we'd see the
main opening beside a cluster of three big boulders.

The guy's "hill" was practically a cliff—it was navigable
with hands and feet, but that was about all that distinguished
it from an unscalable rock face. And the entire mountain was
littered with huge boulders as if the gals had thrown them here
just to get in the way. There was no help for it. We were going
to have to climb that monster.

The worst of it turned out to be hauling our gear up the
mountain. It caught on something with practically every step
we took. And once we got onto the mountain, it was hard to
gauge what constituted halfway up. The floor of the valley
looked as if it were a mile below us in a matter of minutes.
Our other problem was that Robert was an incredibly agile

climber—part of his thief training, apparently—and I was, well, not.

Eventually, he took my pile of gear from me entirely, and that evened us out quite a bit. He slowed down, and I didn't have to call out for him to stop and wait for me nearly so often. We kept having to go around rock outcroppings, and all the sideways traversing disoriented me. Fortunately, Robert didn't seem so afflicted.

Finally, Robert announced, panting, "This is about halfway up the hill. Now, we just have to look around for a cluster of three boulders."

Although it was strenuous scrambling across the face of the hill, it was nowhere near as bad as going straight up. We traversed the hill twice, edging higher each time in search of this supposed cave entrance. I'd begun to wonder if the farmer had played a colossal and rotten joke on us when suddenly I spotted a distinctive cluster of rocks. They sat alone in a little grassy area with no other rocks around them. Each stone was about my height and maybe ten feet wide. And they nestled together in a precise triangle set into the hillside.

"I think I found it!" I called out to Robert. He joined me, and we approached the boulders together. We stepped around to the right side of the stones, and there it was. Between the right-hand boulder and the face of the hill. A good-sized opening, maybe eight feet tall and twice that wide, stretching almost all the way across the back of the three boulders. We stepped into the entrance and immediately noticed white gouge marks in the floor. As wide as my hand and maybe four feet long, they were definitely man-made and definitely fresh. It looked like something incredibly heavy had been dragged across the stone.

We walked twenty or thirty feet into the cave before we had to turn on our flashlights. We donned the miner's hard hats Rhys had given us and turned on their lamps.

"This looks like an old mining tunnel," Robert commented.

It did, indeed. The walls were rectangular and bumpy, like a pickax had been used to chip them out of the mountain. Mother Nature hadn't carved this tunnel.

I took off my glove and ran my hand over the surface of one wall. "This is very old. The rough edges have all worn away."

Robert pointed up at a rusty fixture up near the ceiling. "At some point this place had electric lights." He shined a flashlight up toward the old socket and said suddenly, "Have a look at that!"

I turned my own headlamp up where he pointed and gasped. A very much intact electrical wire ran along the intersection of the wall and ceiling. It was a heavy-duty affair the thickness of my wrist and wrapped in black rubber insulation. Why in the world would somebody run wiring of that scale down into this cave? And recently, to boot.

More cautiously, we moved forward. I don't know how long we walked. I didn't stop to dig under my glove and sleeve to get at my watch. The tunnel proceeded mostly downhill on a very gentle grade. We passed through a few natural chambers, and the hefty wire ran around the edges of them and resumed its course down a tunnel each time.

There was no question but that we would follow that wire wherever it took us. Side passages branched off at regular intervals as if this had, indeed, been a mining operation of some kind.

And then we heard a noise.

Not a big one. But definitely not a sound we'd made. Robert and I froze, turning off our headlamps simultaneously. We stood there in the dark for a long time, just listening. All I heard was an occasional drip. But the sound I'd heard was more like two stones striking one another.

"Let's use as little light as possible," Robert breathed.

Oh, great. Been there done that in the catacombs, and it sucked. And those had been nice smooth tunnels with perfectly even floors. Robert turned on a single penlight and put his finger over the end of it. We gave our eyes a few minutes to adjust to the extremely dim illumination, and we eased forward again.

We heard another sound. And this time, it was definitely coming from well in front of us. Someone was already down here! Robert turned off the lone flashlight—and it wasn't totally pitch-dark! The very faintest of light came from somewhere ahead of us. You have to understand. We're talking degrees of blackness, here. But nonetheless, there was a light source ahead of us.

Robert glided forward one step at a time, pausing between each footstep to listen. This patience must have been part of why he was a successful art thief. Me, I was going insane with the suspense.

That's not why I stumbled when I did, though. Nothing so deep and psychological as that. My foot merely hit a wet spot and slipped when I tried to put my weight down on it. The climbing cleats scraped across the stone until they caught a protrusion and my sliding momentum came to an abrupt and overbalancing halt. Which is to say, I nearly fell on my face and was only stopped from doing so by crashing into the wall.

My metal canteen clanked against my flashlight, and that slammed into a loose stone, causing a cascade of scree to break off the wall and clatter to the floor. All in all, I made a big, damn noise that no idiot could possibly miss.

Sure enough, the faint glow ahead of us was extinguished immediately.

And seconds later, we heard the sound of running footsteps. Coming right at us. Fast.

"Run," Robert bit out. I turned around and, fumbling for my flashlight, headed back up the tunnel. I got my flashlight on and put on a burst of speed, scrambling over the rough floor like a mountain goat with a cougar on its heels.

We kept having to stop at every intersection to check which direction the overhead cable went, and each time we did, I could swear the pounding footsteps behind us got a little closer. Fear gave my feet wings, but there's only so much adrenaline can do for a person.

"Faster, sweetheart," Robert urged me when I began to tire.

We arrived at the first big natural chamber, and I lost sight of the electrical cable. We had to stop and backtrack to the tunnel we'd come out of and follow it around the perimeter again to the correct tunnel. The footsteps—for we could distinguish at least two sets of feet now—sounded really close when we finally got our bearings again.

"You go on ahead," Robert murmured. "I'll stay behind and slow them down a little."

"No!" I exclaimed under my breath.

"They know the way and we don't. We'll never beat them out of here. *Go.* If nothing else, go get help." He pressed the car keys into my hand.

I knew that stubborn set to his jaw. I wasn't going to talk him out of this heroic foolishness. And so, despite my terrible misgivings, I ran.

I didn't get more than a hundred feet or so beyond the big room when I heard shouting behind me. I couldn't help it. I slowed down. I heard Robert's voice taunting the men. The echoes were distorted so I couldn't make out words, but the tone of voice was unmistakable.

And so was the smack of fists on flesh. Oh, God. *They'd attacked Robert.*

No matter what he said, my feet weren't taking me one step closer to the exit and safety. I had to go back.

Now, I wasn't a complete idiot. I kept my wits about me and did two things. I turned off my flashlight and pulled out the pickax. It wasn't huge, but it would pack a mean punch if it connected with someone's head.

My heart racing and my breath coming short and fast, I eased back down the tunnel. And I prayed I wouldn't make any more boneheaded stumbles. Robert's life might depend on it.

A glow lit the mouth of the tunnel ahead. I crept toward it, crouching low. Very carefully, I peered around the corner and into the big room. Three men had Robert. Two were holding him by the arms, and struggling to do so, I might add. And the third man was punching the lights out of the man I loved. It was all I could do not to charge in there, roaring like the mother bear Robert had once compared me to. But that wouldn't do any good. I couldn't overpower them.

And then I looked more closely. No surprise, I recognized one of the men. He was one of the Italian guys who'd jumped me in the park in Paris.

Robert's struggles subsided, and thankfully, the beating stopped. The guy using Robert as a punching bag growled something in Italian to the other men, and they turned and dragged Robert back the way they'd come. Robert made a lot of noise, dragging his feet and stumbling a lot. I don't know if that was because he really had been knocked for a loop or because he suspected I might come back for him and need the cover of noise.

Either way, I proceeded cautiously down the tunnel well behind the foursome.

We passed the spot where I'd stumbled earlier and headed toward the glow, which became stronger and stronger as we approached it. I saw Robert briefly silhouetted in the mouth of the tunnel, sagging between the Italians. My stomach felt full of needles at seeing him hurt and in pain like that.

And then they disappeared from sight. Exclamations in Italian greeted Robert's appearance. I listened closely, and it sounded to me as if there were now four men in there with Robert. But I wasn't sure. Not that it mattered. I couldn't take on four big, strong men by myself.

I took another careful step forward. And another.

Something warm and smooth clamped over my mouth and I leaped straight up into the air. I struggled madly, trying to swing my pickax in the close confines of the tunnel. But my attacker clung to my back like a burr and I couldn't shake him off.

Or rather her. A voice whispered in my ear. "It's Ginny. I'm here to help."

Ginny? The cat burglar type from Rome? What in the world was *she* doing here? How did she find us? Or was she part of the Italian team ahead?

She breathed in my ear again, "We need to rescue Robert before they kill him. Will you let me help you?"

I nodded under her gloved hand. She released me, and then I felt a tug on my sleeve. Back the other way. I didn't want to go outside! I wanted to charge in that room and get my man back!

When I refused to budge, the mouth touched my ear again and whispered a touch impatiently, "There's another way in. Follow me."

Well, okay then. I reached out in the dark and grabbed her jacket. Carefully, I memorized the turns she took in case she was leading me on some kind of wild-goose chase to distract me while her cohorts did away with Robert. Where had she come from, anyway?

There were no cars at the base of the hill, no sign of people having climbed the hill to get to the cave. I was going to be very annoyed if there was another way into this cave complex that didn't involve making like a mountain goat.

Finally, Ginny stopped and turned on a flashlight. She crouched in the tunnel. Using her finger, she drew a rough map in the dust. "Robert's here. We've come around in a half circle like this. If my navigation is correct, all we need to do is turn left at the next tunnel, and it should lead us into the chamber where they've got Robert."

But we'd be coming into it from the opposite side. Maybe, just maybe that would give us some sort of tactical advantage over Robert's attackers.

"How are you in hand-to-hand combat?" Ginny asked.

"Not bad, but not great. I can hold my own. I've had some training."

Her mouth curved up sardonically, "Not to mention that desperation makes a woman mean."

I nodded grimly. "And there is that."

"Let's go have a look at the layout. Then, we'll back up here and form a plan. Okay?"

"Got it."

We snuck around the corner and up a short tunnel, and sure enough it ended in a relatively well-lit chamber. Crouching in the entrance, I peered out into the room. And stared in disbelief. There, in front of me was a crude machine the size of a step van. And mounted on one side of it was a device that could only be described as looking like a giant ray gun. It pointed down toward the floor in the far corner of the chamber, where a large pool of water lay, still and glasslike. If I didn't know better, I'd say it was some sort of doomsday machine.

And given the crackling and popping sounds it was making, it was clear the thing was powering up.

Chapter 19

I may be an art historian, but my dad happens to be an electrical engineer. And like it or not, I grew up around circuit boards and home-built radios and all manner of electrical gadgets. The machine in front of me was very simple. Even my rudimentary knowledge of electronics was sufficient for me to know what I was looking at. An engine about the size of a car looked to be acting as a generator, feeding electricity to a giant capacitor.

A capacitor stores up an electrical charge on some sort of surface—like the parallel array of a dozen or more giant metal plates in front of me, all of which were connected by heavy wires to the back end of the ray gun. The plates had to be ten feet across and at least that tall, separated by layers of what looked like plastic foam or something similar. When the insulating agent is removed rapidly from between its charged surfaces, the capacitor releases its stored energy in one giant surge of power. Almost like a lightning bolt.

In this case, it looked for all the world like that bolt of electricity was going to be directed through the ray gun and toward that pond in the corner. Water is, of course, an outstanding conductor of electricity. That would be why electric razors and bathtubs don't mix, for example. That pond seemed a strange target, indeed, for a machine of this magnitude. What could possibly be so important about it?

I had no idea.

And more to the point, I had no time to consider the question. I caught a glimpse of Robert kneeling on the floor, his fingers laced behind his head. One of the Italians had a pistol pointed at him. But as Robert didn't seem to be putting up any sort of fight at the moment, the gun-toting guard looked fairly casual. He definitely didn't look to be on the verge of executing Robert. Even better, his back was to me.

The other Italians were clustered around the engine end of their gizmo. They all seemed to be looking at a gauge of some kind and then down at their watches. I caught enough of their conversation to decipher that they were trying to figure out how long it was going to take the weapon to charge. Their estimates ranged from three to ten minutes.

That thing was a *weapon?*

It was sure going to kill that pond deader than dead. There had to be enough juice stacking up in that thing to knock out a small city…or a very large power grid.

Of course. My brain finally kicked back into gear in spite of the panic hovering far too close to the surface of my thoughts. These guys would store up a massive amount of electricity and then shoot it into the ley lines as a single electromagnetic pulse. That pond must mark the spot where a bunch of the ley lines came together. And now that I looked again, I made out decrepit carving on the far side of the pond. A rough bowl was carved right into the stone wall beside a large, flat, tablelike rock. Yup, an ancient altar to mark a site of great mystical power. Just like Rhys had described.

And like I already said, water was a tremendous conductor. What better way to send a huge surge of electricity down all the ley lines at once? Zap the whole darned pond!

I had to stop that machine. *After* I rescued Robert.

Ginny—I'd almost forgotten about her—tugged at my sleeve and gestured for me to back up. Reluctantly I followed her back down the tunnel.

"Don't ask me how, but I know the guy with the gun on Robert," she breathed. "He's big and strong, but not particularly trained in combat. He relies mostly on being intimidating."

He intimidated me. I thought fast. "Do you know him well enough to walk in there and start up a conversation with him?"

Ginny looked startled. If she was a thief, she was probably used to thinking in terms of being invisible and working on the sly, not marching in brazenly and announcing herself. But desperate times call for desperate measures. Simply overpowering four men was out of the question. Therefore, we'd have to knock them mentally off balance. Having an attractive woman one of them knew stroll in out of the blue and start chatting should throw them all for a serious loop.

Ginny nodded slowly. "I could tell them I've been asked to come here and check up on their progress. It's flimsy, but it might be just unexpected enough that they'd buy it."

Who did she know that might ask her to check up on guys like these? I didn't voice the question aloud, for there wasn't time to nitpick details at the moment. That machine was set to fire in a few minutes, and I had no doubt Robert was toast as soon as it did.

Ginny whispered, "I'll see if I can draw the other men around to the far side of the machine away from Robert and the guy with the gun. Then, you jump the guy with the gun and overpower him."

Overpower him? Me? I must've looked skeptical because she added, "Robert will help you, of course."

Of course.

She continued. "Use something heavy and conk the guy over the head. Just don't make any noise, or we're all in the soup. Agreed?"

I can't say as I liked that plan very much. The risks were huge to her and to me. But I didn't have any better ideas, and we had only a few minutes to get in there and stop the disaster. Reluctantly, I nodded my agreement to Ginny.

We headed back for the mouth of the tunnel, and I pulled the pickax out of the rope slung across my back. I hefted it warily. Long before I was ready, Ginny straightened up, gave her hair a quick toss and strode right out into the middle of the room. I lurked deep in the shadows, out of sight.

The Italians squawked in surprise, and one of them exclaimed, *"Dottore Moon? Che cosa state facendo qui?"*

My jaw dropped. That guy had just said, "Dr. Moon? What are you doing here?" Doctor Moon? *The* Doctor Moon? That petite brunette was the most wanted art thief in Europe? Was she the one who'd stolen the Black Madonna statue? Was she in league with these Italian thugs? Oh, God. Had I just walked into a trap and sealed Robert's fate, as well?

Should I scrap Ginny's—Dr. Moon's—plan and charge in now to rescue Robert, or should I wait and see what she did? After all, she and Robert used to work together. Did the thieves' code of honor extend to helping out old colleagues in a pinch? Why in the world was she down in this cave, anyway? Was she already here working with the Italians? Had she followed us? The sailor in Italy did say someone small and sneaky had been hanging around the dock all day. *Should I trust her or not?*

"Hey, boys." Ginny drawled in Italian. She sashayed forward, her hips twitching with catlike allure. "How's it coming?"

"What the hell are you doing here?" one of the men burst out.

"Checking up on you, of course," she said smoothly and

with just a hint of menace. "You didn't think our employer would let something this important go unsupervised, did you?"

The Italians didn't miss the threat in her tone. "Everything's fine," the spokesman said.

"Then why do you have some guy kneeling over there with a gun pointed at him?"

"He says he's a geo-something-or-other. Was exploring the cave. Inconvenient, but we've got him handled."

Ginny nodded casually and strolled over to the machine. "And how's this contraption coming along? Is it ready to go?"

"We're powering it up now," one of the men said eagerly. "Your timing is perfect. You're here just in time to see us fire it."

"Of course, my timing is perfect," Ginny retorted scornfully. "Show me how this monster works." And with that, she strode around to the far side of the machine, the three Italians following along as obediently as puppies.

Now. I had my opening. Did I dare take it? I paused, torn in an agony of indecision. To choose incorrectly would cost Robert his life. But then Jane all but kicked me in the behind and I found myself lurching forward.

I regained control of my limbs and eased forward carefully while Ginny continued to talk one of the smoothest lines of bull I'd ever heard. The woman had a golden tongue. I bet she'd pulled off a couple of her thefts simply by talking people into handing works of art over to her. She grilled the men in detail over the machine, keeping them thoroughly occupied while I inched forward into the cave.

I kept to the darkest shadows I could, making my way along the wall toward where Robert knelt. I couldn't see him from here, but he was just around the end of the machine. I thought he might have glimpsed me as I first slipped into the room, but I couldn't be sure.

I froze as Ginny and the men came into view, circling the

machine. I was totally exposed. There was nowhere to hide between me and the tunnel I'd come out of. Ginny said something in animated Italian too fast for me to follow. She took a couple steps toward the far side of the machine. Stopped. Gesticulated with her hands some more. Took another couple steps. It was ever so subtle, but gradually she led the guys out of sight again. Now I just had to hope my thug hadn't turned around to watch.

I heard Robert mumble something to his guard. *Bless him.* He was drawing the guard's attention to himself for me. Smart man. I heard a dull thud. Kind of like a fist burying itself in a stomach. An *oompf* of expelled air accompanied the noise.

I went around the corner low and fast. The guy was leaning over Robert, his fist drawn back for another blow. On silent, furious feet, I darted right up behind him and swung the flat side of the pickax at the back of the guy's head. At the very last second he turned his head—he must have glimpsed the movement behind him. Oh, God. I was going to kill the guy! I tried to pull my swing, to break the force of the impact, but I only partially succeeded.

The blow caught him in the temple, dropping him like a rock. Robert scrambled awkwardly to his feet. He was moving injured. He started to head back toward the tunnel I'd come out of, but I stopped him with a hand on his arm. I pointed at the machine and drew my finger across my throat in a slashing motion.

He shook his head vigorously in the negative.

We had no choice. It would be a national disaster if this thing were allowed to fire. Businesses would fail. Lives would be ruined. The economy would be thrown into recession and chaos. People would *die*. And besides that, he and I both needed to redeem our reputations. And maybe it went even deeper than that. Maybe we both needed to do something heroic and noble to convince ourselves that we were worthy. Worthy of what, I don't know. Just worthy. I didn't have time to reason it out any more deeply than that.

Robert rolled his eyes and took the pickax from me. He lifted it high over his head and took a mighty swing at the ground. Or rather, at the thick electrical cable leading to the machine that was laying on the ground. Sparks jumped like crazy when the blade bit into the thick wire. Thankfully, the ax had a wooden handle, so he wasn't electrocuted when he hit that live wire. Robert yanked the tool free and raised it to swing again.

And all hell broke loose.

The guy on the floor behind us yelled out. Apparently, my blow had only dazed him and he chose that incredibly inconvenient moment to wake up. The other men came charging around the end of the machine with Ginny behind them. I dived for the gun Robert's guard had dropped when I hit him. Robert changed the swing of his pickax and took aim at the nearest guy charging him from behind the machine.

I wasn't going to be able to pick up the guard's gun first. So I did the next best thing. I kicked the guy's hand just as it wrapped around the pistol. I booted the weapon out of his grasp in a high arc. It landed in the pond with a satisfying plop. The guy lying at my feet howled in pain, but still managed to grab my ankle. He gave a good yank and I went sprawling. I rolled over, kicking and hitting for all I was worth. I landed several solid blows in quick succession, and the guy pushed to his hands and knees and tried to crawl clear of my flailing limbs.

I needed something heavy to hit him with. You'd think in a cave there'd be rocks everywhere, but no. The floor was as bare as my living room. Dammit! I swung my trusty rucksack off my shoulder and gave a swing with it. Something heavy and hard inside it connected with the back of the guy's neck, and he dropped to the floor again. This time I hoped he was dead.

"Behind you," a wispy voice breathed from the vicinity of the pond.

I whirled around, swinging my rucksack as I did. I clobbered the guy from the park in Paris in the side. He grunted, righted himself and kept on coming. But that pause gave me an instant to catch my balance. I windmilled my right arm down and back, circling it up over my head and slinging the rucksack down on top of the guy's head. He threw up his arms to ward off the blow, and I let fly with my left foot.

My toes slammed into the softness of his groin until they ground against bone. The guy let out a deafening scream that echoed through the vaulted space. Needless to say, he dropped to the floor. He was going to be incapacitated for a good long while.

I looked for Robert. He was squared off against the biggest guy of the bunch. For her part, Ginny was facing a guy who towered over her, as well.

Abruptly, I noticed an ozone smell starting to fill the air. Oh, crap. The machine was getting close to charged. I looked around frantically for the pickax, but saw no sign of it anywhere.

"Ginny!" I yelled. "We've got to stop the machine!"

She charged toward me, drawing her attacker with her. What was she up to? She took a flying leap that was nothing short of spectacular and landed on top of the engine housing. Another leap, and she was on top of the whole contraption.

"Don't touch the plates!" I shouted. "You'll be electrocuted!" She might also discharge the machine by accident. And even if it were only ninety or ninety-five percent charged, that might be enough to fry the power grid, anyway. I glimpsed her starting to yank wires running from the plates to the ray gun free of their connections, and then the guy who'd been chasing her was on me.

He was big. And strong. And mad. And I was in serious trouble. He knocked aside the meanest, hardest blows I could aim at him and charged me, wrapping his thick arms around me and crushing me to his chest. My arms were forced around the guy's waist, and I could only pound ineffectually at his ribs through his heavy jacket.

It was no love hug, let me tell you. My ribs were so crushed I couldn't even draw a breath. It felt like a thirty-foot-long anaconda had me in its coils. I stomped on his feet, kicked at his knees, and bit at whatever I could get my mouth on, which turned out to be his leather coat. None of it did a lick of good.

The room went gray, and then my vision narrowed down to a tiny tunnel with a bright, white light at the end.

"Ana!" I heard Robert shout hoarsely from a great distance.

"The statue. Use the statue," a voice whispered in my ear.

How? I was being suffocated, here. I couldn't breathe a piece of stone...*but I could hit my assailant with it.* Using the very last ounce of my strength, I swung the rucksack up toward the back of my attacker's head. My forearm and the bag were just the right length to connect with the back of the guy's skull.

The arms around me went slack and the guy staggered back. I drew a great, sobbing breath and swung again. I felt as much as heard the Lady crack inside my bag as it connected with the guy's face. And a piece of my heart cracked along with it. Oh, God. *Elise.*

And then Ginny shouted, "Robert, look out!"

That pesky bastard I'd knocked out twice already was back up. He was charging straight at Robert's back, the pickax raised high in the air. And there was *no way* I could get there in time to stop the blow.

Time shifted into suspended animation. I turned, my mouth opening slowly to scream. My hair floated across my face with the force of my turn, which took a lifetime to complete. "Nnnnnnoooooooo," I articulated as if I had a mouthful of cold molasses.

My hands lifted by slow inches to ward off a blow they could not reach. Robert half turned, his forearm beginning to rise to take the blow. The pickax started its downward arc. Inch by deadly inch it fell, its ten-inch-long spike aimed directly at the center of Robert's forehead. My life—our life—that could have been flashed before my eyes. A beautiful, intimate wedding in the Highlands. Children. Laughter. Quiet moments. An old age rich with wonderful memories. A lifetime of passion so beautiful it could make a soul weep.

And it was all about to end.

But then a dark shape came flying past me, and when I say flying, I mean literally. Airborne. Sailing past overhead. I made out the blur. It was Ginny. She'd leaped off the top of the machine and slammed feet first into the chest of the guy with the pickax. Not only did her boots knock the pickax out of the guy's hands, but the force of her impact threw him backward to the floor like he'd just been hit by a Mack truck. His head made a sickening, crunching noise like a stalk of celery being broken in half. I seriously doubted he was going to be getting up after that hit for a while—if ever.

Time abruptly resumed its normal flow and a pool of blood spread rapidly under the downed man's head. Ginny rolled to the side, holding on to her knee as if she'd done serious damage to the joint.

I spun to face my attacker. He'd stumbled and fallen to his knees. He wasn't unconscious, but he was in no condition to fight. I headed for Robert to check his condition.

And then a beeper went off behind me. Somehow, I just knew that sound meant the ray gun was charged up and ready to fire. I turned around in time to see the guy on his knees stagger to his feet, his right index finger outstretched toward the control panel on the side of the engine. A single thought passed through my head.

Oh, shit.

I made a running dive for the guy's feet. It would've been a blatantly illegal move in my family's flag-football games back home, but fortunately, my brothers and I hadn't always followed the rules. I hit the guy in the side of the left knee. My momentum carried me through both of his lower legs, knocking his feet out from under him. He fell across me heavily, pinning me to the floor. The two of us struggled, but it was mainly about disentangling ourselves, as opposed to an actual fight.

I rolled to my feet first and raised my rucksack and its ruined statue high in threat. Anaconda boy subsided, sitting on his bottom on the floor and putting both hands behind his neck without any prompting. I was tempted to pat his head and say, "Good boy."

I moved over toward the control panel, being careful to keep every last Italian squarely in my field of vision. I had to give them credit. They'd been a persistent bunch.

While I stared down at the panel of gauges, Robert brandished the pickax and kept our foes from getting any cute ideas. I had no idea which button to push to turn the thing off. "Robert, could you finish severing that electrical wire?"

"Sure thing." He swung the pickax several times and neatly severed the incoming power cord.

I frowned. "That'll stop it from charging any more, but it won't make any difference now that the negative charge is stored on the plates. We'll have to discharge this thing or else let it sit for a long time while the ambient air bleeds off the charge. It could take hours or days to bring this thing down to a safe level."

"Why don't we fire it, then?" Ginny gritted out from between clenched teeth, sounding as if she were in serious pain.

It wasn't a half-bad idea. All we'd have to do was aim it at something harmless. Hmm. I had no idea if any of the walls in here were harmless. I worried that ley lines crisscrossed through all of them, en route to their intersection beneath the pond. "What if we point the ray gun at the ceiling?"

Robert and Ginny nodded. I made my way over to the

business end of the weapon. Very gingerly, I grabbed the back end of the gun and tugged down on it. The contraption was incredibly heavy and took all my strength to swing it up and away from the pond. When I had it pointed at the ceiling, I turned to the capacitor to have a look at it.

"This thing is going to give off a gigantic electromagnetic pulse. I don't know how safe it'll be to be anywhere near it when it goes." But I knew how to find out. I turned to the Italian who had answered most of Ginny's questions about the machine. "I'm tying you up and leaving you in this room when we blow Big Bertha, here."

His eyes bugged out.

Okay, then. That answered that. We didn't want to be in the same room with this sucker when it went off. I studied the capacitor some more.

"Maybe if we ease the sheets of insulation out slowly, one by one, we can bleed down the charge on the machine enough to reduce its blast to a safe level," I suggested.

Robert nodded his agreement. "When I first got in here, I thought I saw one of the men using levers of some kind on the other side of the machine to move some big white sheets into slots. I didn't see any more than that, though. I was somewhat occupied at the time."

Yeah. Getting his brains beat out. I glared at his captors as I stomped around the far side of the machine. Bingo. A whole row of long handles pointed up at the ceiling. A sizzling noise greeted the motion as negatively charged ions leaped across the gap to link up with their positively charged counterparts on the opposing plate. One by one, I eased each insulating panel down, gradually bleeding off the stored energy. It took nearly ten minutes, but at the end of the day, I thought the machine was largely powered down.

"I think we could fire it relatively safely now and get rid of the rest of the charge."

Nonetheless, I made Ginny and Robert take cover on the far side of the room while I reached for the silver-dollar-sized red button on the control panel. Here went nothing.

I flinched as a bolt of energy shot out of the ray gun like a lightning bolt into a black night. A crack of noise deafened me, while the flash of light nearly blinded me. As afterimages of that beam of light streaked across my field of vision, I prayed I hadn't just collapsed the entire French power grid. There. With the power cord cut, this machine was now useless. Just to be safe, though, Robert took the pickax to the generator and the control panel. He made short order of the doomsday machine.

I headed for the tunnel entrance where Robert and Ginny had taken cover. They were talking quietly when I approached.

Robert broke off and wrapped his arms around me tightly. "Could you please not fire off any more ray guns any time soon? My heart couldn't take it."

"Neither could mine," I mumbled against his chest.

He said, "Ginny and I aren't in any shape to hike out to the surface alone and call for help. I feel as if I've been worked over with a baseball bat, and Ginny's done something to her knee. She's in significant pain and the joint won't bend at all."

I glanced down and could see the joint swelling like crazy under her pant leg. That and her face was a pasty shade of white and glistened with a thin sheen of sweat. That crazy jump off the top of the machine must have wrenched it somehow. I looked up into the woman's dark eyes. "Thank you. I couldn't have done it without you."

She grinned lopsidedly through her obvious pain. "Then does this mean you'll give me a head start before you call the police?"

She'd realized one of the Italians called her Dr. Moon in front of me, and that, as an Interpol agent, I would undoubtedly know who she was.

"Answer me one thing," I said. "Did you steal a statue recently from Elise Villecourt? She lives off rue de Bassano in Paris."

Ginny seemed a bit guilty. Then she looked me square in the eye and answered without hesitation. "I swear I did not steal it in the first place."

"Then as far as I'm concerned, you were never here. Tomorrow, I'll have to do my best to apprehend you, but for today we work together."

Our eyes met in mutual understanding. She and I were square. She'd likely been sent after me to try to steal the statue, but instead she'd helped me rescue Robert and prevent disaster. And in return, I would say nothing of her true identity or her presence here. Thief or not, I owed her one. A big one. Tomorrow would be back to business as usual. I'd be a cop and she'd be a thief. But today, she had my silence and my gratitude.

We made the miserable hike out together. And yes, there was a back way out. It dumped us on the far side of the mountain, not thirty feet from the road. Two cars were hidden in the brush between us and the tar-and-gravel surface. As annoyed as I was to make the discovery, I was more relieved not to have to climb down the other side of the mountain. I was sore and tired and stressed out, and Robert wasn't in any better shape. And between the two of us we had to all but carry Ginny out. But she couldn't afford to be here when the police arrived.

Across the valley, the lights of a farmhouse glowed into the night. We'd done it. France still had electricity.

Robert and I sat down on a rock and waited while Ginny made her way down to the road. She'd insisted on going alone. We heard the roar of an engine, and the silhouette of a motorcycle disappeared into the night.

Robert grinned. "Nice Harley. Not quite like Penny, but not bad."

I rolled my eyes. "Someday you'll have to tell me all about Dr. Moon."

"Someday. After she's either caught or retired. But there's this code of silence among thieves—"

I put my hand over his mouth. "I know," I said gently. "Let's not think about the past anymore. I'm much more interested in the future."

"That's a deal."

Ginny got an extra few minutes' head start we hadn't agreed to while Robert and I lost ourselves in sealing the deal. But eventually, I used my cell phone to call Catrina and Rhys to tell them where we were and to ask them to bring us help in the form of police and perhaps a helicopter for lifting everyone off the hill.

The operation to retrieve the Italians from the chamber deep inside the mountain took hours. It was well into the night before the doomsday machine was declared fully disabled by the bomb squad, and we were all finally airlifted and driven off that hill.

Robert was treated and released from the hospital with a fistful of painkillers. The guy Ginny had jumped on—the one I'd clocked twice—was in emergency surgery to ease pressure from intercranial swelling. The guy I'd kicked in the groin would probably live to father children, but the nurses told me they'd had to knock him completely out with morphine and valium because he was in such pain. I confess that I experienced satisfaction and not an ounce of sympathy at that news. The other two men were treated for minor injuries and turned over to the police for prosecution. Neither one of them was saying a word to the authorities.

And then it was our turn to deal with the police.

Robert was the easiest to clear. A quick phone call to Elise to verify that he and I had been trying to recover her stolen statue was enough to get any theft charges against him dropped. She told police we'd already been in touch with her to let her know we'd recovered the statue for her and were planning to bring it back to her in Paris immediately.

But then there was the matter of the murder charges against me.

It helped that I was able to produce my original Interpol badge. Its dinged up state seemed to impress the authorities. It took them about an hour, but they verified that it was an authentic badge. François Littmann, bless him, told them in no uncertain terms that I was an Interpol agent whether or not my identity had been erased from the agency's computers by accident. Apparently, he also made a vehement statement to the effect that I was not capable of murder.

It was probably the phone call from President Dupont that got me released, though. Elise wasn't kidding when she said she'd be able to bring her own powerful friends to bear to stop the witch hunt against me. When the police told Dupont that I'd stopped some sort of electrical machine from firing in an underground cave, the president asked to speak to me directly.

I took the phone receiver that the lead detective passed across the table to me.

"Agent Reisner?"

"Yes, sir?"

"France owes you a great debt of gratitude. Of course, given the...extraordinary...nature of the disaster you just prevented, it would not be prudent to make a public display of thanks to you."

I imagine the French people weren't quite ready to hear about ley lines and ghosts and magic. "No public display is necessary, Mr. President."

"I've spoken with the police, and they assure me you have an airtight alibi for the night of Monsieur St. Germain's unfortunate death. The combination of your companion's statement, and that of a security guard at a hospital who remembers you emerging from the catacombs across Paris from the murder scene at approximately the same time of the murder, have convinced police you couldn't possibly be the killer. I have been assured that all charges against you will be dropped."

Of course. The security guard who chased us out of Val de Grace and tried to arrest us! I'd completely forgotten about him.

"My freedom is all the thanks I need, sir."

And that was that. I was no longer a wanted criminal, and neither was Robert. Ginny's name never came up, and the Italians weren't saying a word, so they weren't likely to blow her cover, either.

I was fairly certain the police already had Armande St. Germain's murderer in custody. Between the four Italians who'd been arrested, one of them had to have done it. The cops did tell me they'd picked up some footprint evidence and a couple partial fingerprints both at the murder scene and at my apartment. They believed the two events were linked. When I suggested they try to match the four men they had in custody to that forensic evidence, the police agreed readily.

It was well after midnight when one of the detectives, who were by now treating Robert and me with casual friendliness, stepped into the interrogation room where we were waiting for news and finishing up a late snack of sandwiches and wine.

"You were right, Agent Reisner. We got a match. Two of your guys from the cave match the fingerprints from the St. Germain murder."

Outstanding! Now Robert and I were positively in the clear.

"Who are those guys?" I asked.

"Who do they work for?" Robert added.

The detective frowned. "They had no ID on them and they don't exist anywhere in the police records system. No fingerprints, no photos, nothing. And they're refusing to give us even their first names. Whoever they're working for must be bloody powerful to inspire such loyalty—or such fear—in his flunkies.

"So there's no way to find out who they work for?" I asked in dismay.

The detective shook his head. "Not unless they start talking. And I think the odds of that happening any time soon are zero."

Damn. I looked over at Robert. "We've got to find out who's behind this. We'll all be in danger until we do."

He nodded and put a comforting hand over mine. "All in good time, sweetheart. We'll keep investigating. Just not tonight. Let's give ourselves a little time to recuperate, regroup and do more research. But I promise—I won't give up until we nail whoever tried to murder Elise."

He left unspoken the part where the same person or persons were trying to kill us, too.

"Oh, and you have a visitor," the policeman interjected.

Here? At this hour? Surely Elise hadn't made the trip down her in her fragile state of health. "Is it a woman?" I asked.

"No. It's a priest."

I expected Rhys to walk in the door. So I was stunned when Father Romile—that's right, the librarian from the Vatican—came into the room. My stomach sank. So much for our freedom and bright future. He was going to accuse us of theft and we'd be right back in trouble with the police. Robert and I exchanged chagrined glances.

"May we have privacy?" the priest asked the detective.

"Of course. I'll make sure the intercom is turned off. Give me a moment."

I glanced up at the speaker mounted high in the corner. I almost wished it would stay on. Maybe Father Romile would be more circumspect in the tirade he was about to launch at us.

The cop poked his head back in to let us know all recording and monitoring devices were turned off. And then Father Romile turned to the two of us.

"Is there anything you'd like to confess to me?"

I sighed. "You know we stole the map. We're sorry. Really. But it was a matter of life and death."

He chuckled dryly. "You didn't steal it. We let you have it."

I stared at the little man, whose eyes were twinkling merrily. "You didn't honestly think it would be so easy to waltz out of the archives with a priceless map, did you? We let you go. And believe me, we had a hard time of it, holding off the Swiss Guards until you made it into the museum."

"We who?" Robert demanded. "Who exactly let us have the map?"

"Ah, my son," the priest answered seriously, "The Church is not always of one mind. There are factions within it. Disagreements. You could even say politics."

Where was he going with this line of reasoning? He'd said some startling things the first time we'd talked to him in the Tower of the Winds.

"We, too, are plagued with certain…extremist elements…both within the Church and loosely attached to the fringes of it. When the power outages began and Madame Villecourt expressed her concern that ley lines might be the delivery method of these attacks, we undertook research on our own to see if she was correct."

I don't know about Robert, but I was staring open-mouthed at the wizened man.

Father Romile continued, "I compared every ley line map the archives owns to the sites of the power outages. It became clear right away that whoever was perpetrating the attacks was using a ley line map of some kind. But which one was the question. There are many such maps from many different time periods. The key was to find the right one. Then, you came along a few days later and said that Madame Villecourt sent you. We made a quick call to the airport in Rome to verify that her jet brought you to Rome, and then we took you to the map."

This clever fellow had pulled a whammy on us! He played us as slick as any con man!

He grinned at me, his dentures big and white. "I'd love to see your statue again some time, Miss Reisner. I'm afraid I used it as my excuse to make my exit and startle the two of you into copying or taking the map. But really, I have no objection to Black Madonna images. Yours appeared to be of exceptional quality."

"Unfortunately, I broke her earlier this evening."

"That's too bad."

I unzipped the corner of my backpack and pulled out the carefully rolled up ley line map. "I believe this is yours, Father. And thank you for letting us borrow it."

He laughed and took it back, tucking it into a document tube he pulled out of somewhere on his person. "I'm glad we could be of assistance to you."

It was nearly 4:00 a.m. and Robert and I were seated back in the kitchen of Catrina's farmhouse sipping tea before it finally occurred to me to check on the Black Madonna statue. I knew the lady was broken. I'd heard the pieces of her grinding around in my bag ever since we left the cave. But I hadn't had the stomach to look at her until now. I reached into my rucksack and pulled out a piece of her. It was her head and upper body and all of the baby, except for its chubby little legs. The second large piece of the statue was the lower half of the woman and the rest of the baby. The urn at her feet had broken free.

Catrina gasped and leaned forward to look at the broken statue. "She's beautiful!"

"She was a lot prettier when she was in one piece," I replied wryly.

Rhys picked up the two largest pieces and held them together. "She can be repaired, I think. She won't be quite like new, but she'll look pretty close."

I sighed. "But that won't help the statue's owner. I have a feeling the Lady's magic has been destroyed. This statue won't be able to save Elise's life."

Catrina frowned. "Elise Villecourt?"

"You know her?" I asked, startled.

"She's the one who called me and asked us to help you and Robert. She's an old acquaintance. A long-time patron of the Cluny and a lovely lady." Catrina looked down at the broken statue. "I had no idea she owned a Black Madonna statue like this."

I shrugged. "She told me she puts the Lady away whenever guests come to her home."

"I can see why. This thing is priceless."

Robert frowned. "Actually, my research on the piece shows it to be of moderate value for its age. It's an exceptionally executed piece, but the non-Christian elements—the sword and the urn to name two—not to mention how happy the Lady is, bring down its value as a Madonna image."

Catrina rolled her eyes at him. "Silly man. That's not what makes her priceless. She's a religious relic, not of the Christians, but of the Marians."

I commented, "You wouldn't believe the wild things that have been happening around this statue. I've been having the strangest dreams. And seeing ghosts, and we think she bestows some sort gift of Life upon her owners."

Catrina and Rhys exchanged loaded looks. "You'd be surprised what we might believe about visions and relics," Catrina said quietly.

I nodded. "That's why we were in such a hurry to get her back to Paris. Without the statue, Elise Villecourt is dying. But now—" I broke off, too choked up to go on.

Rhys said quietly, "Let's have a look at the other shards and see if we can put some of them back where they belong. Maybe the effect will still happen if we put her back together exactly."

I reached into the bag one more time and scooped up the surprisingly large number of chips that had fallen off of her. I dumped them on the kitchen table. And it was my turn to gasp.

Rich hues of cobalt-blue and brilliant red spilled out onto the wooden surface.

Catrina and Rhys both came half out of their seats. "Do you know what that those are?" Catrina managed to croak.

I looked down at the colorful bits of stone all entangled in a clump of what looked like wool fibers. "They look like mosaic tiles to me."

Catrina nodded slowly. "Where did those come from?"

"I have no idea. I didn't put them in my bag. Only the Lady, the ley line map and our spelunking gear were in my bag when we went into the cave."

Robert reached out and took the two big pieces of the statue from Rhys. Gently, he tilted them apart. "If I'm not mistaken, this statue was hollow. I bet those little stones were hidden inside her. The wool was probably wrapped around them to keep them from rattling."

My stomach lurched with a burst of hope. Maybe, just maybe, there was hope for Elise yet! If those colorful stones were the source of the statue's magic and not the statue itself, theoretically, we could hand over the tiles to Elise and she'd get better. Eagerly, I expressed the idea aloud.

Catrina shrugged. "I doubt the stones will reverse any aging she has done in the past few weeks. But perhaps they might give her relatively good health and physical comfort for the remainder of her life."

"That's enough for me," I replied.

Robert looked over at Rhys. "Would you mind if we borrowed your car again? We need to get to Paris right away. We have some tiles to deliver."

As I reached out to collect the tiles, Catrina reached out at the same time to reverently touch the collection of tidbits.

But Rhys shot out his hand and stopped her fingers from connecting with the stones.

"Not tonight, darling," he murmured. "You never know what these might do to you."

I frowned, but when neither he nor Catrina offered up an explanation, I didn't push the matter.

Rhys distracted me then by tossing a set of car keys across the table to Robert. "I filled it up on the way home from the hospital. It'll need a quart of oil when you get to Paris."

Robert looked over at me. "Shall we be on our way?"

As we packed up our things, Robert came across his cell phone. He dialed a number on it and waited a long time.

"No answer."

"It is the middle of the night. The person you're calling is no doubt asleep."

He exhaled in frustration. "I've been trying to call him for the past couple days at all different hours, but he never answers. Something's wrong."

"Him who?"

"My client. I need to tell him that not only did I trace the provenance of his statue, I found it and destroyed it, too."

"Perhaps you should just tell him you couldn't come up with anything on it."

He grinned over at me. "Good plan."

"Maybe we should run a provenance search on your client and figure out who he is. See if he's connected to Elise's theft and the attacks on her and us."

Robert's eyes lit up at the prospect. Ah, he was an adventurer at heart. I expected he'd spend most of his life questing after some piece of art or another. And I could live with that. As long as he stayed on my side of the law.

Catrina and I exchanged hugs as I thanked her from the bottom of my heart for her help and hospitality. And then we hit the road. Robert drove, and after a while I dozed off.

And I had one last dream.

A little girl with bright orange curls sat in the grass playing with a half-dozen roly-poly puppies. She laughed with delight as one of them jumped up and licked her face, knocking her over onto her back. The rest of the puppies pounced on her and she squealed with laughter.

From behind me came an answering laugh. I turned, and there was Jane. She looked older, more relaxed, than I'd seen her before. Happier. At peace even. She extricated the little girl from the pile of puppies and scooped her up, swinging her around in the air while the two of them laughed together.

"Mummy, will I ever have a daddy?"

Jane laughed and hugged the child close. "I hope so. But I'm not worried if you don't. You and I, we have everything we need. We have a fine home, good friends and abundant love."

"And puppies!"

"And puppies," Jane repeated, smiling gently.

She turned then, looking over the child's shoulder…

…good grief, directly at me!

"You see?" she said. "It all turned out for the best. I got the child I craved, and she got the love she needed. In the end, love is all that matters. That is the true gift of Life."

And indeed it was. I woke up, my mind clear and my heart at ease in a way they had never been before. As the miles stretched behind us, the events of the past week fell further and further behind me. My fear of being arrested and having my career ruined. My fear of Robert disappearing before we got to spend a lifetime together. My fear of being unworthy of love.

The layers peeled away one by one until there was only the road and the night and the man I loved and me. And that was enough.

Gradually, the sky grew gray in the east, then pink, then blazing orange. And then, finally, the long night was over.

Chapter 20

I sipped at my mango juice, its pungent sweetness rich on my tongue. I set the cold drink on the little table beside me and laid my head back against a fluffy terry cloth towel draped over the chaise. A warm breeze wafted across my skin, and in the distance ocean waves lapped upon the shore. I was relaxed down to the very core of my being.

The woman beside me commented, "This is a magical place, isn't it?"

I opened my eyes lazily and smiled at her. Elise looked worlds better since we'd delivered to her the handful of tiles from the belly of the Lady. The statue had been repaired and looked almost as good as new, but we'd decided to leave the tiles outside her. Elise seemed to think there might be another use for them someday, and we all hated to think of breaking the statue again to get the tiles out a second time.

Elise's hair was still snow-white, but the papery dryness of her skin had eased, and a rosy glow of health was slowly returning to her cheeks. She would never be as young and vital as she had been before the theft, but that joyous charm that had pervaded her being when I first met her was back.

"This is a truly lovely place," I replied. We were at Elise's beach house in Saint-Tropez. It wasn't a huge affair, but its whitewashed stucco walls and red-tile roof opened onto one of the most magnificent white-sand beaches I'd ever seen, and the warm breeze never flagged. Of course, the house was filled with magnificent art that made me cringe to think of it casually hanging on her walls.

"I'm glad you like it," Elise said casually, "since I've willed it to you."

"What?" I exclaimed. I sat bolt upright.

"I've willed it all to you. The penthouse in Paris, the private jet, my ski chalet, the art, the cash, everything."

I took off my sunglasses to stare at her.

"After all, you saved my life, dear Ana. And you did the Marians a great favor by stopping that horrible machine."

Since this conversation was rapidly turning into true confessions time, I asked a question that had been on my mind for weeks. "Elise, are *you* a Marian?"

"I am, indeed," she answered without hesitation. "And my mother, and her mother before her, all the way back to the beginning of the order."

Her answer was no surprise to me. And I suppose, neither was my next question to her.

"You're my grandmother, aren't you?"

"I've been wondering when you were going to get around to asking that one. Of course I am."

"Then why—" I broke off. How to phrase it delicately.

"Why did I leave your grandfather and never let you know of my existence?"

"Well, yes."

"The Nazis worked very hard to uncover old secrets pertaining to medieval legends. In their hunt for the Holy Grail, they stumbled across some of the Marian secrets. And in so doing, they…reactivated certain forces who were historically opposed to the Marian's beliefs. By the end of the war, every Marian—and her loved ones—was in grave danger."

A look of intense pain crossed her face and her voice trembled with grief.

"It was the hardest thing I've ever had to do, but I sent my husband and my son away for their safety. I made Otto promise never to come looking for me as long as our son lived. Even today, my enemies would not hesitate to kill Otto, your father, or you, my granddaughter. I'm sure it's the enemies of the Marians who stole the Lady and tried to kill me."

The idea of being in mortal danger for no other reason than being someone's blood relative was hard to fathom.

Elise continued, "The fact that I have the Black Madonna statue marks me as a Marian. The Lady is one of the great Marian artifacts, and she would never pass out of the hands of the Marians."

Understanding exploded across my brain. "That's why you couldn't tell me about her in the very beginning, isn't it? You took a vow of secrecy not to reveal that you had her, not only to protect the Lady, but also to protect your family!"

"Exactly."

Hesitantly, I asked, "Does being a Marian pass through male children to female granddaughters?"

"Good heavens, yes!" Elise exclaimed. "You're as Marian as I am. Many, many people are. The descendents of the original Marians have had thousands of years to be fruitful and multiply. The sad thing is that very few of them know of their heritage. Over the centuries, knowledge of it has been nearly completely lost. But we plan to rectify that. Soon. The ages are changing and our time is coming."

Something moved within me. A sense of a final puzzle piece dropping into place in my soul. "I'd like to learn more about what these women believed—believe."

Elise laughed. "You've asked the right person that question. I've spent most of my adult life researching that very thing. When we get back to Paris, I'll show you the secret room behind my library. I keep every note I've taken, every book I've ever found on the subject there. It's not everything, mind you. Most of the early Marians' records were destroyed centuries ago, and periodic purges aimed at wiping us out have taken place throughout history. But in bits and pieces, I've reconstructed much of the story."

"Tell me more," I said eagerly.

"All in good time. Here comes your young man now."

I looked up and Robert strode toward us, wearing a pair of swim trunks that made my breath catch in my throat. I hadn't seen or heard Jane since we left Languedoc several weeks ago, yet every night in Robert's arms was more magical than the last. I was rapidly coming to the conclusion that the glorious passion between us had nothing at all to do with ghosts and statues and everything to do with having found our soul mates.

He was speaking on the phone, "So he's completely disappeared? The bank account he set up to fund my search had not been replenished, and nobody's seen or heard from him in weeks?" A pause. "Well, keep me updated, Angus. If he happens to contact the university, it's imperative I speak with him."

I smiled indulgently. Robert was back on the hunt again. This time he was trying to track down the mysterious man who'd hired him to look into the Lady's provenance.

The phone in Robert's hand rang and he answered it quickly. He held it out to me. "Phone's for you."

I put the instrument up to my ear.

"This is Doctor Murieux's office. We have your test results back."

"Great. Does that mean you've figured out why my system has gone so off-kilter? Is something wrong with me?" Ever since the events of a month ago, I'd been feeling off, having trouble sleeping and eating. I thought it was just a touch of post-traumatic stress, but Robert made me go to the doctor and get a full physical.

The nurse laughed. "Nothing is wrong with you unless you call being pregnant a disease."

"Pregnant?" I repeated stupidly. "That's not possible. I have polycystic ovaries—"

"And you are also pregnant, my dear. The doctor would like you to set up an appointment with an obstetrician as soon as possible. I have the names of several we recommend."

"How did this happen?" I asked myself more than the nurse.

"The old-fashioned way, I imagine," the woman giggled.

The Lady. She'd been in our hotel room with us that first night we made love in Rome.

The phone was lifted out of my hand, and Robert tugged me to my feet, lifting me into his arms. He spun me around, kissing me senseless as he did so. I heard laughter—his, mine, Elise's and a familiar, shimmering laugh that I felt more than heard. Even Jane was here to share our joy.

Robert finally lifted his mouth away from mine. "Now you *have* to marry me!" he crowed exultantly.

I grinned up at him. "I was going to do that, anyway. Now I only will do it sooner."

He spun me around again and I hugged him tightly.

Indeed, in the end love was all that mattered. The Lady might have given me the gift of Life, but more importantly, she'd given me the gift of Love.

* * * * *

The secrets of the Marians are still in danger!
Don't miss the next thrilling adventure in
THE MADONNA KEY, *Ginny's story,*
Dark Revelations *by Lorna Tedder.*
Available in November 2007 wherever
Mills & Boon® books are sold.

Turn the page to read a thrilling extract from
Juliet's Law *by Ruth Wind.*
Available exclusively in Mills & Boon® Intrigue
in November 2007!

"Ready?" her sister asked, putting sunglasses on her head.

"I am."

A woman in a yellow jacket moved by the table and gave Desi a long, hard glare. Desi stared right back. When the woman continued toward the cash register, Desi and rolled her eyes at Juliet. "The dentist's wife," she said when the woman had gone outside. "She hates my guts."

"Because?"

"Because she's one of Claude's groupies, and in their eyes, I'm just a mean woman who doesn't understand him."

"Yeah," Josh said, behind them, "you old meanie, you."

Desi grinned, her eyes flashing in a way that made her sister wonder what had forged the bond between these two.

And was there something romantic brewing? "You better believe it, mister."

Did her sister have feelings for this man? He was sort of her type, after all, a rugged Native American, an outdoorsman. He had that adorable daughter who needed a mother.

Josh laughed softly, and Juliet felt the sound run down her neck like warm fingers. She resisted looking up at him, getting caught again in that dark, patient gaze. But even as she resisted, she felt the steady presence of him at her back, solid, steady, calm, and she couldn't help the wave of yearning it kindled in her. It had been a long time since Juliet had felt safe—if she ever had.

Scott was a good man—smart, supportive, ambitious—but she'd never felt sheltered by him. Josh, on the other hand—

With a popping little shock, she heard her thoughts. *Stop it!* She was engaged! It was one thing to admire the long, sturdy thighs of a man, or the grace of his hands. A woman had eyes, after all....

But it was something else again to be thinking of resting against that broad shoulder, to imagine taking a deep breath of relief as that deep laughter rang into the room.

Disloyal. In two directions if Desi was attracted to him, too.

Blindly, Juliet stood and walked towards the door, grabbing a green-and-brown-wrapped mint from a bowl on the counter. "I'll be right outside," she called back. Without waiting for a reply, she rushed out.

The door was in a little foyer with racks of newspapers and tourist brochures on one side. As Juliet rushed through, a man was coming in, and Juliet stepped aside, and—

Slammed squarely into her demons. She was never quite sure what happened, why she was flung back in time, but suddenly, she smelled a musky aftershave and margaritas, and there was a swooshing of all sound, as if her ears were covered. In real time, she ducked her head and managed to stumble around the man coming in the door, ignoring him when he said, "Miss, are you all right?" and got out to the sunshine in the street. Sweat poured down the back of her neck.

But even in the bright sunshine and open air, her throat felt constricted, and her breath came in ragged, tearing gasps. The worst was the sense of mindless panic urging her to *flee! flee! flee!* Her legs burned with the need, her lungs felt as if they would explode. With as much control as she could muster, she grabbed the stone corner of the building and leaned on it, trying not to fight the sensations nor give into them.

A heavy hand fell on her shoulder. "Hey, Juliet, are you—"

She screamed, slammed the hand away. Tried to back off, bumped into the wall.

Saw that it was Josh, and wanted to burst into tears.

He held his hands up, palm out to show he wouldn't hurt her. "Hey, hey, hey," he said. That rich gentle voice splashed into her panic, coating it like chocolate.

And just as suddenly as she'd been sucked into the flashback, she fell back out. With a soft noise, Juliet pitched forward, instinctively reaching for the sturdiness of his big, strong shoulders. Her head landed against his sternum, and she could smell the clean freshness of clothes hung out to dry on a line, and something deeper, his flesh. A gentle light hand smoothed her hair.

"You're okay," he said. "You're okay."

And it was true. After a moment, the dark memories retreated, and she could take a long, slow breath. Raise her head. Only then did she realize how close they were. Embarrassed, she tried to take a step back, and bumped into the wall at her back. "I'm sorry," she said, trying to duck to her left, afraid to look at him.

"Easy." He moved his big hand up and down her arm. "You don't have to go anywhere. Your sister will be here in a hot second."

"I'm—this is…oh, I'm embarrassed." She bent her head. "Thanks. I'm sorry."

"You don't have to apologize." His rumbling voice again rolled down her spine, easing the tension there, and his hands kept moving on her arms in a most soothing way. Steady. Gentle. "You don't have to say anything at all."

Juliet bent her head. He wore dark brown leather hiking boots, sturdy-looking with laces and hooks and eyes and a sole that looked as if it could withstand six inches of ice. Her feet in their thin California boots looked insubstantial, tiny even, and with a glimmer of pleasure, she thought one of the reasons to like a man so big was so that you could feel small next to him. And she was not normally a small woman.

She wanted to offer an explanation, to say something to excuse her weird behavior. The flashbacks were hateful, like a scar, and it made her feel overwhelmed to imagine telling him. Where to start? "Thanks," was all she said.

He released her and in the next instant, Desi came out, offering breath mints to everyone. Juliet moved away, vaguely aware of him watching her. "We'd better get to the courthouse," she said. "Get this taken care of."

"Yep. Let's do it. "

Juliet glanced up at Josh. "See you later."

His eyes were steady and sober and saw far more than she wished. "Right."

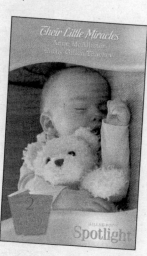

A SEARCH FOR SURVIVORS BECOMES A RACE AGAINST TIME – AND A KILLER

When a plane goes down in the Appalachian mountains, rescue teams start looking for the survivors and discover that a five-year-old boy and a woman are missing. Twenty miles from the crash site, Deborah Sanborn has a vision of two survivors, and she senses these strangers are in terrible danger.

With the snow coming down, not only are they racing against time and the elements – they're up against a killer desperate to silence his only living witness to murder.

Available 21st September 2007

FIRST CAME THE COVER-UP... THEN CAME THE NIGHTMARE

Florida

Investigating the disappearance of her boss, scientist Sabrina Gallows discovers a deadly secret that her employers will kill to keep hidden.

Washington, DC

Congressional aide Jason Brill suspects his boss's friendship with big business may be more of a liability than an asset.

Together, Sabrina and Jason are drawn into a sinister plot that puts corporate greed and corruption above human life. Each must race against time to reveal the truth about this unspeakable evil...

Available 19th October 2007

MIRA

4 FREE

BOOKS AND A SURPRISE GIFT!

We would like to take this opportunity to thank you for reading this Mills & Boon® book by offering you the chance to take FOUR more specially selected titles from the Intrigue series absolutely FREE! We're also making this offer to introduce you to the benefits of the Mills & Boon® Reader Service™—

- ★ FREE home delivery
- ★ FREE gifts and competitions
- ★ FREE monthly Newsletter
- ★ Exclusive Reader Service offers
- ★ Books available before they're in the shops

Accepting these FREE books and gift places you under no obligation to buy, you may cancel at any time, even after receiving your free shipment. Simply complete your details below and return the entire page to the address below. You don't even need a stamp!

YES! Please send me 4 free Intrigue books and a surprise gift. I understand that unless you hear from me, I will receive 6 superb new titles every month for just £3.10 each, postage and packing free. I am under no obligation to purchase any books and may cancel my subscription at any time. The free books and gift will be mine to keep in any case.

17ZED

Ms/Mrs/Miss/Mr ....Initials ....
BLOCK CAPITALS PLEASE

Surname ....

Address ....

....

....Postcode.......................................

Send this whole page to:
UK: FREEPOST CN81, Croydon, CR9 3WZ

Offer valid in UK only and is not available to current Mills & Boon® Reader Service™ subscribers to this series. Overseas and Eire please write for details and readers in Southern Africa write to Box 3010, Pinegowie, 2123 RSA. We reserve the right to refuse an application and applicants must be aged 18 years or over. Only one application per household. Terms and prices subject to change without notice. Offer expires 31st December 2007. As a result of this application, you may receive offers from Harlequin Mills & Boon and other carefully selected companies. If you would prefer not to share in this opportunity please write to The Data Manager, PO Box 676, Richmond, TW9 1WU.

Mills & Boon® is a registered trademark owned by Harlequin Mills & Boon Limited.
The Mills & Boon® Reader Service™ is being used as a trademark.